The
CONFESSION

By Beverly Lewis

ABRAM'S DAUGHTERS

The Covenant • The Betrayal
The Sacrifice • The Prodigal
The Revelation

❖ ❖ ❖

THE HERITAGE OF LANCASTER COUNTY

The Shunning • The Confession • The Reckoning

❖ ❖ ❖

ANNIE'S PEOPLE

The Preacher's Daughter
The Englisher • The Brethren

❖ ❖ ❖

THE COURTSHIP OF NELLIE FISHER

The Parting • The Forbidden

❖ ❖ ❖

The Postcard • The Crossroad

❖ ❖ ❖

The Redemption of Sarah Cain
October Song • Sanctuary* • The Sunroom

❖ ❖ ❖

The Beverly Lewis Amish Heritage Cookbook

www.beverlylewis.com

*with David Lewis

08A

BEVERLY LEWIS

· · ·

The CONFESSION

BETHANY HOUSE
MINNEAPOLIS, MINNESOTA

Published by Bethany House Publishers
11400 Hampshire Avenue South
Bloomington, Minnesota 55438

Bethany House Publishers is a division of
Baker Publishing Group, Grand Rapids, Michigan.

Printed in the United States of America

ISBN   978-0-7642-0464-7

The Library of Congress has cataloged the original edition as follows:

Lewis, Beverly.
  The confession / by Beverly Lewis.
    p.   cm. — (The heritage of Lancaster County ; #2)
    ISBN 1-55661-867-0 (pbk.)
    1. Title. II. Series: Lewis, Beverly, Heritage of Lancaster County ; 2.
PS3562.E9383   C6   1997
813'.54—dc21   97-41118
                                                                        CIP

DEDICATION

To Judy Angle
Thanks for keeping the secret
and
for blessing the idea with prayer,
shaping it with wings.
With gratitude and love.

BEVERLY LEWIS, born in the heart of Pennsylvania Dutch country, fondly recalls her growing-up years. A keen interest in her mother's Plain family heritage has inspired Beverly to set many of her popular stories in Lancaster County.

A former schoolteacher and accomplished pianist, Beverly has written over eighty books for adults and children. Five of her blockbuster novels have received the Gold Book Award for sales over 500,000 copies, and *The Brethren* won a 2007 Christy Award.

Beverly and her husband, David, make their home in Colorado, where they enjoy hiking, biking, reading, writing, making music, and spending time with their three grandchildren.

Author's Note

In writing the following pages, my heart was captured by Katie's emotional pain and her desperate search for truth. Her story now continues, just days after she abandons the Amish community and moves in with Mennonite relatives. And weeks *before* Daniel Fisher's shocking letter ever arrives in Hickory Hollow.

Part I

One can never consent to creep when one feels
an impulse to soar.

Helen Keller

PROLOGUE: KATHERINE

◈　　◈　　◈

I remember everything about my first glimpse of Cousin Lydia's kitchen. It was modern as the day is long and all aglow with electricity.

Being a curious three-year-old, I'd set out to reach the light switch, making determined grunts as I stood on tiptoe, stretching myself up . . . up while peeking around the wide doorjamb to see if the grown-ups were watching.

At last, my little fingers touched the magic. Off . . . and on, and off and on again, I made the long white ceiling lights buzz and flicker, splashing fluorescent gleams onto the floor and the wallpaper. I must've played that way for a good five minutes or more.

It was *Dat* who told me to stop. "Ya mustn't be playin' with the lights, Katie. Ya might burn 'um out," he said softly but sternly. Then he scooped me up in his long arms and carried me to the front room with the rest of my Plain relatives.

Nearly twenty years later, I had to smile at my renewed interest in the light switches found in every room of Peter and Lydia Miller's Mennonite farmhouse. Especially the shiny gold one in the boarding room I now called home.

Being raised Old Order Amish meant I'd never lived

around such fancy things, and for all good reason: the *Ordnung*, an unspoken list of church rules and regulations that had put a damper on my every word, deed, and, ofttimes, my thoughts, too.

I, sadly enough, had gone and broken those laws, several of them—hadn't kept my confession promise to Bishop John, refusing to destroy a forbidden guitar. In return for my wickedness, I was to be shunned all the days of my life.

All my life . . .

If, and only if, I was willing to go to the bishop and repent—bend my knees in earnest contrition, pleading with God and the church membership for mercy—only then could a sinner such as I ever be brought back into the fold of the People.

So Katie Lapp, the secretly "adopted" daughter of Amish parents, was as good as dead. Shunning practices were carried out that way in Hickory Hollow—the way they'd been seen to for three hundred years.

But what of Katherine Mayfield—my real name and the real me? Well, I couldn't imagine *Katherine* thinking twice about a kneeling confession for what I'd done. Not for love nor money. There was too much at stake.

Still, the steady ache in my heart persisted, and sometimes on the clearest of days, from high atop the second-floor landing window, I managed to make out the snowy outline of a distant roof and double chimneys—the old farmhouse where I was raised.

True, Samuel and Rebecca Lapp's sandstone house was just one buggy mile away, up Hickory Lane a bit, though it might've been a good hundred miles on dark December days like today. 'Cause standing here, staring my past in the face, it seemed my whole world might fade to a deep, dark purple if I let it. Stubborn as I was, though, I refused to give in to the searing pain of rejection. And betrayal. Wouldn't let the memories of the shunning drape a dark cloud over my future. In a peculiar sort of way, that was my salvation—that, and my Mennonite relatives.

If it hadn't been for Peter and Lydia, I might've succumbed to despair. But they had a way of treating me like I was really and truly one of the family. Clear from my first day here.

My eyes had begun to open up in more ways than one. The way they talked to God, for instance. Why, it was downright astonishing at times. Oh, I'd heard them say blessings over the meals off and on through the years, but family devotions and the prayers that followed were brand-new to me. Ever so joyful.

And what singing! Three- and four-part harmonies filled the house every evening after supper. My guitar had found a temporary home, and so had my broken heart.

Answering to "Katherine" instead of "Katie" took some getting used to, for sure and for certain. There was no easy way to change something as comfortable as your own first name just because one day you up and decided you were someone new. Still, I was determined to try.

Sometimes Lydia had to call me two and three times to catch my attention. I suppose it wasn't so much the sound of "Katherine" that threw me off—it was latching on to what the name stood for that was the biggest struggle.

For truth, I belonged to someone who'd never known the Ordnung and its confining practices, someone who understood all about the busy modern world I'd missed out on. My birth mother, Laura Mayfield-Bennett—*she* was my true kin. And if I could trust what I'd been told, the woman was dying of some *greislich*, dreadful disease. I needed to act quickly, but the fear in my heart was powerful-strong. At first, it held me fast, even kept me from learning to drive a car or from trying out the telephone hanging high on the wall in Lydia's kitchen.

But there *was* something I didn't hesitate on. Something

13

no amount of fear could keep me from doing. Cousin Lydia drove me to town and dropped me off at the prettiest beauty shop I'd ever seen. 'Course, I'd never darkened the door of one before—just looked from a distance . . . and wished. Didn't have an appointment, but they took me right in and cut and styled my hair just the same.

Glory be! What freedom I felt when the scissors started snippin' away at my long, uneven locks that'd never been cut my whole life long.

Well, the weight of the world fell right off me, in a heap of auburn hair all over the floor. I shook my head and the air swooshed through it, clear to my scalp, and I asked myself why on earth I'd waited so long for something so awful nice.

The answer was bound up in rules and expectations same as my waist-length locks—tied up in a knot under a veiled covering all these years. But there was no need for me to be carrying around a headful of long, too-thick hair anymore. I was free to do whatever I pleased with it . . . *and* my face. Clothes, too. A wonderful-good feeling.

Staring in the mirror, I saw Katherine Mayfield's painted lips smiling back at me. When she whispered, "How do you do?" I heard the refined sound of her "English" voice in my ears. Still, it would take some practice to get it right every time.

I reached up and ran my fingers through my shoulder-length hair; honestly, feeling it so bouncy and free gave me the shivers. The new cut gave me something else, too. A curtain of soft curls!

"You have beautiful natural waves, Katherine," the beautician said with a big smile.

What a day! The curls, so long hidden, had finally made their appearance. I was more than grateful and told her so.

As for Lydia's telephone, I realized I couldn't be waitin' to use it anymore. Couldn't let the fear hold me down, so I got real brave. Five days after coming to live in this fancy house—filled with electricity, microwave ovens, forced air heat . . . and the tallest, prettiest Christmas tree I'd ever seen—I picked up the Lancaster phone directory and made myself read all about how to dial up a long-distance operator.

Then closing the pages, I thought about the sin I was about to commit. Would I never stop straying from the path of righteousness? Seemed to me I'd sinned so awful much, though, what would one more transgression hurt?

A sense of urgency swept over me. My natural mother was dying . . . she wanted to see me. *I* wanted to see her, to know the woman named Laura, wherever she was.

Enough of this pondering over my faults and misdeeds. It was high time to take the first step toward finding my roots. A giant step, to be sure.

I reached for the telephone. . . .

CHAPTER ONE

It was dark and bitterly cold when Laura returned from the attorney's office. She was weary and sighed audibly, bearing the weight of this most recent appointment.

Theodore Williams, her longtime chauffeur, peered at her over the leathered front seat of the limousine. "Mrs. Bennett, are you all right?"

"A bit tired," she replied. "Please don't be concerned."

"Very well" came the deep yet gentle voice.

She allowed herself to lean hard against the backseat, waiting for Theodore as he made his way around to the trunk. Oh, how she longed for the days of mobility, freedom to come and go as she pleased. Could it have been only one month ago she'd braved the cold and the distance, hiring her driver to take her to a remote Amish community in Pennsylvania? She hadn't felt up to such a trip even then, but at least she had been able to get around while there, without much help.

Regrettably, the mid-November jaunt had turned up not a single lead. Her daughter—her only child—had not materialized, even though Theodore had so willingly backtracked to various spots in and around Hickory Hollow before driving home the next day, back to the place of her childhood in the Finger Lakes region of New York.

Yet, in spite of the futile search, she had held stubbornly to one small hope—that an Amishwoman sitting in a carriage in front of a general store might have followed through with Laura's request. She had entreated the elderly woman to deliver her personal letter to one of the many Rebeccas living in the community—specifically, to the *only* Rebecca who would understand the desperate, handwritten plea. The woman whose adopted daughter was to celebrate her twenty-third birthday next summer, June fifth. . . .

The familiar sounds of Laura's empty wheelchair, its thin tires making contact with the cold pavement, brought her from her reverie. She began to straighten herself a bit, sliding forward in the seat as best she could, despite her frail and weakened condition.

In an instant, her chauffeur, dressed in a tailored black suit and overcoat, opened the car door. She lingered a moment, struggling to button the top of her coat against the frigid air as Theodore stood in readiness behind the wheelchair. "Rosie! Miss Judah!" he called toward the house. "Mrs. Bennett has returned."

In the space of a few seconds, the housemaid arrived, followed by Laura's live-in nurse. The two women gently assisted the mistress of the house, easing her out of the black car and settling her into the wheelchair.

Theodore paused judiciously, then—"Shall we go?"

Laura gave a slight nod and was cautiously wheeled over the wide, circular drive—freshly plowed from a recent snowstorm—and into the Tudor-style mansion.

A magnificent Christmas tree stood sentinel in the corner of the expansive entryway, adorned with white doves and lambs to represent divine peace and the Lamb of God respectively. There were lovely cream-colored roses, ivory stars, clumps of dried baby's breath and hydrangeas, and hundreds of twinkling white lights.

Laura breathed in the pine scent, relishing the rich holiday fragrance. *Will I live to see another Christmas Day?* she wondered, glancing away from the enormous tree.

She fought back tears. *Will I live to see my Katherine face-to-face?*

Faithful Theodore guided her chair down shimmering marble halls to the wide French doors in the south wing of the Bennett estate, at which point the venerable gentleman stepped aside, relinquishing the job to Natalie Judah, the nurse. "Do have a good evening, Mrs. Bennett," he said in a near whisper.

"Oh, I will, and you really mustn't worry." Then, motioning for him to lean closer, she said, "Remember . . . not a word to anyone. Are we agreed?"

"As you wish." Before straightening to his full height, Theodore pulled a long envelope from his vest pocket. "Shall I tend to this matter on your behalf?"

Laura had only to nod.

"Consider it done, Mrs. Bennett. Good evening." And he was gone.

Once settled in the commodious suite of rooms, Laura allowed Nurse Judah to assist in removing the wrap she'd donned for her errand. That done, she extended her arm as Natalie checked her pulse with a gentle touch. Frowning, the young RN—dressed all in white, including hose and shoes—then smiled the faintest of smiles and patted Laura's arm. "You've had a strenuous afternoon," she remarked, turning to speak to Rosie. "I think it would be best to serve supper here . . . in Mrs. Bennett's private quarters."

Rosie bit her lip momentarily, then made an obvious attempt to conceal her concern and came near the wheelchair, resting her hand lightly on Laura's shoulder. "I'll see to it."

Laura watched as her nurse set about preparing to administer the regular evening injection of morphine. Reticent and edgy, she stared at the needle. "If you don't mind, couldn't it wait . . . perhaps for just a while?" she asked, not certain why she'd made such a request.

"Oh? Are you experiencing some kind of discomfort? Nausea? Pain?"

The truth was, there had been no ill effects of her afternoon outing. "I'd just like to rest a bit . . . it's been a tiring day," she replied.

"We must be more careful from now on," Natalie reprimanded softly. "You mustn't overdo, Mrs. Bennett."

Laura understood perfectly, for her most recent attacks had come on with excessive fatigue and emotional stress, so much so she had made the decision to move her rooms to the main floor, primarily out of concern for her husband.

A man of disciplined work hours, many of which were spent in his upstairs office suite, Dylan Bennett was easily distracted, and what with her needing constant medical attention, and with Nurse Judah and Rosie coming and going at all hours, she had relocated. More convenient for all concerned. Indeed, *essential* for other reasons unknown to her husband of nine years.

As a relatively new believer—Laura had become a Christian three years prior—she maintained her heavenly Father was in control of her very life and that of her long-lost child's. More recently, she had begun to pray in earnest for God's will as to her and Katherine's reunion—a reunion her husband might not welcome. A solitary afternoon would suffice for such a visit, but she knew in the depths of her being it must be soon . . . very soon, before the crippling disease advanced to claim her life.

The prayers and devotional time she enjoyed with other Christian women—Rosie Taylor, her personal housemaid, in particular—had become a thorny problem, presenting something of a nuisance for Dylan. Her husband, who did not share her newfound faith, had discouraged her from having Bible studies and prayer groups on the premises. Had he put his foot down and absolutely denied her this social and spiritual outlet, she would have obeyed, out of respect. She could only pray that Dylan would never resort to such a harsh measure.

During one such discourse, Laura had to gently remind him that the estate, in fact, was legally hers —her childhood home—having been left to her upon the death of her widowed mother, Charlotte Mayfield, twelve years earlier. The comment was not well received by Dylan, causing more of a rift between them.

Even so, Laura would occasionally invite a church friend or two for an intimate gathering, trusting that someday in God's perfect time, Dylan might join her in the study of the Scriptures. More important, that he would come to find peace with the Savior for himself.

It had not occurred to her, however, that by making arrangements to alter her will, she might be adding fuel to the already stormy debate. In fact, not until Mr. Cranston, her attorney and private counsel, had mentioned it today had she even considered the matter to be an issue. Her ultimate decision was not borne of a vindictive agenda; she was merely following the footsteps of her sensible and loving mother. That was the extent of it.

But she must be discreet. And, for now, Dylan was not to be the wiser.

❖   ❖   ❖

Natalie Judah went in search of her patient's warmest slippers, moving quickly past the lovely dressing room area, complete with jacuzzi bath and vanity, toward the large walk-in closet. On the way, she grappled with her growing emotional attachment to the kind yet determined woman she had been assigned to nurse through a prolonged and difficult illness.

Laura Bennett. A woman with so little life left in her.

Nothing in Natalie's medical training had prepared her for the intense empathy she had come to experience with her first in-home patient, a woman much too young to be dying. In fact, Natalie had found it practically impossible to maintain, as she'd been taught, a semblance of "professional detachment" in the face of Laura Bennett's single-minded goal—obsession, even. So with all the nursing skills at her command, Natalie had determined to do her best to keep Mrs. Bennett alive to realize her fondest dream—to meet the daughter she'd given away at birth, the infant who would by now be a young woman.

Sadly, all this presented a real dilemma. The very objective that drove the poor woman had the capacity to further weaken her, both physically and mentally.

At times, her patient's diagnosis tore at Natalie's heart, for malignant multiple sclerosis was an explosively progressive disease. She did not have to be forewarned as to how the final stages would play out.

◈ ◈ ◈

Laura gazed with interest at the live miniature twin Christmas trees perched on the cherry sofa table across the room on the very edge of her favorite Tibetan damask rug. Red velvet bows and long strands of wooden beads garnished the matching trees, resplendent even without tinsel or lights. She thought of all the Christmases she had missed with her daughter, the never-ending preparations, the gala events surrounding the season . . . hers, completely devoid of the laughter of children.

Had Katherine as a youngster fallen in love with the splendor, the music of Christ's birthday? Laura sighed as her thoughts flew backward in time. What sorts of things did Amish folk do to celebrate? she wondered. Had Katherine come to know the truest significance of the blessed season? Laura could only assume so, for surely the Amish knew and loved the Bible as she did.

Letting her mind wander, she considered the Plain community she'd secretly visited last month while searching for signs of Katherine. What *was* the chance of an Amish family giving up one of their own kin—by blood or otherwise—to spend time with a stranger, and all in response to a desperate plea?

She thought back to the crucial letter, and if she had been able to stand and walk to her writing desk, she would have done so, for in the narrowest drawer lay a copy of her message to Rebecca, the adoptive mother of her child. Still, she knew it by heart—every word of it.

The baby girl I gave to you has been living in my heart all these years. I must speak the truth and say I am sorry I ever gave her away. Now, more than ever, because, you see, I am dying.

Once again, her eyes drifted to the identical Christmas trees. Their bows and beads dazzled her, and she knew why, as a girl, her favorite colors had been red and green. She stared deep into the dense branches, daydreaming of other holidays . . . the breezy, casual days of girlhood, years before her precious baby daughter was ever conceived.

Tears sprang to her eyes. Then, without warning, the colors began to blur. Laura felt the hideous muscular jerking, starting on her left side. Frightened and experiencing intense pain, she placed both hands on her thigh, praying silently for the tremors to cease.

When they did not, she removed her hands slowly from her upper leg, hoping to conceal her true condition from the brunette nurse who had just come into the room, carrying fluffy blue slippers. Laura squeezed her fingers together, locking them into a folded position, and pressed them hard against her lap.

Natalie was not to be fooled, however. "Mrs. Bennett, I really must give you a shot now . . . *before* your supper comes." The soft-spoken woman stooped to remove Laura's shoes, replacing them with her favorite house slippers. Nurse Judah rose and offered a reassuring smile, giving Laura the courage to accept the intimidating injection.

Then, before the drug was ever administered—while the nurse prepared the syringe—the dreadful dizziness began. During the past several days, light-headedness had frequently accompanied the frenzied trembling. It was at such moments she would lose control and cry out, fighting off her pain with the best antidote she knew. "Oh, Lord Jesus, please . . . please help me," she would pray, whimpering.

Nurse Judah swabbed the vein gently. The moist cotton ball made a chilling, unwelcome path along the crease of Laura's arm.

"Can you make a fist, Mrs. Bennett?"

It was all she could do to cooperate at first, but slowly Laura willed her body to relax, and as the medication entered her bloodstream, the morphine began to work its miracle.

After the uncontrollable quaking had ceased, a cloud of exhaustion gathered over her. In the midst of this heaviness, Laura thought of her long-lost girl and feared her own time was short.

❖   ❖   ❖

Theodore Williams made his way out of the house to the limousine still parked in front of the grand entrance. Getting into the car, he thought of Mrs. Bennett's insistence on being driven downtown today. She'd certainly not looked well;

anyone could see that. But she seemed determined, at all costs, to discuss her last will and testament with Mr. Cranston.

Theodore's suspicions could not be quelled—the ailing woman must have it in her mind that she wasn't long for this earth, for it was the urgency in Rosie Taylor's voice, when she'd phoned at noon on behalf of the mistress, that had alerted him.

"Mrs. Bennett will not be satisfied till you agree to take her," the maid had said, stating quite clearly that no one else would do. "She insists on having *you* . . . and keep quiet about it, too." It was the latter remark that worried him greatly.

A more kindhearted lady Theodore had never met, and because Mrs. Bennett was not one to engage in manipulation or deceit, he was moved to help her as he had on at least one previous occasion. The memory served him still—that dreadful day when it was discovered her husband, shrewd man that he was, had been careless with the dear lady's accounts.

It was then that the mistress had taken Theodore into her confidence, a rather rare and ponderous position for an old Britisher solely in her employ. But he'd pulled it off— and quite successfully, too—arranging to drive her to an independent law firm, one completely divorced from Dylan Bennett's own accounts and financial dealings. To this day, and as far as Theodore knew, the man had not the faintest knowledge of any of it. None whatever.

Prudence dictated that Theodore would continue to keep this tidbit as quiet as the present afternoon's journey, when—he had a most ominous feeling—Mrs. Bennett had gone and altered her will.

He parked the black limo beside the white one, then opened his overcoat, reaching into his suitcoat pocket, where he pulled out the long linen envelope, unsealed. He would not investigate its contents, to be sure, and since it was too late to secure it in Mrs. Bennett's safe deposit box tonight, he locked up the envelope in the glove compartment of the car and headed for the gatehouse.

I'll take care of it tomorrow, he told himself. *Yes, indeed. First thing tomorrow.*

CHAPTER TWO

Lydia Miller turned off Hickory Lane and onto the dirt driveway adjacent to the farmhouse. She parked her car in the detached garage bordering the converted barn, where her husband and two of their oldest sons had, years ago, set up a woodworking shop on the main level. She saw that the lights were still on in the office area. Noticing, too, the abundance of light streaming from nearly all the windows on this side of the house—upstairs included—she chuckled, making her way across the snowy barnyard, arms heavy with two sacks of groceries.

Katie Lapp's certainly having herself a heyday, she thought. The electric bill was sure to reflect it.

Approaching the house, Lydia wondered what it might've been like to grow up Amish with few, if any, comforts of a modern home. The mere thought of gas lamps, battery-operated water pumps, and horses and buggies made her grateful for the decision her elderly parents had made long ago—choosing a conservative Mennonite fellowship over the Amish church.

When Katie opened the back door, Lydia almost forgot to address her by the new name but caught herself in time. "How was your afternoon . . . Katherine?"

A smile as bright as a rainbow crossed the young woman's face. "I used the telephone today for the first time. *Ach*, it ain't so awful hard, I guess."

Lydia shrugged her shoulders. "It'll be old hat soon enough."

"*Jah*, I hope so."

Setting her groceries on the table, Lydia turned to the sink and began washing her hands. Then, with Katie's help, she put away three discounted boxes of dishwashing detergent and an array of other housecleaning supplies. "So . . . who'd you call, if it's any of my business?"

"I talked to a lady operator in Rochester, New York . . . I—"

Glancing over at Katie, Lydia hurried to set her at ease. No need for the dear backward girl to divulge the entire phone conversation. "That's all right, really 'tis. You don't have to tell me more."

"Oh, but I *want* to!" Katie closed the refrigerator door and rushed to Lydia's side. "I can't believe what I did today! Honest, I can't."

Studying the young woman next to her, Lydia sensed the yearning. "So, tell me, what did you do?" she asked softly, wondering if her cousin's daughter had already attempted to locate the ailing birth mother.

Katie pulled out a kitchen chair and sat down, touching her long auburn locks, flowing free in wavy curls. Her brown eyes sparkled, and Lydia noticed a trace of eye makeup. "There are forty-eight people with the last name of Bennett."

"Forty-eight? Ei yi yi, such a lot of long-distance calls."

"From what Mamma remembered, Laura lives somewhere near Rochester, I think. A city that sounds something like 'Canada.' "

"Well, have you looked on the map yet?"

"Just the one in the phone book, ya know, to get the

right area code." Katie beamed, looking right proud of her-self—proud in a good way, no doubt—being able to spout off modern things like area codes and such.

"How on earth will you know if you've located the right person?"

Katie nodded. "Could be awful tricky, I 'spect. But I have some *gut* . . . uh, *good* . . . ideas."

Lydia sighed, feeling somewhat relieved. "Then you haven't made any personal calls there yet?"

"Not just yet." The hesitancy in the girl's voice was ev-ident. "I wanted to ask your permission first . . . let you know I'm willing to pay for all the long-distance calls I might hafta make."

"Then we should get busy." Lydia located a book of maps from the shelf under her corner cupboard. "Here, let's have a look-see. Maybe we can find a city in New York that sounds like 'Canada.'"

They put their heads together, leaning over the map on the kitchen table—Lydia's, primly supporting her Mennon-ite cap; Katie's uncovered hair shining, tousled curls spring-ing free, at odds with her upbringing.

After searching and not finding anything, Lydia checked the index for cities in New York. Her pointer finger slid down the page as she calculated each entry. "Here's one," she said. "I wonder, could this be it?" She pointed to *Canandaigua*. "Sounds a bit like 'Canada' to me. And the population is rather small, so there shouldn't be as many Bennetts to call."

Katie laughed. "Ach, you rhymed just then."

"I did at that."

The two women chuckled merrily and set about pre-paring supper. Katie peeled potatoes while Lydia warmed up leftover ham and buttered green beans in the microwave oven.

"Have you thought of praying about your search?"

29

ventured Lydia. "It would be a wise thing to ask our heavenly Father for His guidance. Don't you think so?"

Katie kept peeling potato skins without looking up. "I don't know how to pray thataway. Didn't learn, really. Never thought it was the right sort of thing to be doing, neither."

"Well, I believe I know just the person to teach you," Lydia replied, an excited feeling welling up in her. "Just the one."

Looking up, Katie broke into a shy smile. "Ach, really?"

"I wouldn't fool you about something like that." Lydia turned and went to gaze out the large bay window, framed in hanging ferns. "My husband has taught many a soul to pray, Katie."

"*Katherine*," Katie reminded her.

Lydia was silent. For a moment, she came close to apologizing but let it go this time. She had considered the arrival of Rebecca Lapp's only daughter as somewhat of a mixed blessing. The poor thing was really groping her way these days, insisting on a fancy name like "Katherine Mayfield." Peculiar, it was. This, and the fact that her and Peter's home—dedicated to the Lord's work years ago—and their close proximity to the Amish community, made it rather convenient for the young woman to run from her past and rent a room outside her church district.

Lydia wondered if she was doing the right thing by the shunned girl. And what of Samuel and Rebecca Lapp . . . and their sons? What must *they* be feeling?

The situation perplexed her, and she had the oddest sensation overall. While pondering earlier, she'd wondered why Katie had reacted so harshly to her parents keeping her adoption a secret. Was this what had caused the young woman to deny her own identity? Or was it the shunning— the heartrending way she'd been treated by the People— that had changed everything so?

Lydia shook her head, bewildered. She couldn't get over the young woman's worldly clothing. She'd lost no time in buying a fancy red wool skirt and that shiny satin blouse with swirls of red, blue, and gold flowers, of all things. She figured Katie must've surely shaved her legs, too, because she was wearing the sheerest of hosiery lately. And such a hairdo! All wavy, and oh, so much shorter than any Plain woman—Amish or Mennonite—would ever dare to think of wearing.

Katie's shoulder-length hair bothered Lydia to no end— the girl was constantly fingering it and tossing it about. The usual head covering was missing. Of course, now, what with all of Katie's bright-colored clothes, the veiled cap would look completely out of place.

She sighed and turned from the window, touching the back of her own cap, Mennonite in styling. Surely there was a devout Plain woman—called Katie—hidden away somewhere inside the newly modern girl.

Surely there was.

❖　❖　❖

Katherine's room was high in the house, situated under the eaves, and neat as a pin. The smell of lilac had already begun to permeate the room because of the many hand-made sachets she'd brought with her from home.

There was a down-filled comforter all decked out with sunny yellow tulips, and a white-and-yellow striped bed-skirt that fancied up the four-poster bed. The place was mighty large, yet different from anything she'd ever seen in an Amish household. And the maple furniture, *every* piece—thanks to Cousin Peter's woodworking skill— matched the other: a triple dresser with wide, moveable mirrors; a tall chest of drawers with bright, colorful doilies; and two square lamp tables.

No dark green window blinds, cold hardwood floors, or mountains of Amish quilts. Also noticeably absent was any sign of a cedar chest, where a single woman could store hand-stitched items, awaiting her wedding day.

Katherine brushed aside the annoying thought. She'd gone and run out on her own wedding, leaving a disgusted widower-groom behind. A man who'd turned out to be the sternest bishop Hickory Hollow had ever known—Bishop John Beiler, the imposer of *die Meinding*—the shunning.

Ach! The very thought of it stung her to the core. But she was Katherine now. Body, soul, and spirit.

She stared at the foot of the bed where a hope chest might've been. 'Twasn't so important to have such a thing in a room for rent. Still, she couldn't help recalling the many lovely items she'd made during the years in preparation for her wedded future. All of it, every last hand-sewn piece, she'd packed away in the Lapps' attic. Just thinking of it, she had to laugh—a choked sound—for it was the dusty attic of her childhood home, where everything had begun to crumble and change.

Crossing the room, she went to sit in the upholstered chair near a beautifully draped window. She lifted her tired feet to the hassock and let out a weary sigh. Above her, the ceiling light shone brightly, and she decided as she relaxed that this room was her haven against the world. The world of her People who had pierced her very soul.

Shunned . . . for all time. . . . Once again, she was stricken with the paralyzing thought.

Purposely, she stared at the gold light switch across the room, and Cousin Lydia's words flickered through her mind. *Ask our heavenly Father for guidance*, the Mennonite woman had said.

But Katie—Katherine—had no idea how to do such a thing. Her strict Amish roots went too deep in her, maybe. Still, she mustn't accept that as a reason *not* to pray Cousin

Lydia's way. Besides, she wanted to break all ties with her past, so praying as if you were talking to God . . . now, that would be one way to go about it.

She got up and knelt beside the chair. "Dear Father in heaven, there's a Mennonite downstairs who says I should talk to thee . . . er, you, about findin' my real mother. I do hope thou, uh, *you* won't be minding too much. . . ."

She stopped. Such a strange way to speak to the Almighty. She resorted to beseeching Him in German, as she was accustomed. "*O Herr Gott, himmlischer Vater*," she began.

It was difficult—no, downright bossy—to ask anything personal of the Lord God, heavenly Father, especially since she was in bald-faced disobedience to His commandments. So she didn't make a request at all but recited a prayer from *Christenpflicht*, the standard Amish prayer book, instead of a spontaneous one.

After the prayer was done, she felt as though she'd broken faith with the new person she was attempting to become—Katherine Mayfield.

Before getting off her knees, she spied the beloved guitar lying under the double bed. Retrieving it, she sat on the hassock, exhilaration replacing her sadness as she strummed the once-forbidden strings.

The lively songs she sang were old ones, some she'd made up as a little child. Another was a slower tune, one she and her first love, Daniel Fisher—who'd drowned in a sailing accident five years before—had written together during the last week of his life.

Dan, she truly hoped, would be pleased up there in Glory if he knew what her plans were for tomorrow. He was a spirited fella, Daniel Fisher. Never gave up trying till he got what he wanted. Especially when it came to religion and the Bible.

She remembered him being mighty stubborn for a young

Amishman—liked to ramrod his ideas through to those who didn't see eye to eye with him.

Katherine sang on.

Don't prejudge the dead, she could hear the conscientious voice of Rebecca Lapp, her Amish mamma. Herr Gott was the final Judge when all was said and all was done. The Almighty One was sovereign. Come Judgment Day, *He* would decide what would become of her dear *Beau*'s eternal soul.

Louder she sang, defying the thought of Daniel ever being anywhere but in Blessed Paradise. Never before and never again had someone understood or loved her more. And tomorrow, if Dan was looking down on her, she'd make him grin . . . chuckle, maybe.

She planned on using Cousin Lydia's telephone to dial up that long-distance operator in Canandaigua. She would not give up till she got hold of a woman named Laura Mayfield-Bennett. Laura, who would understand perfectly. Laura, who would recite the day of her daughter's birth and say at last, "Welcome home, Katherine."

What a fine, wonderful-good day that would be.

CHAPTER THREE

❖ ❖ ❖

Katherine waited for the house to clear out a bit before heading to the hall phone the next morning. She'd written and rewritten the directory assistance number for long distance on a scratch pad from the kitchen, anticipating the moment.

But when she walked up the stairs and approached the telephone, she could only stare at it. There were so many things to be thinking about. If she picked up that phone . . .

Hmm. It just might be best not to know anything about her natural mother, really. Might be best to leave well enough alone.

Her dear friend Mary Stoltzfus would say, "Stick to doin' the right thing, Katie." Well, if she was to do the right thing, would she be standing here in this Mennonite house this very minute?

She shrugged off the crippling thought. Her heart, fractured and feeble, insisted on knowing the truth.

But when she got up the courage to dial the number, the electronic answering service came on the line. Katherine waited, insisting on speaking with a real "live" operator.

"What city?" the woman asked.

"Canandaigua."

"One moment, please."

Katherine waited, her breath coming in shallow spurts.

"What listing?" was the reply.

"I need a number for someone with the last name of *Bennett.*"

"Spell it, please."

"B-e-n-n-e-t-t."

"Thank you, one moment." The operator's voice sounded stiff, and Katherine wondered if that was how all of them talked. But she wasn't about to give up. She wouldn't let one uppity operator discourage her.

"There are fifteen Bennetts listed. Is there a *first* name?" the operator asked.

"Please try Laura Mayfield-Bennett. It might be under that name."

Almost instantly, the woman said, "I'm sorry, there's no such listing."

"Oh . . ."

"Would you like to try another?" came the wooden voice.

"No, thank you, but could you give me the phone numbers for those fifteen Bennetts?"

"I am authorized to give only one listing per call."

Only one? Katherine's heart sank. "But it's an emergency. Someone's dying . . . someone . . . uh, it's my real mother, she's dying . . . and I hafta find her."

"I'm very sorry, miss. You may continue to call back, however, if you wish to try all the numbers for that listing."

Katherine resigned herself to the way things must be done. After all, hadn't she always followed the most rigid rules in dress, in word, and in deed since toddlerhood? Why not go along with one more?

The operator gave her the first name—*Arthur O. Bennett*—and the number.

"Thank you," Katherine said and hung up.

Then, fingers trembling, she began to dial, remembering to include the area code.

Such a life these moderns have, she thought. On the other hand, *she* was still getting used to the simplest of conveniences.

Last evening, before retiring, she'd discussed her plans with Lydia and Peter, asking permission to use their telephone again. They had agreed to let her reimburse them for the long-distance calls when the monthly bill arrived. It would take quite a bit of her money, but Katherine thought it cheaper than hiring a private detective. Letting her call long distance like this was one of the nicest things anyone had done for her lately.

She heard the phone on the other end ringing in her ear. Once . . . twice . . . a third ring.

Then—"Hello?" a strange voice said.

"Ah . . . I . . . could I speak to Laura Mayfield-Bennett, please?" Her knees were shaking along with her voice.

"Well, I think you may have the wrong number," the voice replied.

"Oh, sorry." Quickly, she hung up.

Not to be discouraged, Katherine picked up a pencil and drew a single neat line through the name. "I'll just try the next one," she said, as though saying the words out loud might give her a bit more confidence.

But she hesitated, staring at the telephone. She thought of Cousin Lydia's kind suggestion of asking the Lord for guidance. Maybe she oughta get up the nerve to do it. Or ask Cousin Peter before she tried.

When she finally redialed the Canandaigua operator, someone new was on the line, and she had to go through the whole rigmarole again.

This time the name given was a *Clifford M. Bennett*. She dialed the new number. The phone rang and rang—ten times at least—before she halted it by hanging up. So she made a tiny question mark beside that name and repeated the process.

Next . . . *Dylan D. Bennett.*

Quickly, she cleared her throat and took a deep breath, trying to look on the bright side of things. Using the phone like this was a very good thing for her to be doing, she thought. Good practice.

But she wasn't prepared to have someone answer, not immediately on the first ring. "The Bennett estate," a confident female voice answered. "How may I direct your call?"

Suddenly, Katherine felt ill at ease. Her mouth went dry, and she was caught completely off guard, hearing a woman answer the phone this way. She almost wondered if she'd gotten hold of her natural mother by sheer luck!

"Is Laura Mayfield-Bennett at home, please?" she managed.

"I'm sorry, Mrs. Bennett is not available at the moment. May *I* help you?"

Katherine felt her heart racing and sat down quickly. *Oh my, now what?* she wondered. This woman talking to her on the other end of the line . . . this woman holding the telephone receiver up there in New York somewhere . . . she was saying, in so many words, that Laura Mayfield-Bennett—her mother, her real mother—lived there.

The Bennett estate. . . .

"Miss? Is there someone else you wish to speak to?"

"Oh, I'm sorry," Katherine said, rallying. "Yes, there sure is. Could I . . . I mean, would it be all right if I talked to . . . her husband?" She glanced at the name and number on her scratch pad. "Mr. Dylan Bennett?"

"Let me see if he's available." A short pause, then—"May I ask who's calling?"

"Oh . . . just tell him that Katherine Mayfield, his wife's daughter, is on the line. And . . . thank you. I thank you very much, I really do!"

The next voice she heard was mighty professional. The way it sounded took her aback—near frightened the wits out of her. And when she began to explain who she was and why she'd called, she forgot all her well-rehearsed "English" speech, and some of the words tumbled out in Dutch.

"I beg your pardon?" the man said. "*Who* did you say you were?"

"I'm Katherine, jah, Katherine Mayfield. I ain't for certain, but I think you might be married to my *mam.*"

There was silence. Long and nerve-jangling.

"Hullo?" she said. "Could ya please tell her I called—uh, tell Laura, that is? It's ever so important."

"I'm sorry, miss. I do believe you must have the wrong number." The voice sounded oh so much different now. Cold and awful stiff. It reminded her of Bishop John's voice when last he'd spoken to her, informing her of the consequences of the shunning.

"But I don't have the wrong number . . . do I? I mean, someone just told me—someone right before you got on the line—said that Laura, your wife, wasn't taking calls. Does that mean she's getting worse . . . because if she is, I wouldn't wanna disturb her. Not for anything."

"Excuse me . . . was someone here expecting your call?" he demanded.

"Ach, I wouldn't be surprised. Laura . . . uh, my mother has been looking for me. Came to Hickory Hollow just last month, as a matter of fact."

"I see" came the terse reply. "Is there a number where she may reach you?"

"Oh yes . . . yes, there is." Katherine studied the Millers' number printed out just above her on the telephone. Because she had not memorized it, she recited slowly.

That done, she instructed him to have Laura ask for either Katherine or . . . Katie Lapp when she called back. "Because the people I'm staying with sometimes forget my new name, and I'd really hate to miss—"

"Katherine . . . or . . . Miss Katie Lapp," the man interrupted, repeating the names slowly as if writing down the information. "Very well, I'll see that my wife gets your message."

"Thank you"—and here she glanced at her list—"thank you, Mr. Dylan Bennett."

"Good-bye," he said curtly and hung up.

"God be with you," she whispered, still holding the phone, warm in her grip.

What kind of man had her real mother gotten herself hitched up with?

Katherine shivered, recalling Dylan Bennett's voice in her ear. *Such a stern-sounding man*, she thought. Panic seized her, and so as to disconnect herself completely from him, she promptly hung up the phone.

❖   ❖   ❖

Rebecca Lapp had asked the Lord God all too often to bring her Katie back to her. But she knew without a shadow of a doubt it would have to be the heavenly Father's own doing—His and His alone. And there'd have to be a startling change in the wayward girl for her to repent on bended knee.

Ach! Such a willful soul her Katie had become. But neither her daughter's past nor her present had kept Rebecca from dropping to her knees many a time throughout the day—always, though, when Samuel and the boys were out milking or away from the house.

She understood full well that Katie's return to Hickory Hollow would have to be the providence of God, because just last week, Samuel had made a fiery announcement. He'd said no one in the Lapp household must ever utter Katie's name. *"We will not be speaking of her again—not ever again!"*

His decree had come out of personal grief, she understood, and, jah, righteous indignation. Rebecca did not feel unkindly toward her husband for it, yet his words hadn't discouraged her from *thinking* of Katie. Which she caught herself doing ever so often these days. My, oh my, had it been nearly one week now already . . . since Katie had gone to stay at Lydia Miller's house?

Rebecca refolded the kitchen towel and went to sit in the front room. Katie was on her mind a lot, it seemed. And she missed her. Missed her like a cripple might pine for an amputated arm or leg.

Himmel, life had changed so terrible much, she thought. Reaching for her hand sewing, Rebecca wondered if she oughtn't to stop by and visit her Mennonite cousin. A quick visit wouldn't hurt none, especially this close to Christmas. And maybe, just maybe, she'd catch a glimpse of her dear girl at the same time. That is, if Katie hadn't already up and gone to New York.

Rebecca teetered a bit on her hickory rocker before resuming the embroidery work. No, she couldn't do it. Samuel—the bishop, too—would disapprove. Besides, it might be too soon to visit thataway. She must wait out die Meinding, hoping and praying that the harshness of the shunning might bring Katie back to the church and to God.

Yet if the truth be known, she herself was suffering from a wicked sin—jealousy. And not just a twinge of it, neither. Ach, she'd had a greislich time of it, trying ever so hard to turn her thoughts away from Katie and her stubborn desire to search for the "English" woman named Laura Mayfield-Bennett. Such a fancy, modern lady she must be.

Rebecca's mind raced near out of control at the possibility of her precious girl taking up with the likes of a worldly woman. Sometimes she thought her mind might be slipping, and she tried desperately to hide her ongoing obsession with Katie's satin baby gown.

But if she could just touch it, hold it and stroke its gentle folds, then and only then could the past catch up with the present and things go on as always—before Katie got herself shunned and left the Amish community.

Here lately, the haunting cries of an infant had caused her to get up and rush down the hall to Katie's old room. Some nights she sat beside the empty bed long into the wee hours, holding the baby dress next to her bosom. She'd even quit praying in German and told the Lord God heavenly Father that she wished He'd never created her. That she herself had never been born.

Jah, it might've been better thataway. . . .

❖ ❖ ❖

Immediately following breakfast, Theodore hurried to the limo garage behind the estate. He opened the door and, much to his displeasure, discovered the black car was gone, apparently in use. This agitated him considerably, and he walked back and forth on the snow-packed walk, thinking what to do.

Mrs. Bennett was counting on him. He must not let the mistress down, especially not out of pure carelessness—putting that important document in a locked glove compartment. He should have retrieved it at the earliest opportunity and put it elsewhere for safekeeping, as he'd promised.

Back inside, he hung his overcoat and hat in the large utility room near the kitchen. Several housegirls were cleaning counters and sweeping the floor as he came scuffling inside, still wearing his boots.

Garrett Smith, his nephew and head steward, stood in the pantry doorway, consulting in hushed tones with Fulton Taylor, the impeccable butler—Rosie's husband.

But it was Selig, the assistant cook, brewing a fresh pot of coffee, who caught Theodore's attention. "Looks like you could be usin' a strong cup of coffee, my man. Here, try this. It's plenty hot—and black."

Theodore accepted the steaming mug gratefully and seated himself next to the bay window. *Such a thoughtless deed I've done*, he fumed, kicking himself mentally. What if the junior chauffeur needed something from the glove compartment? Why hadn't he taken the unsealed envelope along with him to his room last night?

"Two cubes?" Selig asked, waiting with sugar prongs poised.

Theodore nodded. "The usual, thank you." Lost in his thoughts, he stirred, then sipped the dark, sweet brew.

Moments later, Selig came back to the table, pulled out a chair, and settled into it. "Have you heard? We are to be hiring more help."

"Oh?"

"The master mentioned it to Fulton at breakfast, just before Mr. Bennett left for town."

Theodore shifted nervously. So it was Master Bennett who had been in need of the black limousine first thing. Feeling rather dazed, Theodore asked, "Why more help?"

"It seems Mr. Bennett wishes Rosie to assist Mrs. Bennett exclusively. The mistress, poor thing, seems to be failing rather quickly, and I . . . well, I do believe, if I may be so bold to say it, that the master is quite uneasy these days."

Not knowing how to respond, Theodore said nothing. Dylan Bennett, he suspected, was far more concerned with his wife's money and the status of the estate, should the saint of a woman expire, than with the state of her health. He'd known the man much too long to be fooled by any such benevolent charade.

No . . . something else was in the hatching; he could almost guarantee. As for Rosie having been appointed to tend to Mrs. Bennett, he mused over the apparently thoughtful gesture for a moment and decided that naming Rosie as Mrs. Bennett's personal maid was, quite possibly, the kindest thing her husband had done for her in months. Nay, years. There might be hope for him yet.

Nevertheless, things didn't set well. Why hadn't Dylan Bennett allowed his wife the benefit of Rosie's ministrations when the mistress had first requested her?

None of it made sense, and he glanced at the clock, eager for his employer's return.

Eager? One of the few times, to be sure! Theodore chuckled, unashamed.

Midmorning, Mr. Bennett returned at last.

Theodore waited the appropriate length of time before rushing back outdoors, hauling up the garage door, and inspecting the contents of the black limo's glove compartment.

Reaching inside, he located the important document, then turned it over to determine if it had been tampered with. Difficult to say, especially since the flap had never been sealed, the papers slipped snugly into the body of the envelope instead.

Nevertheless, he could feel his pulse slowing to normal and he sighed, resting more easily. What were the chances of someone searching the glove box? No one but Mrs. Bennett, her attorney, and himself even knew of the existence of the envelope.

But . . . he would be more careful from now on, he promised himself. For Mrs. Bennett's sake, if for no other.

CHAPTER FOUR

❖   ❖   ❖

Dylan Bennett lit up an expensive cigar and puffed for a moment before closing the double doors to his professional suite at the estate. Turning, he walked the width of his expansive office and stood in front of the floor-to-ceiling windows, looking out over acres of rolling lawn, newly draped in a foot of snow, and enormous frost-covered evergreens to the north. A genuine old-fashioned blizzard had presented itself during the night, creating a picturesque winterscape.

He pulled up his swivel chair and sat down, rehearsing the events of the morning. The agency contact had been satisfactory, promising to facilitate what he had in mind, thanks to a resourceful colleague.

Laura's condition was definitely on his side. In actuality—before his very eyes, it seemed—his wife's health had begun to decline. Most rapidly in the past three weeks. Just today, he'd discovered—entirely by accident—exactly what it was Laura had planned at her demise.

He grimaced at the irony of the situation, for the latest version of his wife's bequest was now quite clear. She had named her long-lost daughter the sole heir to her fortune.

Good thing—for him—that the daughter had not turned up. Not unless he took into account the backwoods female who had had the gall to call him, claiming to *be* that daughter. She'd probably gotten wind of Laura's terminal disease—through one source or another—and fabricated the whole thing. Still, where did that leave *him*?

He need not question his fate; he would be forced to scramble for a new residence if that Katherine person ever did appear on the scene. Not that he couldn't afford to settle into something comfortable and elegant, but this place . . . this was home, and he was just stubborn enough not to relish giving it up. No, after nearly ten exasperating years, the Bennett estate belonged as much to him as to his wife, he felt.

He took a long, deep draw on the cigar. *I will not be dethroned,* he decided and began to jot down the specific plot he planned to set in motion.

He was glad he'd taped the phone call from that country bumpkin—the Amish girl from somewhere in Pennsylvania, or so she'd said. Such a brassy creature, calling him here in search of Laura.

What was it—something about his being married to her mother? That Laura had been searching for her? If such a thing were true, and this Katherine or Katie Lapp—as she had so ably prompted him—*had* received word from Laura. . . . Well, time was of the essence. He must act quickly.

Finished with the cigar, he let it continue to smoke on the crystal ashtray, creating a gray haze about him. Then, leaning back, he watched the wispy tendrils curl and climb toward the high, molded ceiling. How like his own gradual ascent to fame and fortune, he recalled with satisfaction. . . .

Laura Mayfield had been so naive when first they met twelve years ago. At twenty-six, she was virtually an innocent, to the point of exuding a refreshing coyness. He remembered this because on occasion she would blush, and over the slightest innuendo. This trait had taken him completely by surprise, perhaps because the girl—having grown up in opulence—seemed reticent to socialize and mingle with high society. She despised crowds—disorganized ones, that is. But the congestion of students in a classroom, for example, was an entirely different story. Stimulating, she'd say.

By sheer accident, Dylan had made her acquaintance at the University of Rochester, during the spring semester. She was taking a class in English literature—for the fun of it— and he a refresher course in economics.

As it turned out, his encounter with Laura had been a lucky break for him, which is not to say there was no attraction between them. He was smitten with her petite figure, her lush auburn hair—and her money. She, after an initial reservation or two, seemed convinced she had found her one and only true love, the man destined by heaven to marry her and cherish her for the rest of their days.

To that end, they pursued their fascination with each other, talking for hours at a time. While Dylan would have much preferred to demonstrate his passion, Laura was a stickler about keeping things on the up and up. Insisted on a "pure and honorable relationship."

Being the gentleman—and the pauper—he was, he'd determined to bide his time. Conquest would be all the sweeter for the waiting.

It was during one of their discourses on soul-fed intimacy that he came to learn of Laura's desire for children. "I want as many babies as we can clothe, educate, and adore," she said with the brightest grin on her guileless face.

"Children?" He'd nearly choked.

"Why, yes. Isn't it a grand thought?"

Anything *but*! Children were a nuisance—a liability in his book. Nothing could be more distasteful than the thought of noisy, little diapered mopheads skittering around underfoot.

No . . . children had never been a part of his agenda. Not even as an addendum. And although it seemed entirely possible that voicing his opposition might very well terminate his comfortable relationship with the beautiful and wealthy Laura Mayfield, he cringed at the thought of satisfying her desire for motherhood. Cleverly, he tempered his response, cloaking his true sentiments, never revealing his plans to have a vasectomy—before the wedding.

It was months later that Laura made herself completely vulnerable to him, confessing her mortal sin. She described —in a rain of anguished tears—how, during her junior year in high school, she had become intimate with her first boyfriend. The outcome was an unwanted pregnancy, a baby girl born out of wedlock. "I gave away my precious baby," she whispered as they sat in his parked car. "I gave Katherine to an Amish couple."

He was floored. "Why *Amish*?"

"It's a long story. One you must hear someday . . . when I'm ready to tell it . . . all of it."

He thought it over. So this was the reason for Laura's obsession with children. He remained silent, saying nothing to arouse her suspicions.

When she began to cry again, he stroked her hand, taking great pains to capitalize on this opportunity. He moved away from the steering wheel and put his arm around her. Sorrowfully, she leaned her head on his waiting shoulder.

Then ever so slowly, he traced the outline of her regal chin and with breathless anticipation, leaned close enough to smell her lovely scent. "I'm so sorry, my darling," he whispered seductively. "What can I do to make you happy?"

Laura, her guard down, smiled through her tears, permitting his touch to soothe her, much to his delight. She allowed him to tilt her face and brush his lips against her delicate cheek. He felt her body relax as he made his goal the crook of her mouth. And he moved cautiously, enticingly, toward her lips, relishing the blissful sighs she made with his each caress.

At last a tiny gasp escaped her, and she turned to him, fully responding with the suppressed desire of one long-deprived. Their lips met, and Dylan's hands cupped her face.

One kiss led to another . . . and another, and he quite happily viewed the situation as a breakthrough. Perhaps now things had the potential of steaming up a bit as they prepared for their marriage.

Laura, however, did not allow him to kiss her again until their wedding night—an interminable wait. The event took place one month after Laura's ailing mother passed away, over two long years after they had first met at Rochester. And with eyes wide and focused on his bride's rich legacy, Dylan moved his meager possessions into the grand estate that was soon to bear his name.

And why not? Laura's notion—renaming the old Mayfield mansion as part of her wedding gift to him—was an ingenious one, and Dylan made no attempt to convince her otherwise. Since he was not interested in producing sons and daughters to carry on his name, what an excellent way to secure his future.

Thus, the magnificent manor had become the Bennett estate, and the master of the house managed his accounts—and those of his wife's—with a passion equal to his desire to dominate the pretty, red-haired Laura.

Two years later, however, when she had not abandoned her maiden name but had insisted on keeping it hyphenated, their romance began to wane. Laura had surprised him, emerging as a much stronger and more dynamic personality than he'd ever supposed. She'd begun to volunteer frequently at one of the elementary schools in town.

Around the time of their fifth wedding anniversary,

when Laura had still not conceived a child, she succumbed to deep depression. Playing it safe, Dylan did not enlighten her as to the reason, letting her think she was barren. Soon after, she ceased her work with children, began to withdraw from life in general, and one day, although she kept her accounts in her own name, willingly signed over all financial records and ledgers to Dylan for safekeeping.

Evoking the past always exhilarated Dylan. Today was no exception. He had triumphed, in a sense, or at least he'd thought so. Had met his financial objectives in less than ten years. Yet now it seemed to appear his wife may have, in actuality, outwitted him in the final round.

He felt as if he'd been whipped. Spying his gym bag in the corner where he'd dropped it yesterday, he wondered if a brisk swim at the club might not do him good—just the thing to boost his spirits.

Thinking again of his scheme—his ticket to this estate and the Mayfield fortune—he put out his cigar and rang for the butler.

Fulton Taylor was quick to respond, waiting in the doorway of Dylan's office suite. "You rang, sir?"

"I did." Dylan leaned back all the way in his swivel chair, inhaling thoughtfully before speaking. "About the matter of hiring an additional housemaid."

"Sir?"

"Since you are to be in charge of interviewing applicants, I intend to trust your judgment implicitly." He studied the tall young man with the dark hair and determined jawline. Dylan's trust was well placed; the fellow had an uncanny ability to size up a person. "I suggest you get on with the business of hiring someone immediately." He swept a glance at the calendar.

Fulton nodded, presenting an air of self-reliance. "Will there be anything else, sir?"

Dylan waved his hand as if to brush the issue from his mind. There were other matters to attend to—more urgent details to finalize and finesse. He dismissed the butler.

Then, turning his chair at an angle, he unlocked the file drawer to his left and reached for a folder marked "Katie Lapp."

CHAPTER FIVE

Mary 'n Katie. *For always*, they'd agreed once.

How well Mary Stoltzfus remembered. She'd made the promise to her best friend, and 'twasn't anything she or anybody else could do now about breaking it. Katie was shunned, and from the looks of it, she'd gone away for good.

And it was no wonder! Bishop John had made it quite clear the sinner was not to be spoken to—not even by her own family! The severest shunning in many years, the worst Mary had known since her earliest years of school. Unheard of for Lancaster County.

The community as a whole had begun to rally, but only at a snail's pace. If the rest of the folk felt the way she did about Katie's leaving, she suspected it could take as long as months or even years to heal over the gaping wounds—long as nobody picked at the scabs.

Mary opened the smallest drawer of her dresser, the only sizeable piece of furniture in the room besides her bed. By lantern light, she located the handwritten address of Katie's Mennonite relatives, Peter and Lydia Miller, the place where her friend had said she'd be staying when she'd come to say good-bye.

"S'pose I could write her," she whispered into the dimly

lit bedroom, wondering what she would tell her dearest friend. Would she say she'd spent most of the week in bed, sick at heart and of body over Katie's leaving? Would she tell her how lonely it was in the community without her pea-in-a-pod best buddy?

The more she dawdled over what to write, or *if* to write, the more prickly she felt. "Probably not a gut idea," she muttered to herself, got into bed, and sat there in the darkness, knees drawn up to her chest. Contact with a shunned person could result in *that* person being shunned, too. The very notion was enough to give a body a case of hives!

An icy finger of fear tickled her spine, and she pulled the covers around her. Before undoing her hair knot, Mary rubbed her bare feet against the icy cold sheets, creating enough friction to warm them a bit. Then, loosening her hair and letting it fall over her back and shoulders, she slid under several of her mamma's heaviest quilts.

She said her silent prayers, thinking about Katie bein' just down the lane, probably cozy as a bear in hibernation, sleeping in her Mennonite cousin's modern house. Central heating and all. . . .

Sometime in the night, with only a sliver of moonbeams to light the room, Mary awakened. For some reason her thoughts turned from Katie's predicament to Chicken Joe and that sweet talk of his . . . how many Singings ago? After that, he'd up and quit her for pretty little Sarah Beiler.

Puh! They'd probably be hitchin' up come next November during wedding season.

The thought of such a thing near broke Mary's heart, but because she was one who wanted to do the right thing by a person, she'd never confronted the fella. Just let things be. Still, it seemed she might never meet someone to love her. Someone who wanted to marry a right plump wife who could cook, bake, and keep house to beat the band.

She rolled over and stared across the room at her "for

gut" Sunday dress and thought of another fella—a grown man, really—who might be feeling just as sad and empty inside as she was this very minute. Someone who deserved far better than to be left standing alone, without his bride, on his weddin' day. Standing there in front of all the People . . . without Katie.

Bishop John had come to mind too many times to count these past couple'a weeks. Mary was ashamed to admit it to herself, but she liked the widower. Liked him too much for her own good, maybe, and if truth be told, had secretly admired him for several years now.

Still, she didn't know how she'd go about handling five children, ages four to eleven, that is if she ever *did* manage to catch John Beiler's eye. Probably wasn't something she should go on worrying over, neither. Probably was no chance in Paradise of the forty-year-old widower pickin' her for his *Liebschdi*. Not her bein' Katie's best friend and all.

The way she saw it, if the Lord God heavenly Father wanted her to get married, well, He'd just have to send along the right man. Because, here before long, she'd be turning twenty-one—awful old to be lookin' to get married, specially in Hickory Hollow. Jah, she'd best keep her dreams about ending up with handsome Bishop John to herself. Nobody'd ever need to know about *that*.

Not even Ella Mae Zook suspected. Hickory Hollow's Wise Woman would not approve, most certainly. And if she ever *did* come to know about it, Ella Mae would be sure to suggest that Mary put the bishop out of her mind straightaway.

Himmel . . . no sense entertaining idle thoughts over something that would never happen, most likely.

She sighed, making an effort to cease her ponderings. If she'd known how to pray her private wishes and dreams to God, she would've. Right then and there. Just like Katie's Mennonite relatives talked so boldly in *their* prayers.

She wondered if Katie might not be doing some of that same kind of praying this very night. Down Hickory Lane, one buggy mile away. . . .

Come morning, Mary awakened with a vexed feeling. She'd dreamed about her friend all night, nearly. What did it mean? That she should go ahead and write a letter to Katie?

After her bread making and baking chores were done, Mary slipped away to her bedroom, where she located her favorite stationery and a fine-tip pen in her dresser drawer. She sat on a cane chair near her bed, glanced out the window, and daydreamed for a bit.

The tall, deep window was the same one where she'd pressed her fingertips on that sad, sad day just last month when Katie had come to see why she'd not attended Sunday preaching. Not being allowed to speak to her friend, the loving, yet agonizing gesture was all Mary knew to do, hoping against hope that Katie would see with her own eyes how very helpless she felt.

In a wink, thinking back to the dreadful scene, she went all tense, almost as if she wasn't able to get enough air to keep herself breathing.

"Oh, Katie, stubborn girl," she murmured. "Why'd ya do it? Why'd ya go and get yourself shunned?"

She stared at the crooked old tree outside. And then . . . obedience to church rules went out the window as she picked up her pen and began to write.

Wednesday, December 17

Dearest Katie,

I've thought a hundred times or more of an excuse to write you, dear friend. I guess I thought maybe it would be all right if I just sent a Christmas card and short note.

It'd probably be best, though, if you didn't say anything about it to anyone.

These days without you have been downright hard on me, Katie—not being able to see you anymore. It's all I can do to keep myself from sneaking off down the lane for a visit. But you know my heart, don't you? You know I miss you and wish there could be a way for you to come back to us someday.

This whole idea of dropping a line to you may not be the right thing. I can't be sure. Well, anyways, Merry Christmas!

> *Good-bye for now.*
> *Your truest friend—*
> *for always,*
> *Mary Stoltzfus*

P.S. Please forgive me for not using your "new" name— Katherine. For some reason or other, I just can't seem to think of you with a fancy name like that. You'll always be Katie to me.

Mary put down her pen and reread the words, glancing over her shoulder. Quickly, she addressed the envelope, copying the Millers' address, then licked the seal, pressed it shut, and ran outside to slide it into the large metal mailbox. She'd timed her letter just right, it seemed, for here came the mail carrier down the long, snowy lane.

Mary smiled to herself, knowing full well she'd be reprimanded for this deed if caught. But how could that happen with the mail getting picked up right this minute?

"Good mornin', miss," the postman greeted her.

"Hullo," she replied, her eyes downcast.

"Have a good day, now." He took her letter and placed the Stoltzfus mail in her outstretched hand. With a flick, he pushed down the red flag and was on his way.

"*Denki*," she called. Then in a whisper—"And thank you for takin' my letter to dear Katie."

❖ ❖ ❖

Sleet fell on Hickory Hollow later in the day. It pitty-patted on the snowy birdbath behind the screened-in back porch of the Millers' house and on the windowpanes out front.

Twenty-four hours had come and gone since Katherine had braved repeated calls to the operators in northern New York. She sat in the corner window of her rented room and watched the weather worsen.

The gloom outdoors matched her mood, and she was thankful for the warm house. In spite of all she could do to ignore the dismal sky and bleak, raw day, the darkness pushed in upon her. Why hadn't her natural mother returned the call? she wondered. What was keeping her?

A troubling thought haunted her. What if Laura's husband hadn't given his wife the message? He'd seemed a bit reluctant, she remembered. And his voice had sounded so very . . . cold. *Like an icicle.*

Was that the reason she distrusted him?

Katherine decided, right then and there, she'd best be talking things over with Peter and Lydia just as soon as they returned.

Meanwhile, she went downstairs to the kitchen and set a pot of broth on to simmer, adding potatoes, carrots, celery, and other vegetables and seasonings. Next, she gathered the ingredients to make whoopie pies—one of her favorite Amish desserts. Wouldn't Lydia be surprised?

More than anything, Katherine wanted to help out. She missed working alongside her mamma, but she knew she daresn't dwell on that subject much or else she'd be of no use to anyone. Memories of her life with Samuel and Rebecca Lapp brought certain tears all too often. Dear, dear Mamma and Dat—how she missed them!

If it hadn't been for Lydia and Peter, she figured by now

she might've gone *wiedich*—mad! What with missing her family and her dearest friend, she felt disabled at times, like someone with a crippling disease. Especially when she thought about getting on a bus and heading for that strange-sounding city—Canandaigua.

Oh, she could see herself storming the door of the Bennett estate—but only in her mind. When it came to actually going there, knowing she would be seeing her birth mother face-to-face, well, *that* was the part that scared her, but good.

Still, something deep inside, something probably connected hard and fast to Laura Mayfield-Bennett, pushed her onward, giving her the pluck to do what she knew she must do.

So in the middle of salting and peppering the stew, Katherine decided she would allow one more day, and at the most two, for a long-distance call to come in. If she heard nothing back from Laura after that time, she'd consider using some of her former dowry money to take a bus and head north.

After a whole day and a half, Katherine had not received a single telephone call. "What do ya think I should do?" she asked Cousin Peter at breakfast.

"Well, if 'twas me, I'd probably head right on up there," he spouted off.

Lydia patted his hand, smiling. "But Katie . . . er, Katherine's *not* you, honey. She's a sensible young lady."

"I honestly don't know how sensible I am anymore," Katherine remarked. "Sometimes I wonder if I oughtn't to just call up that number again, ya know?"

Lydia nodded, looking a bit worried. "I certainly hope your Laura hasn't . . ." Her voice trailed off.

"I've been thinking the same thing," Katherine admitted. "If she's dying, like Mamma said she was . . . well, there's no tellin' how long she has to live." She rose and dished up seconds for herself and her relatives. "Seems to me I oughta think about getting up some courage. I'd hate to miss seein' her alive. Really I would."

Katherine paused, glancing out the window for a moment. "I guess I'm thinkin' that if someone as powerful-close to you as your own birth mother dies before you can ever make peace with her, well . . . *fer die Katz*. It's no good. No good at all."

Lydia sighed. "Far be it from me to disagree." She adjusted her glasses. "So are you saying you might be leaving us?"

Before Katherine could answer, Peter spoke up. "Don't you think somebody—a relative or someone—oughta ride along with you, if you go?" His blue eyes were wide with near-parental concern. "Seein' as how the rest of your family—" He stopped short of uttering the dismal word.

Still, Katherine knew exactly what the tall, blond man was about to say. He was right, of course. She was a shunned woman with no moral support whatsoever. Except for Mary's Christmas card and that sweet but awkward note, Katherine had heard nothing from the Amish community.

She wasn't surprised. This was the way shunnings were. The transgressor went into a tailspin, fretting over his or her loss of family—and the ability to buy and sell from anyone in the community, too. Lots of times, the frustration alone was effective enough to bring a sinner back.

Katherine noticed Lydia's head covering was slightly askew. "There's no rush, really," said Lydia. "You could stay here over Christmas . . . and be thinkin' about what to do after that."

"There *is* a rush, ya know," Katherine reminded her, settling down at the table with her second plate of scrambled eggs. "But thanks for your kindness."

"I'll drive you into town whenever," Peter volunteered. "You just say the word."

"Monday." The word spilled out almost before Katherine realized what she was doing. "I'll call tonight and see about bus fare."

"At least, you'll have Sunday with us," Lydia said, smiling.

Katherine was genuinely glad for that. The Millers' church meeting and Sunday school was like no other. What singing! And, oh, how the people got up and testified. It was like going to heaven before you died.

When Peter offered to help purchase her ticket, she declined. "I still owe you money for all the telephone calls." She paused, looking at one, then the other of her relatives-turned-friends seated across the table. "I owe you both so much," she whispered. "Denki for everything."

"You know you're always welcome here," Lydia said, and Katherine saw that the corners of her eyes glistened.

"I know that, and it means ever so much." She stared at the black coffee in Lydia's cup and struggled to control her own tears. The Millers' kindness and that of her Amish friend—the secret card and note from Mary—were almost more than she could bear.

Quietly, she excused herself and left the table.

❖   ❖   ❖

While her baby slept in his cradle nearby, Annie Lapp thumbed through a pile of Christmas cards. The one from her husband's parents stood out as the loveliest of them all, but when she opened to the greeting, she realized how very odd the signatures looked to her. Ach, there wasn't one thing wrong with the way Rebecca Lapp had signed her and Samuel's names, and the boys—Eli and Benjamin.

It was Katie's name that was so obviously missing, and

that fact alone made Annie remember the events of her sister-in-law's excommunication from the church and the shunning, too—all over again.

She arranged the cards on a string she'd put up across one side of the front room and couldn't help thinking of her dear brother, Daniel. Another Christmas without him.

She sighed. If he just hadn't gotten himself drowned . . . maybe, just maybe, Katie would still be here in Hickory Hollow where she belonged. Instead, word had it Katie was living with Mennonites down the lane, paying rent to them, of all things. *Lydia and Peter Miller. Jah, gut folk. Just ain't Amish*, she thought with a sad shake of her head.

She got up and went to the kitchen, stoking the woodstove, wishing that none of the bad things had ever happened, starting with Dan's death and ending with Katie's shunning—every bit as divisive.

CHAPTER SIX

❖   ❖   ❖

On Sunday, while sitting on a cushioned pew between Lydia and Lydia's daughter-in-law, Edna Miller, Katherine was glad to experience another taste of morning worship at the Hickory Hollow Mennonite meetinghouse.

She sat quietly, reverently, as she had been taught as a child, paying close attention to the still-unfamiliar church trappings about her. All worldly, indeed, her People would say. Running a hand across the soft cushion beneath her, she thought what a stark difference—a nice change, really— from the hard wooden benches she'd been accustomed to while growing up. In front of the church, on a raised plat-form, stood a simple, lone pulpit, centered in the middle. She had known even prior to last Sunday—her first time as a visitor—that the preacher would stand behind the pulpit when he gave his sermon. She'd learned this tidbit of infor-mation from Dan years ago when he'd described the inside of several Mennonite churches. This, after having slipped away to an occasional non-Amish meeting himself.

"Oh, such a joyful time," he'd said about the forbidden services. "The people sing and testify. It's so wonderful-gut, Katie, really 'tis."

Of course, Dan had never gone on to say, "You should

really go and find out for yourself," or "I'll take you along with me sometime." None of that sort of talk. Dan had been careful that way, not willing to risk getting his sweetheart in trouble just because *he* was restless in their cloistered society. Or so she figured.

Still, she thought of Dan as she sat there, the light spilling in through the tall windows on both sides of the church like a divine floodlight. Katherine remembered her darling with an ache in her heart, wondering if they might've ended up Mennonite one day. If he'd lived long enough to marry her, that is.

When the song leader stood up before the people, he tooted softly into his pitch pipe, and the congregation began to sing out spontaneously in a rich four-part harmony.

Under Katherine's satiny sleeves, goose pimples popped out on her arms. Once again, all heaven came down, pouring right in through the lovely, bright windows. A foretaste of Glory filled the place, accompanied by the rapturous sounds of the a cappella choir.

Two rows up and just to the left of the center aisle, four young women sat shoulder to shoulder, wearing matching white organdy head coverings. The teenage quartet unknowingly captured her attention, and although Katherine didn't recognize more than a couple of the hymns, she could see that the girls, who seemed to be sisters, certainly sang with sincerity and total abandon. Hardly even glanced at their hymnbooks, they knew the song so well.

Sharing the hymnal with Lydia's daughter-in-law, Katherine was once again captivated by the musical notation and noticed something else while turning to find the next hymn. The book included gospel songs, too.

"We only sing those songs on Sunday nights or at midweek prayer meeting," Edna explained in a discreet whisper.

Nodding as if she understood, Katherine stared at the key signature of the song they were singing, "Glad Day." She wondered why it was all right with God for Mennonites to write down their music but not Amish. Least not Hickory Hollow Amish folk.

She also wondered why some women in the church wore veiled coverings and others didn't. Why some women dressed in long print dresses with plain-looking white or navy blue sweaters and others looked like tourists and other English folk.

None of it made sense.

She tried to sing along, conscious of the sound of Cousin Lydia's hearty alto voice and Edna's wavering soprano. Each time they came to the refrain, the words *this is the crowning day* stuck in her throat. She'd been taught all her life that no one could truly know the assurance of salvation while alive. You only *hoped* that the Lord God heavenly Father would welcome you into His eternal kingdom on Judgment Day. But to say with all faith you were saved—or to sing words to that effect—was nothing short of boastful.

Pride. The deadliest of sins.

As if to dispute her thoughts, the Mennonite sisters, all four of them, sang the words about going to heaven and what a glad day that would be. It seemed to Katherine they lifted their voices with complete confidence in what they were singing. And she wondered what made the Ordnung so much more important—in Amish eyes—than the Bible itself.

As a child it had all seemed acceptable and right—those regular teachings of the bishop and other preachers. Katherine's best friends were her first and second cousins and classmates at the one-room Amish school—girls and boys in her own church district. Girls like Mary Stoltzfus, who knew her nearly inside out. They dressed alike, wore their hair the same, spoke the same two languages—English and Pennsylvania Dutch—and thought pretty much alike, too.

None of them, except some of the carpenters and

furniture-makers in the community, ever had to associate with outsiders, and they'd been taught that Mennonites, Brethren, and other Christian groups around them were living in sin. If you weren't Amish, chances were good that when you died, you'd be thrown into Outer Darkness or cast into the Lake of Fire. Both, probably. So who'd want to be friends with wicked folk like that?

The Ordnung ruled—shunning or no. And even on this bright and shining day—the blessed Lord's Day before Katherine planned to step into her future, her fancy *English* future—the Old Order reached out to discourage and dismay her.

❖ ❖ ❖

"Tell me one of your stories, Rebecca," Annie Lapp said as she and her mother-in-law sat together in Annie's kitchen.

Rebecca's knitting needles made a soft, rhythmic *clickity-click* pattern in the silence, but she did not speak.

"It's been ever so long since I heard one of your stories," she pleaded.

Still Rebecca declined, shaking her head.

"Storytellin's a gut thing," Annie insisted. "For the teller and for the listener, ya know."

Sighing audibly, Rebecca folded her hands, staring at her knitting. "Jah, I reckon." Yet she made no attempt to start up one of her stories.

Something was terribly wrong with Katie's mam; Annie could see that. The pain in Rebecca's eyes, the bend of her back, ach, how she'd aged. And in such a short time. Annie supposed it had to do with Katie, but she dared not mention the wayward woman's name.

Elam, Annie's husband, had taken a firm stand against anyone referring to his shunned sister about the house—or anywhere else, for that matter. He'd gotten the idea from his father. Both men had decided that neither the immediate family nor the extended family must ever mention her again. Which turned out to be a whole lot of folk, so interconnected were they, what with all the marrying and intermarrying amongst themselves.

Fact was, it had gotten so, here lately, that nobody was talking about Katie Lapp anymore. Truth be told, Annie felt like the People were trying to put the agony—of losing one of their own to the devil—clear behind them. Not out of anger or hatred, no. They were simply trying to go on with the life God would have them lead in Hickory Hollow.

With or without Katie.

"What if I tell *you* a story this time?" she spoke up.

"Gut, des gut," Rebecca replied.

Annie rocked her newborn bundle in her arms, telling her mother-in-law the story she'd never shared before. Not even with Elam.

"It's about a dream I keep having," she began. "I don't understand it and probably you won't, neither."

Rebecca's eyes brightened. "Go on."

"Well, it always starts out on a bitter cold day. Right out of the fog, here comes my dead brother walking up to the house. Marches up the front porch steps and knocks on the door. His frame looks the same, but his face . . . and his eyes . . . well, Dan Fisher looks like he's been gone for a gut long time." She stopped to wrap another blanket around baby Daniel. "It's like he's come back from the dead."

"We all know *that'll* never happen," mumbled Rebecca.

"Still, it bothers me no end havin' that dream keep on a-comin'."

Rebecca looked hollow eyed again. "How often?"

"Couple'a times a week, I 'speck."

"It's just wishful thinkin' is all."

The women fell silent, each with her own thoughts, although Annie wondered whether or not Rebecca's mind might not be clouded up in something other than reality.

"Lord knows if thinkin' could make dreams come true"—the older woman spoke up suddenly, startling Annie with the force of her words—"I'd have my girl back home by now."

Annie gasped outright. She'd never heard Rebecca talk in such an irreverent way. They'd been taught all their lives that speakin' out the Lord's name for any reason but for His honor and glory was downright sinful. And here was Rebecca, sitting in her kitchen, spouting off a near curse. "Mam? Perhaps we oughta be readin' the Scriptures out loud," she suggested quickly.

"I'll not be staying." Rebecca rose. "I best be heading home."

"Wait . . . don't leave just yet."

"It's for the best."

"But we were just starting to visit, and I—"

"What is it, Annie?" demanded Rebecca, turning to stare sharply at her. "You afraid?"

"Afraid of what?"

"That I think you've gone daft over your dead brother?"

Annie got up to put her sleeping little one in his cradle. " 'Course I'm not insane, if that's what you mean."

Rebecca kept walking toward the back door. "There's a fine line betwixt sanity and mental, I'm sorry to say."

The words were strained and ragged around the edges. Rebecca's voice sounded a bit *needlich*. To be so cross was not like Katie's mamma. Not at all.

"Are you all right?" she asked, worried.

"Never better." Rebecca's eerie chuckle was tinged with hysteria—a mixture of wailing and laughter—the high pitch of it enough to raise the hair on the back of Annie's neck.

"Why, of course you've been better, Rebecca. Much, much better." With that, she hurried to the door to help the poor woman with her coat, wishing Christmas wasn't so near.

Something about the Lord's birthday made one want to rejoice—or despair. It was clear her mother-in-law needed some counseling help, and mighty quick, at that. A talk with the Wise Woman might do the trick.

Second thought, maybe *she* would drive the carriage over to see Ella Mae one of these days—tell her about the recurring dream. She wondered what the Wise Woman would make of it.

CHAPTER SEVEN

❖ ❖ ❖

With Christmas only two days away, the Bennett estate was aflutter with activity. Freshly cut greens decorated wide doorways and narrow landing windows. The tangy aroma of pine pleased Laura, and she asked Rosie to wheel her out into the grand hallway.

At one end stood an enormous, fragrant tree, and at the other, parted glass doors led to the dining room, resplendent in bowed greenery and brass candelabra.

Scanning the entrance to the dining room and beyond, she felt as though she were seeing it for the first time. Or, perhaps more accurately, *attempting* to see it, reluctant to admit to herself—let alone to another human being—that her vision was becoming more and more hazy.

Less than a week ago, her eyes had been clear, and except for some occasional smarting behind the sockets, she wouldn't have thought her eyesight to be failing. She wasn't as certain today, however, and contemplated speaking to Nurse Judah about it.

"Is everything all right?" asked Rosie.

No need to alarm her dearest and best maid, and she *was* doing better as far as her leg spasms were concerned.

"I would say this is one of the better days for me . . . in weeks."

Rosie grinned, heaving a huge sigh. "Bless your heart," she said with obvious delight. "I prayed this might be a wonderful Christmas for you, ma'am."

Selig, along with the head steward, rushed past Laura's snug spot in the wheelchair, and she heard their chatter as it faded with their footsteps.

"You won't catch a draft out here, will you?" Rosie asked, glancing down the hall toward the entrance of the house.

"It would be next to impossible—the way you have me bundled up." She smiled at the round-faced woman, her brown eyes dark with concern. "You do take such good care of me, Rosie."

"And what a joy it is" came the meek reply.

Laura felt a soft pat on her arm and wondered if now was a good time to mention the phone call she'd made earlier. "What if I told you I'm thinking of hiring a private investigator?"

"Why, Mrs. Bennett, whatever for?"

"Regarding my daughter, Katherine. You do recall, I trust?"

At that, Rosie came around to stand in front of the wheelchair. "Yes . . . I've heard you speak of her, but why—" She broke off, frowning slightly.

Laura paused. "I had hoped it wouldn't come to this. You see, I have reason to believe that Katherine was never legally adopted."

Rosie gasped. "How could that be?"

"In all these years, I have not received a letter of intent from the couple . . . not that there had to be one for the baby—my daughter—to be raised and loved and—"

"Oh . . . but, Mrs. Bennett, it's nearly Christmas," Rosie interjected. "Perhaps you could wait until after the holidays.

Won't you give it a bit more time?"

"*What* time? I haven't any, have I?" She touched her hands to her knees. "I've lost nearly all balance and strength in my limbs . . . how long must I wait?"

"Three more days?" Rosie implored. "Christmas is upon us."

"Christmas, indeed!" a male voice was heard.

Laura turned to see her husband strolling toward them. "Hello, Dylan," she greeted him.

He was looking fit as usual, dressed in one of his favorite casual tweed sports jackets. But it was the mischievous look in his gray eyes that gave him a boyish appeal. " 'Morning, ladies."

She did little, however, to encourage his outward display of affection—not raising her cheek to his reckless kiss.

He stepped back, his shoes clicking in precision, and folded his arms. "I have a Christmas surprise for you, Laura," he said with a quizzical half smile. "The holidays are a few days off, I realize, but I think you'll understand when you see my present."

She didn't know how to respond, partly because Dylan seemed absolutely overjoyed with the prospect of presenting his early gift.

"Can you be dressed—in your finest—for, say, afternoon tea?"

"Today?"

"This very day." Her husband seemed near to bursting.

Rosie nodded. "I'll see to it that Mrs. Bennett wears her holiday best."

"Good. Take care of it, then." Dylan turned to go, then backtracked and leaned over to kiss Laura's forehead.

"My goodness, the master is jovial today, isn't he?" Rosie said as she wheeled Laura back into her private suite.

"Yes . . . he is. Quite a long time . . . since I've seen him *that* happy." In the excitement of the moment, Laura felt a moment's hesitation. What was the urgency behind the gift? she wondered.

Giving it no further thought, she shrugged the singular feeling away. Perhaps her murky vision had annoyed her unduly.

Perhaps there was nothing to question at all.

❖ ❖ ❖

Natalie Judah arrived a little before the usual afternoon tea, completely out of breath. "The streets are terribly slick," she explained her late arrival. "The weather seems to be getting worse by the minute. And all those last-minute shoppers aren't helping matters a bit." She removed her coat and hung it in the small closet in the sitting area of the cozy room.

"It's a good thing you don't have to go back out tonight, then," Rosie commented, fussing with Laura's hair.

"What a relief!" Natalie sat across the room, watching as Rosie brushed up the thick red mass and secured it with shiny golden combs high on each side.

Mrs. Bennett looked over at her, smiling broadly. "It's such a blessing having you tend to me twenty-four hours a day."

A blessing? Natalie had never thought of nursing in that light. This was her job, and she was more than adequately paid for her services. But there was more—that wrenching compassion for her dying patient. Maybe that's what Laura Bennett was feeling.

"What's the occasion?" she asked, observing Laura's upswept hairdo.

"My husband has a surprise."

"Oh?"

Rosie nodded. "Something that evidently can't wait for

Christmas Eve." A hint of sarcasm edged her voice.

Natalie ignored the comment, glancing toward the hall-way door. "Will Mr. Bennett present the gift here?"

"In this very room," explained Rosie. "And I do hope whatever it is, it won't take too long." She covered Laura's legs with an afghan.

Natalie wondered about Rosie's comment. "Are you feeling worse today, Mrs. Bennett?"

"Not really worse, just . . ."

In an instant, the nurse was on her feet and at Laura's side. "What is it?" She noted the sudden pleading in the sick woman's eyes. And Rosie, who seemed to understand the unspoken gesture, excused herself immediately.

When they were alone, Laura's voice grew soft. "I've been experiencing some discomfort . . . pain behind my eyes."

Natalie approached her patient. "Let's have a look," she said, gently lifting Laura's left eyelid. She examined the eye, hoping for a sign of inflammation or something else. *Anything* but another symptom of the disease's deadly progress.

She found nothing. Stepping back slightly, she studied the woman's pale face, then—"Has this pain come on just recently?"

"I'd say in the past three days or so." Mrs. Bennett went on to describe the annoying sensation of fuzziness as well.

Not a good sign, thought Natalie. It distressed her, hear-ing such bad news this close to Christmas—most likely Laura Bennett's last.

Rosie, feeling maternal toward her charge, who was in actuality eight years older, had returned to stand inches be-hind the wheelchair. Her fingertips were poised on the han-dle grips as the master of the house made his entrance into

Laura's private sitting room. He carried with him a large bouquet of red roses.

Nothing new, she thought. Mr. Bennett often gave his wife flowers for known and unknown reasons. Today, however, it seemed indicative of something—perhaps only a prelude—of what was to come.

"My darling." He spoke in tender tones, coming to kneel before his wife and take her delicate white hands in his. "I don't want to startle you . . ." His voice trailed off, but his gaze was unwavering. "Someone is here to meet you," he continued, "someone you've been longing to see."

Rosie stiffened, glancing across the room at Nurse Natalie, who was staring in shocked expectation. What *was* the man up to?

"Laura, my dear, I believe I may have found your daughter—your Katherine." Mr. Bennett turned and glanced toward the doorway. "She's waiting just outside the door."

A little gasp escaped Mrs. Bennett's lips, and Rosie struggled to subdue her own concern. She sincerely hoped this revelation would not set her mistress back in any way—but then, it wasn't her place to speak up.

Master Dylan paused, perhaps allowing his wife a moment to weigh his words. "Are you ready to meet your only offspring?" he asked. "She goes by the name of Katie Lapp now."

"Katie?" came Laura's faltering voice.

Rosie shot a desperate glance at Nurse Judah, who stood quickly and came to her patient's side, leaning gently on the right arm of the wheelchair. "This is quite unexpected, sir," she remarked, slanting her patient's husband a sideways glance. Then, to Laura—"How do you feel about this, Mrs. Bennett?"

Without warning, the chair began to shake. But it was

not from a tremor brought on by the disease. Laura Bennett was crying, soundless sobs.

Rosie felt a peculiar urge to shield the woman but restrained herself, allowing the moment to unfold. After all, who was she to step in and keep the mistress from laying eyes on her daughter, at long last?

It was nearly Christmas, for goodness' sake. Miracles were *supposed* to happen at Christmastime.

Laura dabbed a tissue at her eyes repeatedly. Then after a time, she nodded—said almost pitifully, "Bring my dear one to me."

Rosie braced herself, planting her eyes on the wide doorway, and gazed at the empty spot. She felt as if she were waiting for the heroine of a play to make a grand entrance. . . .

She was pleasantly surprised when a young Amishwoman, dressed in Old Order garb and head covering tiptoed into the room, accompanied by Master Dylan himself. The slender girl, who couldn't have been a day over twenty, had eyes for Mrs. Bennett entirely. Her oval face burst into a spontaneous yet coy smile. "Hello, Mother," she said.

The master was quick to speak, even before Laura could respond to her daughter's first words of greeting. "Darling, I'd like you to meet Katie."

In spite of her husband's attempt to offer a formal introduction, Laura's gaze never once veered from the Amish girl. "Oh, Katherine, is it you? Is it really you?"

Rosie surrendered her hold on the wheelchair and stepped aside, surveying closely the glint of—what *was* that strange look in Dylan Bennett's eyes? Certainly not glee . . . or was it?

"Oh, do come closer, my dear," Laura said, fighting back tears that only served to cloud her vision further. "I want to have a good look at you. You won't mind, will you?"

The Amish girl came near, and Nurse Judah promptly pulled up a chair for her to sit, facing Laura.

"Denki," came the reticent reply.

Laura noticed Katie's polite nod toward the nurse. Her heart fairly skipped a beat as she gazed happily at the young woman before her.

Katherine, her beautiful daughter, was here at last! Here . . . in this very house!

The young woman spoke again. "Ach, but I want to look at *you*, Mam."

The Plain, simple words seemed to hang in the air. Yet Laura fell silent as fluctuating emotions overwhelmed her. Elation, bittersweet joy. . . .

The two of them—surrounded by Dylan, Rosie, and the nurse—observed each other curiously.

Laura soon found her voice. "Katherine, my precious girl. Oh, I've waited so long, so very long for this day."

Her daughter nodded, smiling sweetly.

Laura's eyes filled with tears, and she brushed them away quickly, fearing she might look up and find that her dear one had vanished. "The Lord has surely answered my prayers," she whispered, reaching for the dainty hand. "How happy I am you've come, Katherine."

"Please, you must call me Katie. It suits me just fine."

So, thought Laura, her birth daughter's Amish parents—the Lapps—had modified the name she'd chosen. Renamed her Katie. Indeed, there was something simple yet charming about it. The short, fanciful name *did* suit her.

"Then, Katie you are," she answered, surprised how the charming nickname rolled off her tongue. It was perfectly right—an acceptable substitute, being a derivative of Katherine, after all.

The notion that she had provided this name warmed her

heart, made her feel more closely connected to this stranger somehow. Gave her a link to the past. A past the two had never shared. Lost . . . lost days. Gone forever.

Still, they had *this* moment. She must cling to that. They—she and this adorable girl named Katie—had *now*. And with all the love she'd carried in vain for her daughter these many years, she decided they would indeed enjoy this time that was every bit as much a *divine* gift as it was Dylan's.

Scarcely able to keep from staring at her child, Laura was struck by Katie's lovely face—the creamy white complexion, picture perfect. And the quiet smile. Everything about her charmed Laura. Yet if there was any disappointment at all, it might've been in the color of Katie's hair.

Laura had always fantasized that her flesh and blood would surely share her own fiery red locks. Still, strawberry blond was most becoming and enhanced the girl's light brown brows and lashes beautifully.

If only she could really *see* this vision of love before her, marred only by the inability to focus her eyes and truly savor her daughter's appearance. "Oh my, there are so many, many things I want to tell you," Laura heard herself saying. "Things that a mother and her long-absent daughter might share."

Behind her, she was aware of Rosie's sniffling, and Laura was quite sure there were tears in her husband's eyes as well. A swell of gratitude to him took her breath for the moment. She must ask him how he'd managed to locate Katherine—and so close to Christmas. But that could wait. "We must take our afternoon tea together," she told the girl. "Just the two of us."

At that, Dylan spoke up, emerging from the corner of the room. "Tea is on the way."

"Wonderful." Laura kept her chin up, looking directly at him, though he appeared as a blur to her fuzzy vision.

Nurse Judah checked Laura's pulse before excusing herself. Rosie seemed more reluctant to leave and leaned over to whisper, "Are you certain I won't be needed?"

"Thank you, but no," Laura said, though a hammer in her heart tripped at an unceasing pace. The pain of the years, the excruciating loss . . . all of it came sweeping through the room, overpowering her. The weight of worry, the haunting memories nearly engulfed her as she sat helplessly in her wheelchair, and for one dreamlike instant, she had to glance around to secure the moment—to reorient herself as to what had just taken place.

It was then she noticed that Dylan had moved to a chair only a few feet from Katie. Why had he remained in spite of her request for seclusion?

She avoided his gaze and turned her attention to the primly dressed Katie, wearing the same shade of blue and the black apron she'd observed on several Amishwomen while in Lancaster County last month. In fact, if memory served her correctly, the color was the same hue that Rebecca, her baby's adopted mother, had worn the day they met in the corridor of Lancaster General Hospital nearly twenty-three years ago.

"Katie, will you consider staying over for the holidays?" she asked, smiling at the prospect.

Before her daughter could respond, Dylan cut in, addressing Katie. "Mrs. Bennett, er, your *mother* and I would love to have you celebrate Christmas with us." He turned, delivering an adoring gesture toward Laura as if the two of them were, in all reality, the happiest couple in the world.

"More than anything, I want you to stay," Laura said, her throat growing increasingly dry as she sat motionless, for all practical purposes, paralyzed. The disturbing, yet not unwelcome tension of the situation—the powerful sense of seeing yet not truly seeing her daughter—left her reeling, breathless.

Dylan seemed eager to dissipate the heaviness in the room. "If you wish, I can have the butler show you to one of our upstairs guest rooms."

"By all means," Laura added. "We'll make you quite comfortable here, Katie."

At that, the Amish girl lit up. "We'll get better acquainted, maybe? Jah?"

"Oh, I do hope so." Deep within her, Laura offered a silent thanksgiving to the Lord for bringing her precious Katie to her . . . right on time.

On time.

So was afternoon tea. Rosie served it, along with pastry delicacies fit for a newly reunited royal family.

Although a thousand questions flooded Laura's mind as they sipped tea and buttered their tarts, she refrained from voicing a single one, uncomfortable with the idea of quizzing her travel-weary daughter so soon upon her arrival. Along with that, despite her appreciation for his gift to her, she was feeling somewhat put out with Dylan, who was clearly becoming an intrusion.

If he were genuinely interested in learning of Katie's prior whereabouts and her past, why was it he continued to veer the conversation away from the very things Laura longed to discover about Katie Lapp? All of it puzzled her, and she felt a panicky sensation come over her, triggering a violent attack of leg tremors.

She cried out, grimacing in pain.

Immediately, Dylan stood to his feet, staring sharply. She was certain he was repulsed, could read it in his eyes in spite of her blurred vision.

When she heard Katie gasp, Laura tried desperately to speak, to smooth over what must be a horrifying moment for the others. But her voice was also shaky.

Nurse Judah took charge. "I'll see to Mrs. Bennett," she said, steering the wheelchair out of the room.

Not now, Laura fretted as she was sped away to her bedroom. When they were out of sight, she clutched at her left leg. *Please, Lord Jesus, not now!*

CHAPTER EIGHT

❖   ❖   ❖

The housemaids and servants seemed to know without being told. An undercurrent of conversation could be heard throughout the Bennett mansion as hired staff flew about making additional last-minute plans.

"It seems Master Bennett has located his wife's daughter. They're getting acquainted in Mrs. Bennett's suite at this moment," Selig was overheard telling the head steward.

"By all means, create an additional place setting," Garrett replied, directing traffic by the mere lift of his brow.

"Anyone laid eyes on the mistress's daughter?" the butler asked.

One of the cooks admonished him with a wave of a spatula. "Talk to your wife. Rosie can tell you what the girl looks like, I'll bet."

"The girl?" Garrett said, holding a round tray in midair. A curious smile played across his lips. "How old *is* she?"

"No one seems to know her exact age," Selig offered from his post beside the cutting board. "But my bet is she strongly resembles Mrs. Bennett."

"One would certainly hope so," said Theodore, who had stepped into the kitchen from the utility room, where he had been observing the banter, rather amused at the playful

speculation going on about him. At his appearance, the pa-
laver did not cease; rather, it continued, and little by little,
small groups of workers could be heard whispering as they
rolled out pies, gathered necessary condiments for the after-
dinner coffee, or dispersed clean linens and accessories to
the guest room.

Searching out his nephew in particular, he spoke up.
"May I have a word with you?" He bobbed his head toward
the hallway.

Garrett, preoccupied with the precise arrangement of
hors d'oeuvres on a brass tray, continued working. "Can it
wait a moment?"

"I'd rather it not."

His nephew peered up at him, looking rather startled.
"Why . . . Uncle, what is it?"

"Drop everything and come . . . now," Theodore com-
manded, and although he hadn't recalled speaking so sternly
to his only living relative, the truth was, he had need of
Garrett.

If only for the sake of extreme curiosity.

Fortunately, Garrett did not take his uncle literally about
dropping *everything*, for the enormous platter was splen-
didly arrayed with before-dinner delicacies—tantalizing in
appearance, and at this point in the planning, quite nearly
finished.

Summoning Selig to take over, Garrett hurriedly wiped
his hands on a towel and followed his uncle into the hallway.
"What could be more important than the hors d'oeuvres?"
he asked when they were alone in a corner of the south corridor, far enough removed from the kitchen for privacy and
close enough to the butler's pantry door in case an escape
was necessary.

"The hors d'oeuvres can wait." Theodore leaned forward, glancing about to check for eavesdroppers. "Now,
what's all this fuss about a reunion with Mrs. Bennett and

her daughter? I've caught nothing but snippets all morning."

A wrinkled frown hovered on the steward's brow. "It seems the mistress's daughter has turned up out of nowhere. Straightaway . . . out of the blue."

"Hmm, quite intriguing, I must say."

"Supposedly, Mrs. Bennett is meeting with the young Amishwoman in her private quarters as we speak." Garrett glanced at his watch. "I mustn't delay now, Uncle," he said, "if tea is to be served on time."

"Very well." Theodore scanned the maze of banisters and landings overhead. Wouldn't do to get caught dawdling in the hallway. Then resting his gaze on his nephew, he dismissed the handsome chap with a wave. "We'll discuss it later . . . *after* tea."

Which was to say that Garrett would surely pay strict attention while attending to tea in Mrs. Bennett's suite, after which he would doubtless report to his uncle.

Returning to his own quarters, he mused over the happenings of the past few days. The missus had looked so pale and wan that day he'd driven her to visit the family lawyer. Surely such a reunion—with the daughter she'd lost—would only serve to sap the little strength she had left.

Had the young lady gotten wind of the fortune she was heir to? Doubtless, she had not, with the will so newly altered. Nor, Theodore felt sure, had Master Dylan. What with his comings and goings—of a dubious nature, to be sure—he'd scarcely stepped foot into the mistress's bedroom of late, not even to inquire after her health. Strange fellow, that.

Still, it wasn't likely that Laura Bennett would have discussed her private concerns with her husband.

Well, whatever happened with Mrs. Bennett and her daughter was entirely their business. Still, if it was any consolation, the day was young. Plenty of time for snatches of information from Rosie and, of course, Garrett himself.

Such revelations might quell his fears for the mistress, or so he hoped.

❖   ❖   ❖

From the bus station across town, Katherine gazed out over the parking lot to the highway. It looked like a sea of automobiles, with not a buggy in sight. A green-and-white restaurant sign blinked off and on, reminding her that she hadn't eaten in hours. But she wouldn't reward herself with a steaming hot meal until her chore was done—locating the proper address for the Bennett estate.

Why wouldn't telephone operators give out addresses? It was the oddest thing and made no good sense, because it seemed to her that if someone could get ahold of a phone number, they should also be entitled to the accompanying address. Unless, of course, there was another reason for the phone company's strict policy.

She opened the medium-sized telephone directory dangling from a chain in a corner of the bus station. Scanning the listing for Bennetts, she spotted the name: *Bennett, Dylan D.* Elated, she jotted down the address on a pad of paper and marched up to one of the ticket counters.

The silver-haired man was eager to help. "*Everyone* knows the Bennett mansion," he told her. "In fact, any cab driver in town can take you there . . . blindfolded."

"Well, that's mighty good news. Thank you." She immediately thought about calling a cab. But the idea of heading out to meet her natural mother, stomach growling and with a dizzy head, was much too discouraging.

The bus trip from Lancaster had been a long, tiresome one. An impulsive peek at the cosmetic case in her handbag told her she ought to freshen up before scurrying across the road for a late lunch.

So she headed to the public rest room and splashed

water on her face, then combed her hair, still marveling at the way it played in soft waves over her shoulders. No more middle part, with her crowning glory all done up in an ugly bun and hidden away under a devotional *kapp*.

But that was then, and this was now. Best to put out of her mind the Old Ways and plan her course of action for the whole new life awaiting her.

The restaurant was abuzz with talk, and even after the cheerful waitress served up Katherine's plate of meatloaf, mashed potatoes and gravy, and corn, she stood around, eager to chat. About the town mayor. About the problems her husband was having at his new job. About everything and nothing at all.

When she paused for breath, and Katherine mentioned that she was planning a visit to the Bennett mansion later today, the waitress perked up her ears. "Really? You're going out to see the Bennetts?"

"Well, actually it's *Mrs.* Bennett I want to see." She realized she'd lowered her voice and was actually whispering. "I heard she's been awful sick. Is it true?"

"That's what's going around about the poor thing. She's failing fast . . . advanced MS, I've heard."

Katherine felt her heart constrict. Ach! She must hurry, must get herself emotionally ready to meet her mother. Before it was too late.

Seemingly encouraged by Katherine's comment, the waitress continued. "Here lately, there's been talk that the Bennetts are taking applications for some more hired help." The friendly server snapped her chewing gum and bent over the table to swipe at a spot of water.

Katherine noticed, too, the woman's made-up eyes and bright red lipstick and wondered if her own lashes might be in need of a touch-up. Wearing cosmetics was a new, almost frightening, experience, only because she was still learning how to apply it correctly and in the most becoming manner, but she loved every little aspect of it. Occasionally, she even went to bed without removing her face rouge and powder, for no reason other than she'd been deprived of indulging in it her entire life. That and jewelry . . . and having a beautician cut and style her auburn hair. Oh, glory!

She'd kept these secret desires hidden away all through her childhood and teen years—the longing for such things as fine jewelry, beautiful hairdos, and lovely clothing. Such *worldly* things, the Amish would say.

Glancing down at her smart silk blouse and wool skirt, Katherine smiled to herself. She'd decided days ago she had much catching up to do. And here she was . . . on the verge of stepping into Laura Bennett's elegant modern world.

Still daydreaming, she touched the thin gold chain at her throat, thrilling at its icy coolness beneath her fingertips. What would Rebecca Lapp, her adoptive mother, say if she could see her now, dressed this way? For a moment she felt a stab of conscience, a prickle of remorse over leaving the dear Amishwoman who had loved Katie . . . Katherine . . . as her own.

Then she shrugged the troublesome thought aside. No need worrying about what the People thought. Not anymore. The Plain life was behind her, all but forgotten, or so she wished. A path strewn with pain . . . truly all that was left of her past. Hadn't all of them—Mamma and Dat and the boys—accepted the harsh shunning without so much as a question, turned their backs as if she no longer existed? They'd *let* her go—as much as sent her away. . . .

"The Bennetts seem to need help out there at their place," the waitress was saying. "You interested?"

Reining in her attention to the conversation at hand, Katherine replied, "What sort of a job would it be?"

"Far as I know, a housemaid's position."

"A maid?" Katherine wasn't sure why she was interested

in hearing someone carry on so about the Bennetts, but she was. If truth be told, she felt more comfortable sitting here in this restaurant, while a mere stranger rattled on about Katherine's natural mother and the estate where she lived, than with the unsettling thought of actually heading out there and meeting Laura Bennett face-to-face.

The late afternoon sun shone boldly on her back as one customer after another left the dinerlike atmosphere. She found herself caught up in conversation with her new waitress friend and ordered some pie with ice cream for dessert, unaware of the sun's steady descent toward the fading horizon.

The cab driver knew exactly where to take her when she was ready.

In the distance, the sky had already begun to turn a rosy hue in the silent moments before dusk. Katherine was mighty pleased with herself for having stumbled onto the too-talkative waitress, who seemed privy to far more information about Dylan and Laura Bennett than she'd first let on.

Thinking she'd been downright lucky—fortunate without trying, really—Katherine congratulated herself on getting an earful, the lowdown, on the Bennetts from an outsider's viewpoint. And all this without ever having to reveal that she was related to Mrs. Bennett.

She slid down a bit in the seat behind the driver, craning her head around so she could see out the back window. Then, looking up through the glass, she spotted one star after another making its evening appearance.

How many stars had she and Daniel Fisher counted in the sky over Hickory Hollow one long-ago evening? Two hundred or more, she remembered. But with the recollection came grievous pain, and she sat up, reaching for the handle on the guitar case, determined never to let anything happen to the instrument that had brought Daniel so much joy. Forbidden, true, yet he'd kept it hidden away from the eyes of the bishop and his own father and mother, unlike her own blundering attempts to conceal her rebellion. How he'd managed all the years before his nineteenth birthday, Katherine didn't know. Yet he had, and because of the circumstances surrounding her shunning, she would never *never* part with the glorious stringed instrument. It belonged to her—now and forever.

Daniel hadn't intended to flaunt his disobedience while they were courting—she was mighty sure of that. He had just done his best to follow the music in his heart. Nothing else seemed to matter much, not even the Ordnung, or what the church members set down as rules for living.

That's just the way Dan Fisher was, all right. Stubborn and bright, all stirred up together into one fascinating, spirited human being. And on top of everything else, what a wonderful-good song maker he was!

She glanced back up at the Big Dipper, thinking that her one true love would be mighty pleased with her quest to find Laura Bennett. Pleased enough to want to write a new song, maybe, if he were alive.

Well, she'd be singing her own song about it soon enough. That was for sure and for certain.

❧   ❧   ❧

The butler thought it a grand idea to make small talk with Mrs. Bennett's newly found daughter as they ascended the staircase to the Tiffany Room, the finest guest room in the house. After all, here was the mistress's beloved child, in the flesh, come home for Christmas; no sense being stodgy about it. The girl ought to feel genuinely welcomed and accepted by *all* the members of the staff.

"Is this your first visit to Canandaigua?" he asked the

young Amishwoman with the lovely strawberry blond hair.

"Yes, it is."

"Well, I hope you'll enjoy your stay." Fulton carried her luggage into the room and set the pieces down near the large closet. "Help yourself to everything and anything. One of the maids will be up in a few minutes to check on your needs."

"Denki."

"That's Dutch, isn't it?" he asked, to make polite conversation.

"Jah, for 'thank you.' "

"Ah . . . so it is." He noted the newness of the suitcases, curious that they seemed entirely out of place with the rest of her Plain appearance. Without any further comment, he excused himself and left the room.

It was the soft appearance of the woman's hands that caused Dylan's alarm. "Amishwomen use their hands for everything from chopping wood to scrubbing floors, or so I'm told. We must do something about *these*—roughen them up a bit," he suggested, still studying them. "Everything else is going so well, I'd hate for your hands to be our undoing."

Alyson Cairns flirted playfully. "My boyfriend won't be very happy if he finds out about the older man in my life."

Dylan stepped back, surveying her Amish getup. "Your young man will have you back in good time."

Her sparkling eyes, devoid of the slightest hint of makeup, tantalized him. "So . . . when did you rush up here and hide away in the closet?" she asked.

"Never mind that."

"Lucky for you your fussy butler didn't decide to put away my suitcases." She eyed the closet door, slightly ajar. "Now, exactly when is my signature supposed to appear on the dotted line? I can't stay around here forever, you know.

It's Christmas, for heaven's sake!"

"Heaven, indeed." Dylan perched himself on a chair, scrutinizing the actress standing before him. "We have a deal . . . it wouldn't do for you to become too hasty."

"Or greedy?" Her grin was discerning.

He ignored the implication. "You're taking orders from me until every last detail is accomplished." He leaned back, bracing his hands behind his head.

"And after your wife kicks the bucket, then what?"

"You'll get your cut, don't worry," he said, pondering yesterday's brief conversation with Laura's physician. The doctor had appeared highly concerned. And, yes, he'd assured Dylan that everything possible was being done to make her comfortable as the illness ran its deadly course. "Everything *humanly* possible," the doctor had reiterated. "There's always the hope of divine intervention, certainly, which is precisely what we must believe for if your wife is to survive the holidays."

Just the information he needed. Laura was not long for this world. Most likely wouldn't last past New Year's. Without question, her soul would fly straight to heaven, on angel wings. The woman was a saint. No need to concern himself over the spiritual side of things—if it turned out he was wrong and there really *was* a God. That is, unless He *did* intervene, and Laura didn't depart this life on schedule. . . .

He watched as the young woman knelt to open her suitcase. "I need a break from these Amish duds, Mr. Bennett." She eyed him meaningfully. "But I *don't* need an audience . . . if you know what I mean."

Alyson was surprised when he left with only a mild protest. She'd expected worse.

And now that he was out of the room, she wished she hadn't been in such a hurry to get rid of him. She'd needed more time to get acquainted with the traditions of the Old

Order Amish. The initial coaching session had been nearly overwhelming. All those rules and regulations! How did people put up with it? She was to dress, speak, and behave as a young Plain woman, yet she'd had only a "crash course" in the little time since the contact with the talent agent hired by Mr. Bennett.

Still, the money—or the promise of it—was incentive enough. Not to mention the challenge of the role. She'd give the performance of her life, Plain or not!

CHAPTER NINE

❖　❖　❖

Katherine paid the cab driver and turned around, facing the stately mansion. Its stone exterior was embroidered with sections of thick ivy, multitudes of vines, dried up in the dead of winter, ascending lifeless, yet aligned, to meet the moonbeams.

From her spot on the pavement, she took in the massive outline—adorned with numerous chimneys—now ominous and dark against a moonlit sky.

Lingering there, she felt as if her eyes and her very soul were being drawn to the place. Years of forbidden cravings culminated in one sweep of the eye. "Himmel! What a place!" she whispered.

She could scarcely wait to explore its elegance. First, though, she must get inside. To pass over its threshold . . . what glory!

Clutching her suitcase in one hand and the guitar case in the other, Katherine made her way across the circular driveway, guided by lantern-shaped lights near the entrance. In a moment of near panic, she hesitated at the portal. *What am I doing here?* she wondered. *How will I ever fit in with these rich folk?*

In that instant, her life seemed to pass before her—from

earliest recollections as a young girl growing up Amish on a dairy farm in a remote area of Lancaster County, to the present and her chic, modern look.

I do hope Laura Bennett will approve of me, Katherine thought, still uncertain. More than anything, she didn't want to come across as a country hick—had practiced long and hard to overcome any such traits of speech and manner, in fact.

Squaring her shoulders, she gave her hair a light toss. A dog howled in the distance, sending a shiver down her spine. She reached for the brass knocker and held her breath at the sound of footsteps.

The door opened, and a tall man, looking for all the world like something out of a store catalogue, stood straight and still, eyeing her curiously. "Good evening," he said, bending stiffly as if he were afraid he might break.

"Hullo," she replied. "I wonder if I might be able to see Mrs. Bennett."

The man stared at her, yet it was not a rude, cold stare. More of an inquisitive look, really. "Whom may I say is calling?"

She was about to speak up, to tell him, without boasting, that she had traveled many miles to see her mother for the first time, her natural mother—Laura Mayfield-Bennett. But her thoughts, yes, even the breath she'd drawn ever so deeply, giving her the pluck to go through with it—all of that—was halted when a round-faced woman wearing a short white apron and a big smile appeared beside him at the door.

"Fulton, show the girl in . . . bring her in out of the cold. She's come about the job, of course . . . and must think she's going to get it, too, for she's brought along all her worldly possessions, it seems."

Whether she was mumbling to herself or to the man she'd called Fulton, Katherine couldn't be sure. But she took note of the glance directed at her guitar case and clung to it all the more. But from the way the perky little woman addressed the towering fellow, still standing in the doorway—just the way she worked him over with her eyes—led Katherine to believe they were husband and wife.

The maid, who, by now, had introduced herself as Rosie Taylor, bustled her into the house, helping her with her suitcase and guitar, then promptly handed them over to Fulton.

Katherine had to chuckle silently at the way things had worked out just now. Here she was, inside her mother's house, without ever having said who she was or on what business she had come.

For a fleeting moment she thought perhaps the situation had been providential—something she had been taught to believe in from her earliest years as a little Plain girl.

No time for reminiscing, though; Rosie and Fulton whisked her off to the kitchen, where a chair was pulled out for her beside a long table. A single-page application lay in front of her, but only after she'd removed her coat and gloves did Katherine reach into her purse to locate her ballpoint pen.

"May we have a look at your referral?" Rosie began when she and Fulton were both seated opposite Katherine.

"I don't have anything like that with me." Katherine was beginning to feel uneasy. Maybe her thoughts of Providence had come too soon.

"Aren't you the woman sent over by the agency?" Fulton asked at once.

"Agency?"

"We *always* hire from the employment agency," Rosie explained. "They screen each of our applicants beforehand."

"Oh . . ." Katherine looked over at her tattered suitcase and the guitar case propped up against the butler's pantry. *Now what?* she wondered. Should she tell them she had no desire to be a maid anyway—that her one and only hope was to meet her birth mother?

"We must stick by our policy, you understand," Fulton was saying. "You'll have to go downtown and be interviewed."

"Well, I really hadn't planned to . . ." She paused, measuring her words. Was now a good time to reveal her identity?

Fulton cocked his head, and Katherine felt as if the man were studying her. "We're all quite busy at the moment—unexpected company, and at this time of year." He sighed. "It would be best for you to contact the agency," he repeated as he stood to his feet. "Now, if you'll excuse me, I'll see you out."

"Oh . . . sir, can't you *please* let my . . . that is, Mrs. Bennett . . . know I'm here? Won't you do that?" She felt as if she were begging.

"Under no circumstances must the mistress be disturbed. This is a very special occasion," Fulton went on to explain. "Mrs. Bennett has just received her only child—a daughter she'd given up as an infant. They're dining together at the moment."

"Her . . . *daughter?*" Katherine's words caught in her throat.

"Yes, indeed," Rosie spoke up briskly. "And the timing couldn't have been better, with Christmas just around the corner."

The timing is dreadful, Katherine thought, standing and reaching for her coat. Had she gotten the wrong phone number clear back at the Millers' place? Was this some bad-awful mistake?

"You look pale," commented Fulton. "Are you feeling quite well?"

"Fine . . . I'm fine," she said, biting her dishonest tongue. *How can this be?* she wondered, thinking back to

Rebecca's conversation with her at the farmhouse. The Wise Woman, too, had spoken of Laura Mayfield-Bennett . . . hadn't she? Katherine's thoughts lingered on Ella Mae who had certainly seen the handwritten name on the fancy envelope. Hadn't she also vouched for the fact that the wealthy Mrs. Bennett had been out searching for her daughter in and around the Lancaster area?

Rosie excused herself and hurried out of the room. Fulton, whom Katherine had decided must be the butler or someone important, seemed mighty restless, as if he were needed elsewhere in the house. Anywhere but here, apparently. After all, she had been a waste of his time—an applicant without the proper referrals.

"I'll find my way out," she offered, feeling disheartened by the way things were turning out. "But I'll be needing a cab."

"Oh yes, certainly." He located a telephone book, then apologized for any inconvenience, and sped down the hallway.

While she was preparing to use the phone, two young men flew past her into the kitchen. "We could use a bit of help," the older man said, opening one of the several refrigerators and motioning to her. "I'm Selig, assistant cook. And you are?"

"Katherine," she said quickly, purposely leaving off her last name.

He shook her hand but seemed preoccupied. "A pleasure . . . Katherine. Good to have you aboard."

She was opening her mouth to explain, but when he insisted she take off her coat and lend a hand by slicing and warming a tray of bread, Katherine did as she was told.

"Wonderful," Selig said. "You've come in the nick of time."

"But—"

"We're obviously a bit shorthanded due to the holidays,"

the younger man explained while placing crystal goblets on a wide slate counter nearby. He stopped briefly to extend his hand. "Garrett Smith, head steward . . . at your service."

"Hullo," she replied. They'd mistaken her for the new housemaid, for sure and for certain!

Grinning, Garrett resumed his work. "I suppose you've heard—the daughter of the house has come home for the holidays."

His words pierced her soul. How many times must she hear this miserable news? What if she were to barge right into the mistress's cozy supper . . . to lay eyes on Laura May-field-Bennett for herself? What about that?

These were reckless thoughts, for sure. But how was she supposed to feel, for goodness' sake—hearing that someone had taken her place?

Determined to keep her helpless, angry feelings in check, Katherine followed instructions, cutting the loaf of bread on a large cutting block with an electric knife. After that, she placed the ample slices in the warming oven. Good thing she'd had opportunity to use such modern contraptions while cooking in Lydia Miller's kitchen. She tried not to think of the hours of time she might've saved had she grown up with electricity, for bread making had forever been a daily chore in the Lapp home.

When there was a lull between Selig's and Garrett's prattle, Katherine spoke up. "The mistress's daughter . . . uh, have either of you seen her?"

"Ah . . . she's pretty enough, I suppose," offered Selig. "Plain, really, though I presume that's the Amish way."

"She's *Amish*?"

"Quite," Garrett replied, going about the business of pouring beverages in the ornate gold-trimmed goblets.

"So . . . she dresses Plain, then?" Katherine ventured, her heart in her throat.

"Totally," Selig said with a grin on his face. "Somewhat

of an eccentric style, I must admit. Especially with that formal little head covering of hers."

The mere mention of the cap took Katherine back to the days leading up to the shunning. The final battles—whether or not to wear her covering in her adoptive father's house— had been such a sore spot. As it turned out, he had required her to wear it, against her wishes, really, during one of those last days at home.

At Garrett's chuckle, Katherine's thoughts flew to the job at hand. "Mrs. Bennett's daughter could use a sound dose of makeup, if you ask me."

Katherine felt her cheeks warm with his brief, yet ardent scrutiny.

"I do believe *you* could teach Katie a thing or two," he observed.

Katherine froze, nearly dropped the platter of warmed bread. "Did you say 'Katie'?"

Glancing up, the head steward nodded. "Interesting name, isn't it? Her last name's Lapp."

"Sounds Dutch to me," Selig offered before dashing off just as several housemaids darted past with trays of dishes, probably the main course plates and silverware.

"What do *you* think?" Garrett asked. "Does the daughter's adopted name sound Dutch to you?"

Her mind whirled. Should she tell this young man why she'd come? Tell him that her given name—her former name was also Lapp? That she'd abandoned the name Katie because of her need to be Katherine . . . wholly Laura Bennett's daughter?

Ach! How had things got so *ghuddelt*—tangled—so quickly? And how was it that Laura Bennett's daughter should have the same adoptive name as Katherine's own?

"Well, what do you say? Dutch or not?" Garrett persisted.

"It's Swiss, most likely . . . one of the more common

names for Pennsylvania Amish," she blurted.

Raising his thick eyebrows, Garrett appeared amused. "And how do *you* know about Amish names?"

"Oh, if you listen good, you pick things up." She'd almost said "gut" and was mighty glad she hadn't. The last thing the head steward should know was that there were, in all truth, *two* women claiming the name of Katie Lapp, under the Bennetts' regal roof.

Part II

It is not the criminal things which are hardest to confess,
but the ridiculous and shameful.

Jean-Jacques Rousseau

CHAPTER TEN

Most of the lights were on inside the New Jersey bungalow when Daniel Fisher arrived home. Even the matching floor lamps on either side of the sofa remained lit.

Looking around as he stepped into his plant-filled vestibule, he wondered if *every* light in the place had been left on. *Wonderful*, he thought. The new cleaning woman had followed his instructions to a tee.

Whether working late on blueprints at home or arriving there after-hours from his drafting office, Dan insisted on being surrounded by light. Too many years of coming home to a dark farmhouse, maybe.

It wasn't only that he required light for his detailed renderings. No, it was much more than that. He'd discovered something extremely reassuring about rooms being lit up from early evening on. Because it was at night, when the sun toppled over the horizon, that he missed Pennsylvania—*home*—most. Missed his parents and brothers, and Annie his only sister, and most of all . . . Katie Lapp. His sweetheart girl would be worried sick if she knew he was living out in the modern English world, far away from Amish society. But she, along with his family and friends, believed he was dead. Drowned at sea.

They deserved the truth. He'd decided this on more than one occasion through the years, yet had never been able to come up with a plan. At least one that would not cause severe complications as a result of his "resurrection from the dead."

To mark the Christmas season, he'd begun to grow a beard. Though facial hair was indicative of a married Amishman, he felt it might ease his way back into Hickory Hollow when the time came. Stubble now, but the sure promise of a full beard as bushy as his father's, all in preparation for a possible meeting with the man he'd wronged.

He emptied his pockets of loose change and his keys, then reaching for the hall switch, he marveled once again at the ability to disseminate light at will. With the mere flick of a finger!

For five satisfying years, he had enjoyed such benefits yet hadn't consciously taken modern technology for granted. Nor did he wish to, though at times he agonized over the guilt of it. The deeply ingrained taboos, church rules, and regulations. . . .

He had not been raised with electricity or fast cars. His father's father and three generations of men—great-grandfathers before him—had lived their lives according to the Old Ways, *das Alt Gebrauch.*

Yet his emotions often became jumbled when he thought of his father . . . the prospects Jacob Fisher had had for him. In an Amish household, the youngest son was expected to take over the family farm at the appropriate age. Daniel had chosen another path for his life.

Surprisingly, in spite of all that had transpired between them—the passionate arguments over doctrine and such—he did not foster bad feelings toward his strict father. He had forgiven Jacob Fisher years ago.

Now the time was ripe to offer his father the same opportunity. And to speak the truth of what had happened on that fateful day in Atlantic City.

Dan glanced around his comfortable rental home, sparkling with holiday lights and trim. Too many Decembers had come and gone since his "accident." Home fires burned brightest at Christmas. As for Katie, she was still to him the dearest girl in all the world.

His thoughts flew back to their first Sunday night Singing together. Back when Katie had just turned sixteen. . . .

The sky was filled with a thousand stars that early June evening. As if someone had sprinkled out a silo full of them all over the heavens. Daniel, eighteen, was hoping—without letting on to anybody—that Katie Lapp just might be coming to Singing. Her first ever. And if she did, she'd be riding over with Benjamin, her eighteen year old brother, in his open buggy, the way all the older teen girls in Hickory Hollow showed up for such things.

He remembered the *Neilicht*—new moon—shining its crescent-shaped light down on the barn, 'cause he kept peering out through the loose, rickety boards every chance he could, looking for her. Looking and waiting . . . wishing there'd been a big yellow full moon high in the sky to spotlight beautiful red-haired Katie.

Ach, the Mennonites had yard lights—made perfect sense to him. 'Cept he was Amish and none of that kind of thinking was bound to do a body good. Electricity was wicked, in any way, shape, or form.

Ach, Katie, he thought. *Where are ya? What's takin' your brother so long?*

When would Ben ever figure out how to gallop that young driving horse of his? Puh, he'd best be taking some lessons, and from somebody who knew how to get a pretty girl to Singing on time.

Pacing back and forth, trying to pretend nothing special was on his mind—least not one certain girl—he picked up a long piece of straw, stuck it in his mouth, and sauntered over to yak at Chicken Joe. Now, here was a boy who never seemed to have a speck of trouble finding a girl to talk to or take home after Singings.

"What's got ya frettin'?" Chicken Joe asked.

"Didn't say nothin' was."

"Mighty restless you are."

"Not any more than anyone else around here." He glanced over his shoulder at the young men milling around, probably fifty or more of them. All wearing wide-brimmed straw hats, which they never took off, not even in warm weather.

Chicken Joe grinned, showing his upper gums. "She'll be comin' soon. You know she will."

Daniel bristled at the comment. Chicken Joe had no right to say anything like that. To pop out with something so bold. The fellow was brazen and even worse, a flirt. Biggest one around.

For himself, Dan had decided long back, about the time he was turning fourteen, that he wouldn't so much as wink at a girl lest he liked her enough to kiss her. 'Course, he wouldn't go doing any such a thing for a long time from now. Still, he knew exactly how he planned on treating Samuel Lapp's daughter. Treat her right fine, like the vivacious beauty she was.

Standing next to a hay baler, he and Chicken Joe talked up a storm for the time being. They'd worn their "for good" clothes, all spiffed up with tan suspenders, white shirts, and black trousers. Only one reason for it—two, really. First off, 'twas their Old Order custom. That, and dressing nice made the girls look twice.

A group of boys scuffled around in the haymow overhead, stirring up dust. Dan figured they'd had a drink or two before coming. Bishop John would frown mighty hard if he got wind of it, because Hickory Hollow's bishop was stricter than most, no getting around it.

When Katie did finally arrive, he stood back, waiting a bit impatiently for the Singing to get underway. Then, sitting on a hay bale in the farthest corner of the barn, he watched Benjamin's sister without ever being noticed. Watched her good, as discreetly as possible, of course.

A group of young married couples sat in one section of the barn. They got the songs going, starting out with one of Dan's least favorite, a slow hymn from the *Lieder Sammlungen*, a small songbook for such an occasion. Thing was, the hymn lasted a good eleven minutes, and he hoped it would be the only one like that. Jah, he liked attending Singings, and not just to see all the pretty girls in his church district and SummerHill's; he enjoyed the music. More than most. Raising his voice in unison with a hundred other Amish young people was good enough reason to come any day, to his way of thinking.

Still, Katie was the main reason tonight. Sitting over there under the hayloft with the other unmarried girls, smack-dab next to one of her cousins, why, Katie looked almost angel-like. 'Course, he'd never so much as laid eyes on a heavenly creature, but that didn't mean she didn't look like one all the same, wearing her good purple dress, same color as the whole row of girls with her.

On second thought, maybe it was the color of her hair that made Katie special. He hadn't quite figured out just exactly what attracted him to her, really. It was simple to see that her hair was as close to the rust red of a robin's breast as hair could be, even though he'd overheard her telling Elam, her oldest brother, that it was *not* red, it was *auburn*. And she'd been mighty firm about it, too. The girl had a powerful-strong personality, he'd noticed. But that didn't stop him from liking her. Maybe even made him fancy her more.

Daniel chewed on his straw and grinned to himself. Any

girl spunky enough to voice an opinion about her own hair color, now, that was the type of girl he'd want to invite for a ride in his new rig. Reason being, there'd be plenty to talk about with a young woman like Katie Lapp.

And talk they did. That warm summer night, with honeysuckle wafting through the air, that night of Katie's first Singing, he took her home. Many more buggy rides were to follow. Occasionally, another boy might beat him to it, talking to Katie first, asking her to ride home. But it didn't take long, maybe two months or so, for him to latch on to her. 'Cause once he took notice of her head bobbing to the rhythm of the songs, her brown eyes bright with the melodies, from then on, he knew she was the one he wanted for his girl. And someday, his wife.

Music made her smile, same as him. Which was saying a lot, 'cause when Katie smiled, the whole world lit right up. Like a hundred and one fireflies. And oh, so much more.

❖   ❖   ❖

Feeling right at home in the kitchen, Katherine accomplished a great deal while the butler and his sidekick were absent. The trappings of a place like this spurred her creative abilities and, with no coaxing from anyone, her hands had found plenty to do. She'd put together several pies—a coconut custard pie, for one—and had them tucked away in the oven when Fulton Taylor reappeared.

"Goodness me, are you still here?"

She hoped he wouldn't force her out; she'd been right good help, if she did say so herself—especially with whatever strange things were going on in the Bennetts' lavish dining room. "Mrs. Bennett's daughter . . . uh, Katie, I believe . . . well, I just wondered if she might be wanting a taste of a real Amish dessert. Something she might be accustomed to back home, you know," she explained her secret conniving.

"Amish, indeed." The butler's smile didn't quite manage to reach his eyes. "What recipe did you follow?"

Katherine tapped her temple. "Oh, one I seemed to have remembered from childhood." Now, why had she gone and said a thing like that? Next he'd be asking where she'd grown up, where she'd come from.

But the butler surprised her by saying instead, "What an excellent idea!" His eyes softened as he spoke. "How very kind of you."

"Thank you," she said, meaning it. Hopefully, he had seen how proficient she was, how completely at ease she was in the kitchen. Now maybe he'd agree to hire her.

Rosie swept into the room just then, wearing an equally astonished expression on her face as she sniffed the air. "What *is* that glorious aroma?" Switching on the oven light, she peered through the glass door. "Quite amazing . . . the pies look and smell absolutely scrumptious."

Fulton spoke up. "And authentically Amish."

Katherine thought there was a smidgen of satisfaction in the butler's voice. She held her breath, hoping against hope that she might be allowed to stay on, might be hired as the housemaid they seemed to need so desperately.

Neither one of them inquired as to how she had come upon the pie recipes. However, they *did* say they were willing to accept the extraordinary desserts as a token substitute for the "proper" agency referral.

Grinning, Rosie opened a drawer nearby and handed her a frilly apron, headpiece, and hair netting. "You'll wear these at all times . . . while on duty, of course. It works best to wind your hair up in a knot under the netting." Then explaining that her husband, Fulton Taylor, was the final authority on employees, Rosie suggested she fill out an application "first thing in the morning, when things have settled down a bit."

"Thank you," Katherine said. "I'll try not to disappoint you."

"Now"—Rosie glanced over her shoulder—"while your pies are baking, I'll show you to your room."

Katherine thought about the song she was sure Daniel would want to be writing about now. Up in the heavenlies . . . Clutching her suitcase and guitar, she followed Rosie Taylor to the long, beautiful staircase.

◈   ◈   ◈

Daniel pulled out a piece of linen stationery from his desk drawer and pondered what he might say. Annie would be shocked to receive a letter from her dead brother, no doubt. He feared the poor girl would collapse.

He would state clearly that she keep the letter confidential, not show it to Dat or Mamma. There was much to be arranged before they should be told their son was alive.

Tuesday, December 23

Dearest Annie,
  For several years now, I have wanted to write a letter to you.

He reread the first line and decided it didn't suit him. Shouldn't he warn his sister to sit down? Tell her that what she was about to read might startle her?

Annie had always been a sensitive sort of girl, so perhaps it was a mistake to approach her this way. The wheels began to turn, and he realized he ought to determine, at least, if she was still living at home. Whether or not she was married. He would have to investigate. Surely someone would know the status of his only sister.

And while he was at it, he might as well inquire about Katie Lapp. Darling Katie . . . the girl he'd loved so long . . . now a woman.

Rethinking the notion, he realized anew that he couldn't bear to have word of Katie. Was it possible she had remained single all these years?

Better off not knowing, he decided.

With a vengeance, he crumpled the beginnings of his letter and pitched it in the wastebasket next to the desk.

❖   ❖   ❖

As rooms go, the one directly above the kitchen was snug and cozy—elegant, too. A timid flame burned in the white-tiled fireplace behind an ornate Victorian fire screen.

"You may hear a bit of kitchen noise occasionally," Rosie commented, "but not much more than you'll be making down there yourself. Which is to say, the live-in staff are up and about early, at the crack of dawn, so to speak."

Katherine nodded. "I don't mind early rising. I'm used to it." She realized she'd done it again—opened herself up for questioning. But good-natured Rosie only smiled back.

Katherine was informed of her duties and told that the schedule for the day of Christmas Eve and the rest of the week would be set in the morning. "Fulton will slip the docket under your door before you're up and about. He'll also give you final word on employment here—after he reviews your application."

"Thank you again for giving me this chance to prove myself." Katherine wanted to embrace the dear woman, whose hair had begun to gray at the temples. Embrace her and tell her how very grateful she was. But she kept her composure, as well as a respectable distance.

It was then that Rosie's eyes caught hers, and for a moment the two women were silent. Awkward seconds passed before Rosie whispered, "I do believe you're a godsend, Katherine."

"I'll try to be useful."

Rosie continued to probe deeply with her clear brown eyes. "I'm counting on it." And then she was gone.

Relieved beyond words, Katherine stood at the foot of the black iron bed, observing layers of homespun linens and colorful quilts neatly placed over the sheets and bedskirt. Several handmade damask-napkin pillows were scattered over large, plump shams. She ran her fingers over the gilding highlights on the footboard.

"I'm a princess in a castle!" She spun about, hugging her arms to herself.

Aware of a delicate scent in the room, she instinctively went to the refinished antique pine dresser. Opening the top drawer, she spied two sachets of potpourri—one in each of the front corners.

"It's lavender!" She held one of the tiny cloth bags against her face, letting it linger there, recalling the very first sachet she'd made as a girl, for her own dresser drawer back home.

Then spurred on by the discovery, she opened each of the four drawers in the old dresser, removing two sachets at a time. Carefully, she spread the tiny potpourri pillows across the wide bed, remembering that as a girl, she had often lined up her faceless Amish dolls this way, humming or singing as she played.

Scurrying across the room to the highboy on the opposite wall, she found, to her heart's delight, seven additional drawers' worth of the dainty, lovely things. Caught up in the thrill, she scattered them on the dresser top, one by one—touching, smelling, examining each little treasure. They were all different in color yet similar in fragrance, and she decided after a closer inspection that the hands which had lovingly created her satin infant gown nearly twenty-three years ago surely had sewn these sachets.

Taking a backward step, she felt for the edge of the bed and sat down—Katherine Mayfield, the brand-new maid in the Bennetts' wonderful-good mansion. Caressing one of the little lavender cushions, she allowed herself to recline fully and stare at the ceiling, at the decorative molding high above her head. How far she'd come for this moment. And how far she had yet to go. . . .

Finding the sachets—a beautiful link between herself and her natural mother—helped ease her apprehensions somewhat. Had she stumbled onto something, something better than ever? If, of course, the mistress of the house *was* her true mamma. . . .

Ach, she had scarcely anything to go on, nothing tangible, really. Even the sweet-smelling little pillows weren't proof enough; lots of folk used such pretty things to freshen up their closets and drawers.

Pressing the miniature bag to her face, she wondered if she had in all actuality come to the right place. She continued to wonder, stewing over past events as she lay there, eyes boring a hole in the brass chandelier centered in the ceiling.

One thing she knew to be true. Only one. Laura Mayfield-Bennett had once come to Hickory Hollow looking for a young woman named Katherine. Yet how many Amish communities were there in Pennsylvania? Hundreds? Maybe more?

How had Laura known *where* to look in Lancaster County? She hadn't, of course.

Jumping to conclusions, Katherine allowed a bothersome thought to make a home in her head. *What if* I'm *the impostor? What if everything up till this moment has been nothing more than a dream?*

Urgency swept her inside out, and she longed to find out who the mistress of the house was, really. She must know, too, once and for all, if *she* or the woman named Katie Lapp belonged to Laura Bennett.

Nothing . . . *nothing* must keep her from finding the truth.

CHAPTER ELEVEN

Katherine hoped her guitar playing wouldn't disturb anyone. She'd waited till the first hint of light had pierced the darkness, had gone into the private bath, drawn the tub water, and closed the door. Sitting on a petite boudoir chair beside the fanciest dressing table she'd ever seen, she strummed softly.

The tune she created was not joyful, not the kind of melody she'd imagined herself humming in these early-morning moments spent within the walls of the Bennett estate. The morning of Christmas Eve!

A melancholy refrain poured forth, capturing the emotions of this her first daybreak in the beautiful house. She entertained the same old nagging doubts, asking herself the question: Could there be someone else named Katie Lapp—another Amish girl about her age? But even as she pondered it, she hoped . . . and as Cousin Lydia would say, she *prayed* it wasn't true.

Laura had gone to Pennsylvania, had given a letter to the Wise Woman, Ella Mae Zook, who, in turn, had passed it along to Katherine's Amish mamma. Rebecca had been the one to tell her of Laura's terminal illness, that Mrs. Bennett was eager—before she died—to see her flesh-and-blood daughter face-to-face.

The notion occurred to Katherine that she must inquire as to Laura's health. Why hadn't she thought of it before? But, of course, what with all the commotion last night— being mistaken almost immediately for an applicant sent from an employment agency—there hadn't been a minute to ask.

Besides, Fulton and Rosie had seemed in a dither at the time, tending to their own personal duties and trying to determine, no doubt, why a woman carrying a guitar and a suitcase had appeared on their doorstep without going through the proper channels.

Should she just assume Laura was her natural mother? Should she also suppose that another young woman was posing as Katherine while calling herself Katie?

And why would someone go to the bother of dressing Plain, playing a role that belonged to another? Who would want to be Katie, an Amishwoman, when *Katherine Mayfield* was the name sewn into Laura's infant daughter's dress?

Baffled, she put away the guitar, eager to bathe and dress for the day. Eager for some straight answers.

❖   ❖   ❖

Laura dozed, satisfied that the daughter she had so longed to see again was alive. Not only alive but right here under her roof, consenting to remain through Christmas.

In the haze between sleep and wakefulness, the slightest twinge of disappointment pricked her. She recognized the struggle between her mind and her heart. The dream—what it would be like to finally meet her dear girl, imagining how she would look, what they would say to each other—all of it—had been altered in a single day.

She felt somewhat let down but assumed this experience was normal. After all, hadn't they enjoyed a delightful supper hour together? And the surprise dessert—something the newly hired help had created for the occasion. How delicious it had been!

The taste of the Amish dish still lingered in her memory as did the look of pleasure on Katie's face when the pie was served. Laura would never forget this evening with her beloved daughter, who was so quaintly dressed in her adorable Amish attire.

Yet it was the oddest thing—the young woman's Pennsylvania Dutch accent. If Laura was not mistaken, it sounded far different from the dialect of the Plain folk she'd met in Lancaster last month.

Something else troubled her, something she wished she could grasp more fully—the fact that Katie and she were far from bonding, even after having spent hours together. They simply had not clicked upon first meeting, as she had always believed they would.

She forced away the vague, elusive inclination, praying that her instincts were off. Perhaps the heavy medication was at fault. Yes. That was probably all there was to it.

Laura lay quite still, listening. Was it her imagination, or was someone playing a guitar in the predawn hours? She strained to hear more clearly, thankful that her ears were functioning better than her eyes.

Faintly, she was able to make out the sounds of a human voice—a woman's voice. Was it her daughter? Was *Katie* singing?

But, no, the sound was coming from the other wing of the house. The room over the kitchen. The domestic quarters upstairs. . . .

The haunting music surrounded her subconscious memory with distant recollections of a mother's soprano voice, clear and true.

How she missed the shrewd yet compassionate lady. And how wise she had been. Charlotte Mayfield had repeatedly warned her about Dylan Bennett, cautioned her while they were dating. "Your father, bless his soul, will turn over in his grave if you end up with that man," she'd said.

But young Laura, caught up in the romance, had argued repeatedly for his sweet, endearing ways. "Dylan is so handsome . . . so wonderful. He won't hurt me, Mother, not the way Katherine's father did. Dylan's a gentleman."

So she'd waited until her mother died, marrying Dylan Bennett against the woman's wishes. As for Laura's father, he'd adored her; she'd always known that. Had her parents lived to see this day, they would have thrown a lavish feast. Would have invited as many guests as the mansion could accommodate.

Instead, Laura felt isolated, alone with her joy. She experienced a pulsing void, wishing her parents were here to dote on Katie, to open arms wide to their only grandchild.

Dylan's hovering annoyed her. Why had he allowed her so little time alone with Katie? Perhaps that was the very reason she and her precious child had not been able to connect, neither emotionally nor spiritually.

At any other time, she wouldn't have reacted so negatively to Dylan's constant attention, but time was running out! Too, they were no longer the dearest of friends . . . or lovers. Hadn't been in years. Not in any sense of the word. Yet Dylan was pretending they were a couple. A loving husband and wife, welcoming home a cherished child.

She considered the strange situation. Why would he behave in such a way? Was it because he had been instrumental in locating Katie? Because he felt responsible for the reunion going well?

Feeling convicted, she prayed for a sweeter spirit. What if her husband was softening toward her? Attempting to make amends for his past misdeeds in these last days of her life?

Love can change a person, she'd told her mother one night when Charlotte had begun criticizing her fiancé. But the very things that had concerned her mother during the courtship had grown into insurmountable marital problems. Dylan had *not* changed for the better. On the contrary, he had become even more controlling.

Now, as she lay in her gleaming brass bed, the trappings of wealth and loveliness about her, she remembered Dylan's countenance as he observed her with Katie yesterday. Was it genuine compassion she had seen in his eyes? Or something else?

Anger welled up. This was the same man who'd tricked her into thinking she was barren, purposely denying her the children she'd always longed for. Repeatedly swindled her out of money, misrepresenting her separate accounts, forging her name on legal documents.

In spite of her husband's wicked ways, she had never considered turning him in to the authorities, or divorcing him, although the latter had crossed her mind on occasion.

"Love him to Jesus," Rosie had once said in a fervent prayer. Yes, she'd offered herself up for Dylan, had travailed in prayer on behalf of his salvation. Yet how difficult it was to extend unconditional love and acceptance to a man who'd so wronged her. To a man whose very life seemed driven by domination and deceit.

Had she not known the love of the heavenly Father, the grace of His Son, she wondered how she might've responded to Dylan all these years.

In sickness and in health. . . .

She had made her marriage vow to only one man. She intended to keep it.

Thankfully, the legal problems had been solved by her recent visit to Mr. Cranston's office. After much prayer, she felt justified in changing her will. Not out of revenge or hatred—it was simply expedient that she do so. This way she could die peacefully, knowing the estate would remain in the family.

Breathing deeply, she allowed the guitar music to soothe her as it came trickling down through ceiling vents, carrying her back to dreamland.

❖ ❖ ❖

Finished with her bath, Katherine brushed her hair, gazing into the large vanity mirror on the dressing table. She must wind her hair back up into a bun; it was required. Ach, the irony of having to look so plain again, having to wrap a netting around her beautiful curls while living in this fancy place. She touched her hair lovingly before proceeding with the bun and maid's cap.

She smiled cautiously for the gilded mirror, wondering what might be taking place back in Hickory Hollow today, what with Christmas Eve just hours away.

Were Dat, Eli, and Benjamin out gathering up fresh branches and pinecones for the house? Would Mam be decorating the wide windowsills in the front room with the greenery? And the work frolics . . . were the women congregating first at one house then another for hours of cookie baking?

She sighed, knowing this kind of contemplation could only cause her pain. Still, she couldn't resist the memory of Mary Stoltzfus. How was *she* getting along?

Katherine worried that her friend might think it rude

for her to have ignored the thoughtful Christmas greeting.
But she knew better. Of all people, Mary most assuredly
would understand. After all, there was a powerful-good
reason for not sending a letter back to Hickory Hollow.
The fear of causing trouble for Mary, on account of the
shunning.

Forcing her thoughts back to the usual cheery atmosphere of a Lapp family Christmas, Katherine recalled
playful, happy chatter, the brisk ice-skating parties on the
pond out behind the house, and the *Grischkindlin* exchange with Samuel and Rebecca Lapp. Other folks
brought gifts, too.

Her mind whirled and in that split second, a crush of
emotions sent her spirits spiraling downward. But not for
long. Wasn't she right where she wanted to be? Wasn't she
glad to be finding out who Katherine Mayfield really was?
Who she might've become had she grown up here in this
elegant world?

No, nothing in Hickory Hollow could call her back now,
nothing at all. The People had rejected and betrayed her.
Her *own* family, the only family she'd known.

"Today I'm going to meet my real mamma," she whispered to the oval mirror, hoping it would be so.

Turning sideways, she surveyed her fancy apron and
maid's cap. Done up under the netting, her beautiful new
hairdo didn't show at all. Not a bit. Sighing, she hurried to
make her bed and straighten up the room.

Just as she was preparing to head downstairs, the schedule for the domestic staff sailed under her door as Rosie had
promised. Katherine gave the page a once-over and determined that the entire staff was obviously shorthanded over
the next ten days, during the holidays. What luck! Or was
it that heaven was truly smiling on her?

When it came time to serve either tea or the main
meals of the day, she would offer her assistance in hopes

of discovering the absolute truth about Laura Bennett's health.

❖   ❖   ❖

Breakfast was over at the Samuel Lapp home. Rebecca quietly cleared the dishes, rinsed, washed, and dried them, and listened in on her husband's conversation with Eli and Benjamin.

"What Jake Stoltzfus does is his business," Samuel told his sons.

"But what about gut land? Soon there ain't gonna be enough to go around here in Hickory Hollow," Benjamin pointed out.

Eli snorted. "What are you worried for? You'll never have to be thinkin' about such things as that."

Rebecca turned sharply to peer at her son's face. Eli, jealous? What an ugly thing it was, she fretted to herself. She was about to reprimand her twenty-six-year-old son but hadn't the chance, for Samuel spoke up first.

"Both you boys'll be getting married, probably, come next November. You'll be needing a place to farm with your wives and later to raise your families."

Eli and Ben were silent. Rebecca wasn't surprised, for it was their custom to keep all engagements secret till the second Sunday after fall communion, when the bishop announced those couples who planned to be married. The special event was called the "publishing" of couples. For her sons, the time was a good nine months off. Still, she knew why it was that Samuel was pushing them for answers.

"I'd hate to think of you headin' off to Indiana just 'cause Jake's thinkin' of going," Samuel continued.

Why were they talking like this? she wondered. Benjamin needn't worry about not having enough land to farm.

The youngest son usually ended up with his father's main house and the acres surrounding it. And Eli . . . surely Eli wouldn't wanna up and leave.

"Can't go divvying up the land, Dat." Eli shook his head. "Ben's gonna need every inch of your forty-five acres to keep things going here for you and Mam."

Rebecca noticed Samuel's concerned look. Her husband didn't say what she was sure he was thinking. That they'd be moving over to the *Dawdi Haus* come next fall, so Ben and his bride could settle in here at the main house. Time to be thinking about slowing down some, anyways. Especially since the strangest things had started going on with her here lately.

Samuel knew all about it. He'd caught her playing with the satin baby gown more than once—touching it and talking to it like a precious little infant was a-lying in her arms.

Made her go nearly berserk at times, teetering back and forth between thinking that the little dress—hidden away for her eyes only—was a soothing balm for her soul and, other times, wondering if it hadn't come straight from the pits of hell.

She dried her hands and left the room to go find it. Growing more and more dear to her every day that passed.

Her Katie . . . gone. Darling baby daughter of her life . . . shunned. Living out somewhere in the modern world, looking for someone else to call Mamma.

Well, it was more than she could bear. Missing Katie and longing for her company, her sweet voice, seeing her grow up Amish and then losing her near overnight to a complete stranger had been too awful much.

Once in the bedroom, Rebecca located the tiny satin garment. Inside her pillowcase. She'd been keeping it hidden there, away from Samuel's eyes.

She headed for her daughter's old room just down the

hall, where nothing ever changed. Things stayed exactly the same in Katie's bedroom. Her scant possessions, like her abandoned head coverings and choring clothes, comforted Rebecca. They reached out to her in her deep grief. She hadn't told Samuel just yet, but sometimes, when she held Katie's baby dress close, she could hear the real cries of an infant. . . .

How long she sat there, she didn't know, but when Benjamin hollered up to her, saying a group of women had just arrived to bake Christmas cookies, she near leaped out of the chair.

"Himmel," she muttered, rushing down the hallway to her and Samuel's bedroom. There, overcome with frustration, she stuffed the little dress back into the pillowcase. How could she have forgotten about the holiday work frolic? Wiped the planned event clear out of her mind.

The womenfolk would wonder about it, all right. Call her *ferhoodled*, most likely.

She shuddered to think what Samuel might say. How on earth would she convince him *this* time that she was just fine?

Jah, fine and dandy she was . . . everything was wonderful-gut. No big thing.

Her face would wear the biggest smile she could muster. Her eyes would sparkle as she greeted her kinfolk and friends.

Still, there was no getting around it. She'd forgotten, but good.

❖ ❖ ❖

Nurse Judah calculated the morphine dosage and prepared the syringe, uneasy about this powerful narcotic to control Mrs. Bennett's pain. It was bad enough that the dear lady must endure the baclofen drug pump, implanted into the skin of her abdomen, dispersing a muscle relaxant directly into her system.

"How are you feeling this morning, ma'am?" she asked, helping Laura sit up in bed.

Her patient did not reply at first, so she waited, allowing Laura ample time to put on her dressing gown, with Rosie's help. "Oh, I'd give almost anything to be rid of this blurred vision," Mrs. Bennett said softly. "It's terribly annoying. . . ." She paused. "I disliked causing such a scene yesterday."

"Please don't be upset," Natalie assured her. "Your daughter is aware of your condition. I'm sure she understands."

Laura nodded. "It's just that I wouldn't want to frighten her away."

Natalie's heart went out to the frail lady. Mrs. Bennett's long-absent daughter had returned just in time for Christmas, and now the poor woman was scarcely able to see the girl, let alone deal with the horribly painful spasms and ever-weakening muscles.

Disappointment was evident in Laura's pale, distressed face. The flare-up had brought the initial visit with her daughter to an abrupt end.

Later, when the shot had taken effect, Natalie and Rosie helped bathe and dress the mistress of the house. Mrs. Bennett's fine motor coordination was rapidly deteriorating, and once again, Natalie could see the tenacious grip malignant MS held over its victims.

"Katie will be down for brunch," Laura mentioned, her eyes brightening a bit. "At least we'll have Christmas Eve together."

Natalie frowned. What was Mrs. Bennett thinking? She couldn't give in to her illness . . . not yet.

Vague as her perception was—Natalie couldn't actually put her finger on it—something wasn't quite right about yesterday's reunion. It just didn't add up.

For one thing, Dylan Bennett had hovered about; the man bothered her to no end. And Rosie had pointed out something else—Katie Lapp's hands.

One would presume that an Amishwoman's hands would be callused from gardening and washing dishes and doing laundry. Katie Lapp's hands, on the contrary, looked like a model's. Anything but the hands of a hardworking Plain woman.

"After today," she heard Laura say, "I don't care what happens. The hospital is certainly an option; I won't put up a fuss. But . . . today . . . I want this day with Katie, alone."

Rosie's eyes widened. "But you're going to have a wonderful holiday. I know you are."

Putting on a smile, Natalie agreed. "Wait'll you see what Selig and the others are planning for Christmas dinner."

"More . . . more of that coconut custard pie, I hope," said Mrs. Bennett.

Natalie smiled. Laura wasn't thinking in terms of dying, not with an appetite for dessert!

She made note of the morphine dosage on the medical chart and replaced it on the top shelf of the linen closet. She could only hope that the narcotic wouldn't begin to suppress respiration. But she was well aware of the vicious cycle, once it started.

"Where *did* Selig get that wonderful pie recipe?" Laura asked from her wheelchair.

The woman had turned to face Rosie now, Natalie observed, and from where she stood, it appeared that Mrs. Bennett was fairly comfortable. For the present, no sign of pain or spasms.

"The new housemaid could tell you," Rosie said. "*She's* the one who made it."

"Oh? A new m-maid? What her n-name?" Laura stumbled over the words.

"Katherine," said Rosie.

A pained expression crossed Laura's face and for a moment, Natalie thought the woman might cry. Rosie must've noticed it, too, for she diverted the subject quickly, calling attention to several small gifts under the twin trees in the sitting area.

But it was Natalie who kept thinking about Mrs. Bennett's apathetic attitude. She'd said she wouldn't make a fuss about going to the hospital. Seemed so out of character, too dispassionate for the mistress—yet a common psychological symptom of her disease.

This troubled Natalie greatly. The woman had just met her daughter—the only child she'd ever borne. And now she seemed ready to give up her fight? Was the illness taking over?

◈   ◈   ◈

After brunch, when the dishes and leftovers were cleared away, Katherine sat down at the table to fill out the required application form. Birth date, place of birth, social security number. Simple enough. Quickly, she wrote the information, secretly hoping someone—perhaps Laura Bennett herself—might have a look at it.

When it came to her signature, she paused and glanced at the top of the page, suddenly realizing she had written only "Katherine." No last name. No middle initial.

It would be dishonest to make up a name. Yet she could not risk losing her job or the chance to determine if Laura Bennett was truly her mamma. So she jotted down "Marshfield," middle initial "L"—for Lapp.

That done, she was promptly assigned to clean the Tiffany Room—to remake the guest bed, tidy up the bathroom, and lay out fresh linens.

When she knocked on the door, the woman who called herself Katie Lapp was absent from the room. Most likely downstairs with Mrs. Bennett, having a chat—and enjoying a cup of coffee or tea. Katherine would ask if she might help remove the tea service later.

For the present, she was tickled pink to have Katie's room all to herself. It would give her a chance to look around.

Chapter Twelve

❖ ❖ ❖

Pausing to catch her breath, Mary Stoltzfus leaned against the windowsill in the Lapps' front room, watching a fall of heavy, wet snowflakes shower down from a thick gray sky.

How much more of this? she thought, for it had been snowing now, days on end. The weather affected her mood, though she wouldn't have complained about it for the world. The land was in need of moisture for the crops, come spring. The Good Lord knew all about that.

She moved away from the window, thinking of Katie. How *was* she? Was she wishing she could write and answer Mary's letter?

Knowing in her bones that Katie had likely struggled over this very thing, Mary knew it wasn't prudent for her friend to be corresponding with her in any way—not even by postcard. Not because she didn't *want* to—but because she'd be fearin' for what might happen to Mary if she *did*!

Thinking that way lifted Mary's spirits a little. But not enough to join the crowd of women in the kitchen. She and her mother and grandmother—along with a number of others in the community—had come to bake Christmas cookies here at the Lapp house. For Mary, it was one of the first times back at Katie's former home since the shunning decree.

She heard the chatter and laughter in the kitchen, and glancing back, decided there were so many of them, nobody'd even notice she was missing, probably.

She wondered if Katie might not be feeling the selfsame way today. Maybe even remembering long-ago Christmases spent in Hickory Hollow, speculating about what the People might be doing; whether or not they were thinking of her. After all, there were so many of them in the church district—a good two hundred and fifty-some folk. What did one lost sheep matter?

Did Katie ever think of Bishop John? Did she ever wonder if *he* missed her?

Well, if it had been up to her to respond outright to such a peculiar question, Mary would've had to say that the man did appear to be a bit downtrodden. Not completely defeated, mind you. But that sad look in his eyes, and the way he carried it around on his face everywhere he went, that's what gave his feelings away.

More than anything, she longed to ease the pain in those lovely gray eyes, erase the burden in his soul. John Beiler needed someone. So did his five little ones.

Ach, the thought of jumping into a ready-made family, large as it was, near scared her to death. But the power of love could change all that, she knew.

If only the bishop had an inkling how often she thought of him. If only he had the same feelings. . . .

The bishop was a man chosen to lead the People. What sort of woman would allow sentimental notions over a man of God? Especially a man still getting over being spurned on his wedding day.

Yet romantic whims cluttered her head all the same—spinning round and only halting when she made a conscious effort to make them stop.

◈　◈　◈

He deliberately bumped his feet together as he came into the kitchen, muttering to himself.

"What's-a-matter with Jacob?" his big sister asked.

The Beiler children gawked from their places around the long table, where they sat making Christmas cards for each other.

"Looks to me like he's got trouble walkin'," said eight-year-old Levi, the bishop's next-to-oldest son. "Didja lop off your toenails too short?" he asked his little brother, chuckling.

"Don't be making fun," warned Hickory John, the oldest. Then to Jacob, "Are ya hurt?"

Jacob glanced at Levi out of the corner of his eye. He wasn't no baby, but—"Jah, I am . . . I'm hurt clean down to my big toe."

Nancy motioned for him to come sit beside her on the wooden bench. "Let's have a peek at them wounded piggies."

Susie, age six and two years older'n him, started giggling.

"Keep your mind on your work," Nancy reminded her.

Jacob was awful glad for a big sister like Nancy. Maybe because she reminded him of his mamma. 'Course, he really didn't know, since he was too young to remember her when she died.

He felt his foot relax as Nancy unlaced his heavy shoes and pulled the left one off first. "Which hurts the most?"

He shook his head. "They *both* hurt, and now I can't walk much. And my heart's beating hard down there." He pointed at his bare foot.

Levi and Susie snickered, covering their mouths.

"S'not nice," Nancy reprimanded. "Think how you'd feel if someone made fun of *your* toenails!"

The children, Hickory John included, howled in a fit of

laughter, and they might've kept it up if their father hadn't spoken up just then.

"It's awful nice to hear my family makin' ready on Christmas Eve," he called to them from the utility room.

Jacob heard *Daed's* work boots drop to the floor, one at a time. "I chopped off my toes nearly," he hollered out to his father. "And Levi's tormentin' me."

"Tattletales go to hell," whispered Levi.

Nancy grabbed hold of his ears, covering them. But it was too late. He'd heard the wicked word. Levi had just said the word that meant the Bad Place—where the devil lived. T'wasn't no gettin' around it this time. Levi'd have to have his mouth washed out with soap. Served him right, too. He was always spouting off things that got him in trouble with Daed.

Just yesterday, Levi had gotten his behind swatted for saying the same word about Katie Lapp. That she would burn in that brimstone-hot place for getting shunned. For leaving Hickory Hollow.

'Course, Jacob had no idea what being shunned was all about. But since he'd never had a chance to say good-bye to the pretty redhead who liked to hum a lot—that happy-go-lucky lady who was gonna be his new mamma—since she'd just up and disappeared, well, he figured maybe Katie had gone down there where Levi said. After all, she'd run away on her wedding day, hadn't she? What kinda silly woman would do such a terrible, awful thing?

Most of 'em, Hickory John said, *wanted* to get married. Couldn't hardly wait to. Like that Mary Stoltzfus. He'd never heard *her* humming, but he thought she might be a nice wife for somebody. Thing was, she was plump as a dumplin'—a wonderful-gut sign, seemed to him. Besides that, Nancy and Hickory John were whispering something about Mary first thing this morning, before Daed called the family to prayer. Nancy said she heard Mary's cousin say that Katie's best friend was thinking of dropping by with some angel gingerbread and sour cream chocolate cookies. Comin' over here to bring treats for Christmas!

Well, if that be true, Jacob decided he'd be real nice to the round-faced girl. She might be feeling just as bad as he was about their Katie having to go down and live with the devil, probably.

◈　　◈　　◈

Dylan spent the morning going over several end-of-year financial records. When he was satisfied with his progress, he made an impromptu call to Laura's doctor, informing the man of Nurse Judah's suggestion that hospital arrangements be made should the need arise.

The conversation was brief. It was quickly decided that a private room would be available and waiting.

Around midmorning, Dylan was somewhat startled to receive an unexpected visitor. Rosie Taylor. "Do come in." He motioned her into his office.

"Are we quite alone?" She closed the door.

Dylan nodded. "What's on your mind?"

"Christmas Eve dinner, I suppose. I'm wondering how we might make it more comfortable for Mrs. Bennett." She paused for a moment, looking rather chagrined.

"Go on."

"Your wife has asked that she and Katie be allowed to dine alone . . . in her private suite, that is."

He picked up a pencil and twirled it between his fingers, suppressing the urge to chuckle. So the two of them were getting along famously, it appeared. "Not a problem," he replied. "Is Katie with Mrs. Bennett now?"

"She is."

"Very well. You'll see to it, then?"

"Consider it done." Then, before leaving, she posed an

interesting question. "Where is it you'll be taking *your* dinner, sir?"

He hadn't thought of it, really. But eating alone in the enormous dining room, elegant as it was, seemed out of the question. Not on Christmas Eve. This night was a time for family, for sharing one another's company, wasn't it?

If his wife chose to exclude him . . . well, he might just make other plans. He stood up and addressed the matter at hand. "If Mrs. Bennett prefers to dine *without* her husband . . . fine. I'll have the meal brought up to me."

"Here, in the office?"

"On second thought, perhaps I'll go *out* for dinner," he said, offering Rosie his most congenial smile.

He was almost certain this tidbit of information would throw Laura for a loop. Rosie would rush downstairs and report what he'd said about dining out . . . alone. And Laura would feel terribly guilty, excluding him this way; after all, her Christian conscience would not permit her to ignore a man who'd gone out of his way to bring a beloved daughter home for Christmas.

She'd come around. Most certainly, his wife would insist on inviting him to join their intimate soiree. Of this, he was soundly certain.

❖ ❖ ❖

She knelt on the floor, pondering whether to open the suitcase. Did she dare snoop? The thought poked at Katherine's conscience. 'Twas not the right thing to be doing—intruding on someone's personal privacy this way. And it was the last thing she would've done . . . under any other circumstance.

But knowing what she'd just discovered about Laura's illness—that the mistress was truly dying—how could she resist?

It was Garrett who'd told her. While they were in the kitchen earlier this morning. "Very ill," he'd replied to her question about Laura Bennett's health. "Nurse Judah has made preliminary plans at the hospital. It's that serious."

"You mean . . ."

"She's dying, yes. Mrs. Bennett, sad to say, may not see the light of New Year's Day."

The steward had been ever so kind to tell her, she thought. Gently he'd broken the news, as if shielding her, their newest staff member, from the grave situation.

And now here, before her, lay the Amish girl's suitcase. It seemed almost providential somehow. Carefully, she opened the lid.

One glance, and she discovered the most immodest clothing she'd ever seen. Yet the skimpy garments couldn't really be classified as clothing, could they? The red sheer top and scant underpants were the farthest thing from any nightwear *she'd* ever worn. Still, she held the silky things, unable to put them down, her eyes searching the suitcase for more evidence.

When she spotted additional non-Amish attire, she felt decidedly uneasy. Nervously, she rearranged the items just as she'd found them, then closed the suitcase and went about cleaning the room.

She'd heard of Amish teenagers purchasing fancy underwear, sometimes even English clothes to wear when they were in town on weekends. That type of thing happened usually only during the *Rumspringa*—"running around" years—when strict Amish parents seemed to look the other way, letting their young people have a taste of the modern world.

But this woman, *this* Katie Lapp, was long past all that. Of course, Katherine would know for sure if she caught a glimpse of the woman, or if she could see for herself if Katie wore a cap. If so, that would mean the young woman had indeed been baptized into the Amish church and had no business hiding such fancy, wicked things!

Katherine was soon back downstairs, offering to help clear off the mistress's dishes. "The guest room is finished," she told Rosie, "and I have a little extra time now."

"Very well, but take care not to interrupt Mrs. Bennett's conversation with her daughter."

"I'll be quiet." *Quiet as a field mouse,* she thought. And her heart leaped up as she scurried down the hallway toward the suite, following Rosie's directions.

Oh, to see my birth Mam face-to-face! she thought. *What a wonderful-good Christmas present that would be.*

But someone's voice intruded on her thoughts. Someone calling, "Excuse me!"

She turned to see Fulton, the butler, running down the steps. "Yes, sir?"

"Are you busy at the moment?" Whatever he needed seemed terribly urgent.

"I . . . I s'pose I'm not." She said it reluctantly, right away hoping the words hadn't come across as grouchy.

"Good. Then come with me."

Katherine obeyed, casting aside her dearest wish in response to Fulton's request. She followed him to the kitchen, her mind whirling.

So close, she thought. *Ach, so very close!*

❖ ❖ ❖

Dan prayed silently as he sent a fax to the Lancaster County Court House. Although he'd decided to check the public record as to requests for marriage licenses over the past five and a half years, his conscience pricked him like nettles.

Within the hour he had the information he needed. The only thing lacking was the street address where his sister Annie now lived with her husband, Samuel Lapp's eldest son, Elam—a fellow he'd run buggy races with years ago. They'd attended farm auctions, often playing vigorous games of corner ball with other Amish teens. And there were those too-serious games of baseball during recess at the one-room schoolhouse.

So . . . Elam Lapp had ended up with his sister. He shouldn't have been surprised, really. Katie's big brother had always taken a shine to Annie. From the earliest days, he'd watched them play together at picnics and barn raisings—and, later, make eyes at each other at the Singings.

Turning off the computer, he dismissed glowing memories of Christmas in Lancaster County.

And of Katie.

❖   ❖   ❖

By lunchtime, the women had made thirty dozen cookies. Rebecca apologized over and over for having other things on her mind. For completely drawing a blank about the morning's plans.

"It's understandable," said Ella Mae Zook. "You've been through a painful time, Rebecca."

"We *all* have," Mary Stoltzfus remarked. "Losing someone you love is the hardest thing in the world."

Annie Lapp nodded solemnly, buttoning her wrap.

Rebecca followed her daughter-in-law to the back door. "Must ya go already?"

"Jah, Elam's baby-sittin' little Daniel, and he'll be more than ready for me to take over, for sure." She clucked, her eyes twinkling. "You know how awkward Elam is with infants."

Rebecca nodded. She'd seen her son trying to burp the new baby. "We'll look forward to seein' ya tomorrow noon, for Christmas dinner, then."

"I'll bring the pies." Annie leaned over to kiss Rebecca good-bye. "Anything else?"

"Got everything pretty near under control, denki."

"Gut, then. Merry Christmas, Mam." Annie turned to go.

Glancing out the kitchen window, Rebecca watched as Annie and the other women made their way to the parked carriages. Thankfully, Samuel and Eli were busy with the womenfolk's driving horses, bringing them back one at a time from the barn where the animals had been watered and fed.

Rebecca turned to face the Wise Woman at last. "Painful's not the only thing about this situation with my wayward daughter," she said, waving her hand distractedly. "I've near lost my mind over my shunned girl."

Ella Mae came and wrapped her arms around her, and for one of the first times since Katie had fled Hickory Hollow, Rebecca felt free to pour out her woes, sobbing as she did.

When she was through, she blew her nose and sniffled a bit. The elderly aunt just sat quietly, as if waiting for Rebecca to pull herself together. "There's been lots better Christmases than this," Rebecca blurted.

"And there'll be lots worse, probably."

"Can't see how that could be," she mumbled into her hankie.

"None of us do, really, I 'speck. It's mighty hard trying to see anywheres past our noses when it comes to problems, but 'this too shall pass.' Remember that, Rebecca. Ain't nothin' put on ya more than you can bear. The Good Lord said so."

She nodded in agreement but scarcely believed a word of it. Aunt Ella Mae had never gone through suffering as miserable as having a daughter shunned. Never.

"I've thought of going over to Lydia's for a visit, since

it's Christmas and all," she found herself saying.

"Wouldn't recommend it, Rebecca. Doubt the bishop would, neither."

Rebecca was going to be honest even though it could turn around and get her shunned if she wasn't careful. "No, but I can't help thinkin' I'd sure like to see my girl one more time, at least. Not talk to her—just gaze on her."

"I know you would, and I'd go with you if ya thought it might look better . . . less suspicious," Ella Mae offered.

"You'd *do* that? You'd come with me?"

"Ain't got too many years left on this here earth. S'posin' I can take a risk . . . if *you* can."

Rebecca allowed the old woman to hug her once again.

So it was settled. She'd hitch up Ol' Molasses this very afternoon and drive on down the lane to see Lydia Miller . . . and whoever else was home.

CHAPTER THIRTEEN

Katherine felt awkward about eavesdropping on the kitchen conversation, but she rolled out the pie dough, listening anyway.

"Mrs. Bennett has requested a portrait be made of herself and her daughter," Garrett remarked to Rosie. "A special Christmas and welcome-home gift all wrapped up in one. A splendid idea, don't you think?"

"Well, that all depends. The mistress may not be up to posing for it today. She's had to rest . . . had to postpone her visit with Katie, even."

"Is that so?" Garrett seemed surprised. "Then what of the portrait?"

"Couldn't say. All I know is she's retired for the afternoon and is skipping tea in hopes of feeling a little stronger tonight."

"Poor thing," the steward muttered. "And we had all hoped that seeing her daughter again would be just what she needed to turn the corner."

"What she *needs*," declared Rosie, "is a miracle!"

So do I, thought Katherine, her chest tightening. Oh, she just had to see her real mamma before something dreadful happened.

What if she dies tonight? What if I never get the chance to tell her who I am? She resisted the horrid thought and those that followed. How frustrating, how painful, to miss out on getting to know Laura Bennett, the woman she was sure was her mother.

Waiting until talk of the oil painting had diminished some, Katherine inquired about her application form. "Has Fulton decided anything permanent about me yet?"

Rosie smiled. "He's upstairs just now. But you should be getting your formal acceptance any moment, I would think."

"I'd be most grateful," she murmured and resumed her work, filling the pie. As she did, her thoughts took wings, and she saw in her mind's eye a little girl, pulling a chair across the kitchen floor to the countertop. The youngster crawled up on the chair and stood tall as she could, watching her mamma make pies. With great interest she remained there until Rebecca asked if she wanted to help pinch the crust down around the edges. Of course she wanted to. And she had. She'd done a right fine job of it, too, her Amish mamma had said.

Katherine stared up at a row of gleaming copper pots hanging from the massive hood over the gas range. What was Rebecca doing today? Was she entertaining the womenfolk . . . making pies?

She wished she'd quit thinking about Hickory Hollow so much. *This* was her home now. This beautiful, fancy place.

❖   ❖   ❖

Fulton Taylor, a man of few words, rang the bell, summoning his wife. Rosie arrived swiftly, somewhat out of breath, he noticed.

When they were alone, he showed her Katherine's application. "What do you make of it?"

Rosie took the sheet from him and followed his pointed finger as he read the name out loud. "Katherine Marshfield. Seems a bit odd, don't you think?"

"Hmm, Marshfield. It does seem rather strange."

"Who *is* this new maid we've brought into the house . . . so close to Christmas?"

Rosie shook her head. "I don't know, Fulton. But there's something peculiar about her. That is, something about her that reminds me of someone."

"You may be right." He nodded thoughtfully. "Though who it could be escapes me. . . ."

Rosie jumped in. "Just this morning, Nurse Judah mentioned how unusual it was that the new maid's last name so nearly resembles the mistress's maiden name—*Mayfield*."

"The name is one thing . . . but the birth date . . . quite another."

"What do you mean?" Rosie peered at the application, getting her nose down close to the paper. "Dear me, I need my reading glasses. Can't see much of anything without them."

He rattled off Katherine Marshfield's date of birth. Then—"What do you remember of Mrs. Bennett's journal? Didn't you record some entries for her a while back?"

"Only when she was feeling her worst. On three separate occasions, I believe."

"And wasn't there a place in the journal for important dates?" he asked, feeling edgy now. "I rather remember your mentioning it."

"Yes . . . why, yes! June fifth is a most important date in Mrs. Bennett's book. I noticed it in all three entries. Her baby daughter was born that day."

His wife's face flushed with color, and he watched as she rushed to the desk drawer. Still holding the application, he waited for her to locate her bifocals.

Rosie hurried back to his side to study the page. Her

forehead creased with deep lines as she read. "It looks like . . . can it be? Katherine Marshfield's birthday is the same as Katie Lapp's!"

They were silent, staring at one another, mouths agape.

It was Rosie who spoke first. "The Amishwoman doesn't look the least bit like Mrs. Bennett—not at all. The thought struck me straightaway."

"Both are redheads," he observed.

"But nothing close to the same color."

He went to sit on their double bed, saying no more.

Rosie hovered near. "Something smells rotten to me. I intend to investigate. Are you in?"

"It may be best to wait," he suggested calmly. "Let things play themselves out . . . without interference from us."

Rosie squinted at the application once again, shaking her head before removing her glasses. "Why not push for answers? Today . . . before the artist comes to paint the Christmas portrait."

He folded the application in half and placed it inside his white butler's jacket. "Keep your eyes and ears open, Rosie. But say nothing at all, do you hear?"

His wife grinned back at him. "Yes, sir." She saluted him comically.

"Very well, then." And he was off like a drum major to oversee supper preparations.

❖   ❖   ❖

Lydia Miller was quite astonished to find Rebecca Lapp and the woman's great-aunt standing on her back steps. "Welcome," she said, opening the door wide.

"Merry Christmas, Lydia!" they called out in unison.

"And a Merry Christmas to you," she replied, showing them in.

Once their wraps were off and they'd gotten themselves

settled in her living room, Lydia offered her visitors something warm to drink. "Hot chocolate, maybe?"

"Tea for me, please," said Ella Mae.

"Hot cocoa would be nice," replied Rebecca.

Scurrying off to the kitchen, Lydia wondered what was on their minds. Goodness' sake, it was Christmas Eve, or at least would be in a matter of hours. And the cold . . . the ladies had braved the harshest winds and dropping temperatures to make this trip.

"It's been such a long time since we've come," Rebecca commented when Lydia was back from the kitchen.

Lydia sat down in an overstuffed chair. "What's kept you away?" She felt suddenly awkward. Shouldn't have said it that way, probably.

She noticed Rebecca's sidelong glance at Ella Mae and realized that Katie's mamma must've caught the message. "Oh, I didn't mean to say anything hurtful, not at all," Lydia spoke up quickly.

"You're an awful kind woman to take my girl in like this." The words seemed to stumble out of Rebecca's mouth. "I couldn't have hoped for a better place . . . not if I'd planned it myself."

Lydia couldn't be sure, but she thought the woman's lips trembled. "Peter and I . . . we were happy to do it. Glad to help Katie out . . . anytime."

She could've said more, much more. Could've asked why they'd shunned the young woman so harshly, not allowing the People to speak to her. But she kept her lips shut. This was none of her business. What the Amish did in the Hollow was not her concern.

Now Rebecca seemed to be fidgeting, looking about the room with anxious eyes. Was she searching for Katie? Was this the reason for the visit?

Lydia's heart ached with the desperate situation at hand. Should she say anything? she wondered. Should she break the disappointing news to her poor, dear cousin that Katie was already off to New York?

When the water was hot enough, she excused herself and went to the kitchen. What would the Lord have her do or say to Rebecca?

It was very nearly a prayer, her thought was. More than anything, she wanted to lift the dejected woman's spirits. Set her heart free of worry, free of care. If the Amish allowed part-singing, now would be a good time to burst forth with hymns of praise, thanking the Creator God for His tender mercies over the lives of His children. She thought of such a hymn and hummed it silently.

Soon the hot drinks were ready. She found her favorite hand-painted serving tray—so nice and sturdy it was—and placed three cups on it. "A little something to warm you," she said, heading back into the living room.

She served them, yet prayed without speaking, asking the Lord for wisdom and guidance while her Amish relatives sipped hot cocoa and tea here in her house. Here, without their dear Katie near. On a quiet Christmas Eve afternoon.

Rebecca felt the heat seep through her ceramic mug— not plastic as were her cups at home. Was Katie also enjoying the fine and fancy things here at Cousin Lydia's?

Gazing around the room, she realized that her wayward daughter had for sure and for certain gotten a taste of the English lifestyle. She noticed the wall-to-wall carpeting, the comfortable sofa and chairs, even an overstuffed footrest, of all things! And there was the electric lighting, with a right fancy glass lamp next to her on a round wooden table— something Peter had made with his own hands, probably.

Framed family photographs and paintings decorated the walls, and, ach, those worldly floral drapes at the windows. . . .

'Twasn't the first time she'd laid eyes on Lydia's frills and things. Shameful, these Mennonites . . . branches off the original Swiss Anabaptist faith. Too bad they hadn't followed Jacob Ammann's teaching back in the late 1600s and "stayed in Jesus." Too bad they'd gone and let electricity and cars corrupt their lives.

Nevertheless, her Katie had run to this Mennonite home. She'd come here and rented a room, told her mamma all about it before ever leaving the Amish farmhouse. Yet being the obedient woman she was, Rebecca had heeded the stern shunning decree given by Bishop John—harshest one she'd known in all these parts. Only other place she'd heard of not being allowed to talk to a shunned party was somewhere out in Ohio.

"I suppose you want to know how Katie, er . . . Katherine is doing," Lydia said out of the blue.

Because she had been ordered by Samuel not to speak their daughter's name, Rebecca thought most carefully how she should answer. Oh, how desperately she wanted to talk about her daughter. To know how she was doing here. She felt as if something were filling her up, wanting to spill out of her, something starving deep within. "It would be awful nice to know, jah," she answered. "Is she well?"

"To tell the truth, Katherine's had the hardest time dealing with her pain, but having the guitar did help her out quite a bit, I think," Lydia remarked. "Singing is good for the soul."

"Oh" was all Rebecca could say. Sounded like an insult to her, and she hoped Lydia wasn't going to dicker over doctrinal differences. Now wasn't the time.

Lydia continued. "Katie's gone, left yesterday—headed up north to find her natural mother, but you probably figured that was gonna happen sooner or later."

"Jah, I did." She looked down, shaking slightly, and welcomed Ella Mae's gnarled hand on hers. The warm and tender touch reassured her, let her know that someone cared. Someone wise and old loved her in spite of the actions of her headstrong daughter.

"I believe your Katie will be all right," offered Lydia, coming over to stand beside her. "Peter and I have been praying. So are many others. God cares for His own."

Rebecca nodded. She wouldn't let on to a Mennonite that the Lord God heavenly Father was listening in on *her* prayers more than He'd ever have time for Lydia's. Reason being, the Millers and their church friends and relatives had left the faith of their fathers. How on earth did they expect God almighty to hear and answer prayers from the lips of unrepentant souls?

"Well, I hope ya have a nice Christmas with your family." She forced a smile for her cousin.

What she really wondered was how Katie would manage, off in some strange place for the holidays. 'Course, she said nothing of the kind, didn't even ask to be reminded of the exact city the girl was headed to. Wasn't any of Lydia's business how or what she was thinking concerning her daughter most nearly every hour of the day . . . and night.

"Will Elam and Annie be having Christmas dinner at your place?" she heard Lydia ask.

"Jah, they'll be spending all day tomorrow with us— baby Daniel, too." She turned to the Wise Woman, just then realizing that Ella Mae had said not a word the entire visit.

The old woman let out a gargled sigh and smiled. "Better hope for clear weather so's everyone can get to where they wanna go."

Rebecca noticed the snow was still coming down awful heavy, and she placed her mug and spoon on the coffee table in front of her. "Looks to me like we'd best be headin' on home."

"Do keep in touch," Lydia said. "And don't wait so long between visits."

Rebecca helped Ella Mae up out of the cushiony seat.

The elderly woman stood tall, not without several squeaky grunts, however. Then waiting for her aunt to stand in one place for a moment, regaining her equilibrium, no doubt, she offered her arm. The last thing she wanted was for Ella Mae to fall and break another hip. Not at her advanced age. Not on Christmas Eve.

"Are you ready?" she asked the Wise Woman.

Lifting a finger, Ella Mae paused a moment before speaking. A strange film came over her eyes. "The Lord blesses those who bless Him—and you, Lydia Miller, have taken a young one into your care." Then she quoted from the Scriptures in her husky little voice. " 'Inasmuch as ye have done it unto one of the least of these my brethren, ye have done it unto me.' "

The verse pricked Rebecca's heart. Like sharp stones stuck inside an old work shoe, they stung her.

CHAPTER FOURTEEN

❖ ❖ ❖

It was Rosie who first noticed the backs of Katie Lapp's hands. She had just wheeled Mrs. Bennett into the sitting room, where appetizers were soon to be served. Surprised that Katie had not so much as turned to acknowledge her mother's arrival, she went over to where the woman was standing before one of the tiny Christmas trees. "Your mother's feeling some better since she rested."

Katie did not respond. Holding one of the lavishly wrapped presents, she seemed lost in thought.

As Rosie rescued one of the delicate tree decorations dangling from a low-lying branch, she got a closer look at the young woman's hands. *Odd*, she thought. They appeared to be terribly rough and raw, where just this morning they had been white and smooth as silk. One of them was bleeding slightly—on the middle knuckle.

"Miss Lapp?" said Rosie.

"Oh, uh . . . I'm sorry. Must've been daydreaming." Katie seemed startled. "Did you say something?"

"Well, I noticed the cut on your hand and thought to offer you some salve. Nurse Judah must surely have some around here."

"Oh, it's nothing," Katie said, her face showing more

awareness now. "Rough hands come from doing chores all day long. You can imagine."

Rosie didn't believe her, not for one second. Nary a flaw had she seen on the woman's hands earlier.

"Don't the Amish have *any* modern conveniences?" she asked.

Katie smiled, showing perfectly straight white teeth. Almost too white, too perfect. "Nothing to write home about."

"Excuse me?" Rosie said, glancing at Mrs. Bennett who seemed content enough to sit where she could admire her daughter. Thankfully, the mistress was too far away to catch their whispered conversation.

"I'd rather not talk about my life with the Amish," Katie said abruptly.

The response took Rosie aback. Lowering her voice again she went on. "Are things going well for you in the Amish community?"

"Good as can be expected" came the reply. "But I'm here to spend time with my mother. At least for now."

Rosie nodded. "Yes . . . yes. Your mother." She turned and paused to glimpse the lovely, frail lady in the wheelchair situated near the mahogany mantel.

Almost unconsciously, she began to compare the two women—the set of their eyes and the color of their hair—as Katie made her way across the room to Mrs. Bennett. Without being conspicuous, Rosie studied the young woman who still seemed rather muddled. Or was it something else . . . reluctance to join them, perhaps?

The more she observed, the more she wondered if it was possible Mrs. Bennett's daughter resembled her natural father instead of the mistress.

She dismissed the idea as ridiculous. Anyone could see that Katie Lapp was not the mistress's daughter. Had not a single physical trait in common. Saddest of all, Mrs. Bennett might never see the truth for herself. Not the way her eyes seemed to be failing a little more each day. Nor the way she'd freely consented to hospital admittance . . . whenever the time came.

The young Amishwoman had not a speck of Laura Bennett in her! Not her gentle spirit, her sweet ways . . . not a bit of it.

Rosie wanted to announce a prayer meeting on the spot, wanted to call down the heavens. Poor Mrs. Bennett would need the Good Lord's help for the days ahead—not only to come to grips with her dying but to deal with something far worse. The fact that an impostor, in the form of a quaint Amish girl, was living right here in her own house!

But who was to reveal the deceit, get to the bottom of things? My, oh my, how would the bitter truth affect the dear missus herself?

◈   ◈   ◈

Dylan noticed her immediately upon entering the parlor area of Laura's suite. She very nearly blended in with the Christmas trees on either side of her. Would have, too, had she not been wearing that frumpy black apron over her long green dress. *Amish green* the seamstress had aptly described the fabric wrapped around the long bolt at the fabric shop.

He noticed, too, her slumped stance . . . the droopy face. Was she missing Christmas with her boyfriend?

He wanted her to stand erect, to behave as if she were enjoying herself. Excellent posture and a pleasant facial expression went a long way toward playing a convincing role. She was being paid well enough!

"It's nearly Christmas Eve, isn't it?" he announced, fingering the lapels of his suit coat. The question was rhetorical—mindless small talk—primarily for Laura's benefit.

Perhaps she would feel a stab of guilt for not including him at her party and relent.

He was well aware of her lovely attire. She was dressed to the nines for an evening of exquisite dining and intimate conversation with "Katie," the clever actress otherwise known as Alyson Cairns. Had Laura had a change of heart about wanting him seated at her table?

The actress strutted over and sat down across the sofa from him, casting occasional shy glances around the festive room. Those innocent expressions seemed only to emerge when either Rosie or Laura spoke to her, he noticed. The sensual parting of her full lips and those smoldering eyes— they were for him. Embarrassing, though it was.

What was going through her mind? he wondered. Certainly not the task at hand—portraying herself as an innocent Amishwoman . . . Laura's daughter. He frowned, hoping she was not discouraged with her role.

Had it not been for the fact that the hired model was wearing the homespun getup he'd acquired from the best seamstresses in town, she might've been any young college student.

For a moment, he recalled Laura in her prime—before the disease had left her gaunt and hollow eyed, a shadow of the vibrant beauty she'd been.

Several times he caught "Katie" looking back at him as he attempted a lively conversation with Laura, juggling the frequent asides with Rosie and now Nurse Judah, who had come in from the hallway to join the group.

It struck him that Laura seemed fidgety. Had she been adequately medicated? This was not a good time to risk a lighter dose, what with those horrid tremors and contractures erupting seemingly out of nowhere. Perhaps he should have a word with Natalie.

He was about to motion the nurse to join him in the hall when Rosie spoke up. "We'll be having the appetizers served here in a few minutes, sir." She eyed Dylan with dark, probing eyes, growing even darker as she stared pointedly.

So that's how they're going to play this, he thought, pulling his gaze away from Rosie and purposely concentrating on Laura.

He waited.

But her eyes remained fixed on her lap, more precisely, her hands. Yet he continued to regard her. Would she speak up—invite him at the last minute? Now was her chance if ever there was to be one. She could show her true colors, display her undying devotion to the man who'd brought her Amish daughter home to her.

The waiting turned awkward; an annoyingly empty space of time ensued, one devoid of a response.

So be it. She'd dug her grave . . . let her lie in it. This he thought without remorse.

"Do have a wonderful evening, all of you." His words slipped out, smooth and measured. He dared not look at "Katie" now. Neither Katie nor Laura.

His wife desired an evening alone with her daughter, and he presumed to know the reason. For questioning, no doubt. For gaining an understanding of Amish life and its peculiar customs. For catching up on all she'd missed through the years.

He almost sneered as he contemplated it. Thankfully, he'd already anticipated the cozy scene between mother and daughter. And Katie Lapp—model and actress—had been well rehearsed for just such a quiet evening alone with Laura. He had been over this business—what to say . . . how to respond—a million and one times with her.

Tonight was the night. With or without him at the table, his wife's supposed daughter was on the verge of pulling the entire woolen cloak over the eyes of the soon-to-be-deceased mistress of the Bennett estate. Conning her way into Laura's good graces, she would inherit Katherine's birthright, which would, in due time, be transferred to Dylan's own hefty accounts.

He could scarcely wait for a report of the evening. A play-by-play would be most entertaining, indeed. He stood and excused himself. Then, planting a guileless grin on his face, he went around the wheelchair, leaned over, and gave Laura a tender kiss on her cheek.

Not exactly a victory kiss, he thought. Oh, but very close. *That* kiss would be forthcoming.

"Good night, my darling," he crooned. "Have a marvelous evening . . . both of you."

"Thank you" was all she said. Her manners were intact, obviously. Yet he knew without a doubt that she was most eager to get on with becoming better acquainted with Katie. Was ready for him to be gone, on his way.

Irritated, he rushed up to his office and rang for a chauffeur. He'd misjudged the final outcome of the evening entirely. Thought he had Laura figured out better than this. "Fulton," he thundered into the intercom, "have Theodore bring a car around to the front."

"Theodore's busy presently, sir."

"Oh?"

"I believe he's en route with Mrs. Bennett's commissioned artist—a Mr. Justin Wirth."

"Yes, yes, I know of him." He was now feeling annoyed at Fulton, of all things. One delay after another.

Justin Wirth, indeed. His sickly wife was certainly cunning when she wanted to be.

"Shall I page Rochester for you, sir?" asked Fulton.

"Rochester will do." The new driver was rather young. Not his first choice on any given day.

Intent on getting out for the evening, Dylan was rather looking forward to a fine dinner and a few drinks. Heaven knows he needed a diversion.

Looking out over the grounds, he watched the snow as

it fell. Heavier now and falling fast. Would it never let up? Just as well. There'd be no arguing with Alyson over staying on for Christmas if she was snowed in. Boyfriend or no.

Laura's "heir" would have no recourse but to fulfill her contractual agreement. In short, play the part to the finish.

❖   ❖   ❖

Besides wanting to figure out a way to get herself into Laura's private suite, Katherine was eager to lay eyes on Katie Lapp. She knew, from recent experience, that she wouldn't sleep a wink tonight if she didn't get herself some answers. At least a sensible explanation to set her mind at ease.

Therefore, she must determine if the Katie woman strolling the corridors of this house wore the Amish devotional cap. Finding out for sure had become an obsession as she spent her day working in the kitchen, assisting in dining room preparations for the feast, and, in general, filling in wherever Garrett or Fulton needed help.

An unexpected turn of events came early in the evening when Selig asked for help shaping and rolling the hors d'oeuvres. "I'll need someone to take this platter to Mrs. Bennett's sitting room shortly." He looked right at her. "Katherine?"

When she realized he was addressing her, she replied, "Me? You want *me* to take the appetizers to the mistress?"

Selig nodded. "They're hors d'oeuvres, Katherine."

"Yes . . . I know." Out of the corner of her eye, she noticed one of the housemaids coming out of the pantry. Rosie Taylor. The woman wore a most suspicious smile on her face and tossed a conniving glance at Selig as she bustled into the kitchen.

Putting two and two together, Katherine felt just as she had the first time the wind had caught hold of her covering, making it stand straight out behind her little-girl head. Tendrils of loose hair had tickled her face that day. She was *schtruwwlich*, for sure and for certain. But never mind her unkempt hair; she had experienced total exhilaration.

She felt the selfsame way now. Her Christmas Eve wish might be coming true after all. Katherine Mayfield, fancy English girl at heart, was about to lay eyes on her one true mamma.

Glory be!

CHAPTER FIFTEEN

❖   ❖   ❖

The smell of fresh pine was heavy in the air as she carried the silver tray down the marble hall. Her heart pounded so hard she thought it might lift the ruffle right off her maid's pinafore apron.

Ach, she hoped her hair was in place, lipstick on straight. How many times had she imagined this moment? Too many to count.

And the dream last night, that unrelenting nightmare. . . . She must've dreamed it half a dozen times.

Always, she was on the wrong side of an enormous door. That door, how it towered above her. Yet she could hear the sound of Laura's voice behind it, inviting her, nay, *pleading* for Katherine to come inside.

The door represented a blockade, as honest-to-goodness real as any she'd suffered in life. Yet the vision had persisted, its message one of despair. She had been kept from her real mamma by a door—a door of secrecy, a door of deceit.

She shivered, thinking of the lengths her Amish parents had taken to hide the satin baby gown . . . to keep the secret hidden all the years of her life.

Now . . . *now* she stood before a pair of wide French doors. Glass, with lovely rounded transoms overhead. Just inside, four women sat around a roaring fire, two of them with their backs to her, talking softly. A nurse, a maid—Rosie—a young Amishwoman, apparently, and a patient in a wheelchair . . .

A sob caught in her throat. The woman in the wheelchair—was it Laura Bennett? How could it be that she looked so young and so very ill at the same time?

It was Laura's hair that captured her attention. Caught it and pulled her gaze so intensely she found herself longing to touch it. What of the texture? Richly auburn in color, yet was it thick—so heavy at times the tresses weighed heavily on her scalp?

The woman's profile seized her as well. She couldn't take her eyes off the fine nose, the delicate chin line.

So many similarities. . . . Why hadn't anyone noticed?

Katherine tried desperately to control the joyful tears that threatened to spoil her view of the gathering. It was all she could do to keep the floodgate in check. But she knew if she gave in to one little drop, there'd be more tears than a body could count.

Taking a deep breath and refusing to cry, she gradually regained her composure. She did it partly by turning her scrutiny away from the mistress and concentrating hard on the youngest woman of the group—the one wearing the Amish dress and unusual cap—the strangest getup she'd ever seen. Was this the woman who called herself Katie Lapp?

She wanted to step in closer, see if the clothes might be similar to the ones worn by other church districts in Lancaster. Then she remembered she was supposed to be serving appetizers, not gawking at strangers, for pity's sake!

Overcome with rapture at seeing Laura even from this distance—the gladness all mixed up with apprehension—she was stopped suddenly by a slight commotion. The Amishwoman had gotten up out of her chair and was hurrying over in Katherine's direction. The young woman looked frantic, as if, for all the world, she needed some air.

Pushing past her at the threshold, Katie Lapp nearly knocked the tray out of Katherine's hands. "Excuse me" came the muttered words.

Katherine peered over her shoulder, wondering what was going on. Had someone said something to upset her? "Are you all right?" Katherine asked, turning to inquire.

"Just feeling a bit . . . uh . . . oh, I don't know. It's getting too hot in there—so close to the fire."

Strange, she thought, *no one else is complaining*. In fact, when Katherine glanced back at the cozy threesome remaining—Laura Bennett snugly wrapped in an afghan— there was no evidence to suggest any of the other women were suffering from the heat.

"Are you *sure* you're too warm?" she pressed.

The woman seemed to force a smile. "Maybe more lonely than anything."

"Lonely?"

"You know, homesick. For my family. We Amish are very close-knit."

Katherine was caught off guard. She understood that feeling, all right. The woman looked so absolutely miserable. "Is there something I can do for you?"

"No, there's nothing anyone can do. But it would be wonderful to get my hands on a phone somewhere." Her eyes lit up as she spoke. "That would be real nice."

Katherine's ears perked up. The Amish didn't use phones for the sake of carrying on a conversation or visiting. They got in their carriages and went off to see their friends and relatives. The bishops liked it that way—kept church members more closely connected.

She was about to explain but caught herself. Shouldn't be letting on what she knew about Plain life. Wouldn't be right smart.

"There are plenty of telephones in the house," Katherine found herself saying instead.

"Oh, I know. It's just that . . ." Obviously frustrated, Katie flung her arms wide, bumping the tray. Quickly, the women righted it.

"Here, let me take this for you," the young woman offered, "since I ought to get back in there anyway."

"Oh no, it's my job." While still holding the tray, Katherine got a closer look at the woman's dress. It *buttoned* down the front, of all things. Lancaster Amish used hooks and eyes, sometimes straight pins, but never, ever *buttons*!

Then, somewhere between supposing and knowing, she got a bright idea. Squinting out at the thick snow flurries, she said, "*Des is bidder kalt haus.*"

Katie looked at her with a wary expression in her eyes. "What did you say?"

"I'm sorry, I thought you spoke Dutch," Katherine replied, her heart in her throat.

Katie mustered up a feeble "I used to."

"Well, then?" Katherine realized she was in way over her head, as Dat would always say.

For the longest time, Katie stared at her. "My family hasn't spoken Dutch in years," she scoffed. "We ain't Old Order anymore."

"Oh? What *are* you, then?" Katherine insisted, thinking she'd rather be asking, "*Who* are you?"

Without warning, the young woman lunged for the appetizer tray, and without a backward glance, marched into the sitting room.

Katherine stood there aghast—angry, too—unable to comprehend what had just taken place. But one thing she understood, for sure and for certain. This Katie Lapp was no more Amish than the man in the moon!

❖   ❖   ❖

Theodore didn't ever remember a time when the roads had been this treacherous. At every intersection he applied a pumping motion to the brakes to avoid slipping and sliding. Thankfully, the streets were abandoned, as even those shoppers who had procrastinated till the eleventh hour had finally made their purchases. A few huddled here and there, waiting in shop windows for the bus or a taxi.

Clocking his speed, he noticed the limousine was inching along at about nine miles per hour. Maybe less.

"We're going almost as slow as a horse and buggy," he said, chuckling to the passenger in the backseat. "Appropriate, I suppose, as we've been entertaining an Amishwoman at the estate."

Theodore glanced into the rearview mirror at the young man.

Justin Wirth was nodding. "So I hear." He paused a moment, then—"I was surprised, and saddened, to hear of Mrs. Bennett's failing health. She seemed quite well a few months back."

"It's terribly unfortunate, and I'd be the first to say that the kindhearted mistress doesn't deserve such a debilitating illness."

"Seems to me that finding her daughter might serve to raise her spirits."

"One would think so."

"How good of Mr. Bennett to locate the girl," Mr. Wirth remarked.

Theodore gripped the steering wheel. "Mr. Bennett, you say? *He* was the one to locate the Amishwoman?"

"Didn't you know?" came the reply. "Why, when Mrs. Bennett phoned me, she seemed quite pleased."

"Indeed?" He felt as if he might not be able to pry his hands free from the wheel.

So Dylan Bennett had been responsible for finding Katie Lapp. Of course—it made sense. *Perfect* sense. He pondered the situation. The man was worse than devious. *Worse.*

Why hadn't he put two and two together?

◆ ◆ ◆

Natalie wheeled her patient into the bedroom to administer the evening shot. Supper would be served in a few minutes, and she was encouraged by the way Mrs. Bennett seemed to be feeling tonight. Rather a surprise after her exhausting morning.

"Mr. Wirth is an absolute wonder," the mistress remarked. "Braving the weather on a night like this . . . and coming out on such short notice—Christmas Eve on top of it."

It was obvious Laura was pleased. The color had risen in her face, and Natalie noticed a renewed sparkle in the brown eyes.

"You're very lucky, I'd say," she replied. "The mother-daughter portrait will be a lovely gift for Miss Katie."

Mrs. Bennett turned abruptly. "You don't think she will mind, do you?"

"Having her portrait made? Why should she mind? She'll love it."

Mrs. Bennett smiled. "Good."

"Your daughter seems to be having a wonderful time."

"Well . . . it's taken longer for the two of us to warm up to each other than I'd ever anticipated. Perhaps because we have so many years of catching up to do."

Natalie was careful to guide the needle, inserting it into the bulging vein. Mrs. Bennett winced, and Natalie regretted for the hundredth time having to inflict yet more pain on the gentle woman. A soul who never complained, unlike many MS patients who often became irritable and hard to handle.

"Your pain's nearly over," she said softly.

"I know," said the mistress, blinking. "Yes, I know."

The words and the inflection in the weak voice took Natalie by surprise, and without further delay, she unlocked the wheelchair. "We have a party to attend," she said, willing the lump from her throat.

"And a portrait to sit for," Mrs. Bennett added, more brightly. "A portrait with my own dear Katie."

Things seemed to be working out between the mother and daughter, after all. Surprisingly, Katie's interest in Laura had taken a sudden turn, almost to the point that Natalie wondered what had been said or done to liven things up between them.

Oddly enough, she felt she could accurately pinpoint the moment when everything had begun to change. Katie had come in from the hall, carrying the appetizer tray. She'd served her mother first, then glancing over her shoulder, seemed to be looking at someone.

Turning, Natalie had noticed the new maid, apparently too shy to enter the mistress's private quarters. For a moment, the young woman had gazed longingly from beyond the glass doors. And when their eyes met, Katherine had scurried away.

❖   ❖   ❖

Rosie observed the artist briefly as he set up his easel and canvas in the sitting room, off in the corner, to be sure; nevertheless, his paints and brushes and things were already scattered across the drop cloth beneath.

What an interesting turn of events, she thought. *A mother-daughter portrait sitting on Christmas Eve.*

Wouldn't Mr. Bennett be surprised when he returned? The man was accustomed to having his way about managing the affairs of the estate—not giving in to what he would surely consider a whim of his dying wife. Rosie sincerely hoped Mrs. Bennett's decision to hire the artist would not cause more conflict than merriment for the holidays.

She shoved the gloomy thought aside and went about her duties, assisting in serving the mistress and the woman called Katie Lapp.

The table was tastefully furnished in every respect. Small in comparison to the immense formal one in the dining room, yet charming, enhanced by the mistress's favorite nineteenth-century floral dishes featuring a poinsettia and holly motif over a tablecloth of ecru lace.

The servants had had to scramble to put together this impromptu supper setting, but nary a complaint from Selig or Garrett about the change in plans, Rosie noticed. The mistress was a jewel of a lady, she was. They all loved her unreservedly and would never leave her—not as long as she drew breath. But she'd not think of that—not now.

Without purposely eavesdropping, Rosie caught snatches of conversation as Garrett held and served abundant food platters and matching service dishes for the mistress and her guest. Rosie would assist Mrs. Bennett by feeding her.

"What was it like growing up without electricity?" Mrs. Bennett asked her daughter.

"Ach, not so bad" came the reply. "We made do with oil lamps and lanterns."

Mrs. Bennett leaned forward. "Did you ever entertain secret thoughts, ask yourself how it would be to plug in a radio or television? Or to operate a computer or cook on an electric range in your own home?"

"Not that I remember. But I did always think it would be *wonderful* to live in a mansion like this."

Rosie chuckled quietly. The unlikely twosome were getting along famously . . . *now*. Still, she noticed how vague Katie's answers seemed—responses most anyone could give at the drop of a hat.

164

In the midst of this congenial conversation, she puzzled over the new maid—Katherine, who seemed to know all about making coconut custard pie, Amish style. Katherine, with hair the identical color of Laura's.

Perplexed, Rosie left for the butler's pantry. She must speak with Fulton as soon as possible.

CHAPTER SIXTEEN

The longer Laura posed for the artist, the better she liked what was evolving on canvas. Justin had already begun to create a warm holiday setting, sketching Laura first and leaving a blank space for Katie. "For later," he told her when she casually inquired.

Did he think she might die before he finished? A reasonable assumption, to be sure. The more she thought of it, while sitting as still as the medication would allow, the more she was fairly certain that *was* the reason Justin concentrated so carefully on her outline alone.

Feeling perkier than she had all day, Laura listened closely as Katie spoke of her life, growing up on an Amish farm. "We were always up by four-thirty every morning, even Sundays. After all, someone had to milk the cows."

Laura found herself laughing along with the woman. She'd turned out to be so very talkative and charming. Laura couldn't quite fathom the difference between the original shy, almost sullen Katie, and this vivacious creature seated across the table from her.

"Tell me about your church services. What sort of music do you sing? Or is there music at all?"

Setting down her fork, Katie smiled. "We don't have instrumental music at church. Someone leads out in a song from the hymnbook, and the rest of us join in."

Laura nodded, trying hard to imagine only a cappella singing for the worship. "Do you sing in English?"

Katie shook her head. "Never."

Impulsively, she asked, "Will you say something in Dutch for me?"

The girl turned pale. "Oh, I mustn't speak it to outsiders. The bishop wouldn't approve."

"The bishop?"

"He makes all our rules—what we can and can't do around non-Amish folk."

Laura reached out to touch her elbow. "Well, I'm not just *any* English person, am I?"

Smiling, Katie agreed that she was not. "But it's best I don't break the rules."

Laura folded her hands in her lap, eager for more information about doctrine and religious beliefs. She was met, however, with obvious resistance each time she quizzed her daughter. Katie was clearly uncomfortable. "Very well. Let me tell you something of my own beliefs—my faith in Jesus Christ, my Savior and Lord."

Katie was polite enough to listen, although Laura suspected along about dessert time that her girl was truly bored with the Scripture references and favorite Bible passages she had been quoting. It was evidenced by the way Katie began to fidget and lose eye contact with her, something Laura had so enjoyed earlier in the evening.

"There is only one reason I wish to bring up spiritual matters," she found herself explaining. "I lived my life without Christ for thirty-six long years. Are you familiar with the hymn 'Amazing Grace'? Well, God's love is all that and so much more, and only because I love you, Katie, do I share my personal experience." She took in a deep breath, and praying a silent prayer for guidance, she forged ahead with her personal testimonial.

When she finished, Katie spoke up. "I've never heard such a thing. God's Son coming to earth to die . . . for me?"

"The first time I heard it told, I, too, could scarcely take it in."

The younger woman looked pensive. "But I don't see how I could just throw away my Amish belief," came the tentative reply. "My parents . . . my *adoptive* parents would be so hurt. And my brothers and sisters . . ."

Laura felt weak suddenly. "I don't expect you to believe the way I do just because we've found each other. Please understand that."

Nodding, Katie spoke in a near whisper. "You don't know how hard it's been to leave my family and friends to come here . . . even for this short time."

"I understand, and I appreciate it very much." She sighed, turning the conversation toward Katie's adoptive family. "How many brothers and sisters do you have?"

"Five sisters and four brothers. Most of them are grown and gone."

"So . . . your parents had children before . . . before the stillbirth?" Laura recalled the first moment of meeting. How devastated and forlorn the Amish couple had looked, there in the corridor of Lancaster General Hospital. The day was as fresh on her mind as if it had happened yesterday.

Katie's expression changed; she seemed stunned for a moment.

"Perhaps I shouldn't have mentioned—"

"No, no, it was just such a painful time for my parents," the girl said with little emotion. "I first heard about it when I was ten."

"I see." She wondered if Katie had also been informed of the money hidden away in the folds of the baby blanket. The money and the note—showing how much Laura, as an unwed teenage mother, had cared and loved her newborn baby. She hesitated to bring it up, lest the adoptive parents had seen fit to keep that part a secret. Perfectly acceptable, of course. Sometimes undisclosed family secrets were better left alone.

Still, she wondered when the right moment might present itself to speak about the future. The moment she would inform her daughter of her rightful inheritance.

Glancing away, Katie remarked, "Look, how pretty!"

Laura turned slightly in her chair to see Justin adding a hearty Christmas tree branch on the canvas background. "Mr. Wirth is an excellent artist—the best—wouldn't you agree? That's why I hired him to paint this portrait."

"How long before it's to be finished?" asked Katie.

"The artist will stay on here through Christmas week. And when the project is complete, the portrait is my gift to you."

Katie's eyes lit up. "For *me?*"

"That and so much more." Was now the time to tell her?

A burst of gladness swept across Katie's face. "You're the most generous woman I've ever known . . . Mother." Without warning, the girl stood up and planted a kiss on Laura's cheek.

"You've been in my heart these many years," she said, choking back the tears. "When we are completely alone, you'll hear what I have planned for you."

Laura continued to observe her daughter throughout the course of the evening. How her face shone . . . and what radiant love in her eyes!

Indeed, the girl seemed almost giddy with delight.

❖   ❖   ❖

Rosie managed to track down Fulton and bend his ear with her concerns about the supper conversation she'd overheard between Mrs. Bennett and Katie.

"I scarcely recognize that Amishwoman anymore," she said when they'd stepped out on the screened-in porch for a quick chat. "She's changed entirely."

Her husband listened, though seemed restless to get back to work. Then, lowering his tone, he said, "I've been noticing *Katherine* much more than Katie, and I think you and I were on to something before. The new maid has obvious physical traits, if you grasp my meaning."

Glancing about nervously, Rosie agreed. "I have an idea," she whispered. "Do you think we should allow Katherine to help serve dessert tomorrow? Mrs. Bennett's annual birthday cake for Christ?"

Fulton pondered for a moment. "It's worth considering."

"Well, shall we plan on it, then?" she asked, happy with the idea that a tradition started by Mrs. Bennett three years back might, in fact, be the perfect moment to usher in the new maid—at least get Katherine *inside* the private quarters. A marvelous opportunity for the two women to behold each other . . . at last. Perhaps then she and Fulton would be able to confirm their growing suspicions.

Fulton rubbed his chin. "By all means, instruct Katherine not to converse with either the mistress or Katie, except as needed for courtesy's sake. Then we'll see what happens."

Like a schoolgirl on the trail of a mystery, Rosie put her hand to her throat. "Oh, I do hope this works out. Nothing would please me more."

Flushed with anticipation of the daring scheme, she hurried inside.

❖   ❖   ❖

While the mistress and Katie dined in quiet splendor down the hall, the servant staff and Nurse Judah gathered at the long kitchen table—an antique—bearing intricate carvings along its sides, and far removed from Mrs. Bennett's intimate suite.

It was to be a quick supper. Enjoyable, though.

Katherine hadn't remembered seeing all the domestic help in one room before, least not all at the same time. Wasn't as if she were being presented formally to them, but it came mighty close.

Several, including Nurse Judah and Garrett Smith, shook her hand, welcoming her to the "busy Bennett place," as Garrett put it. And she wasn't absolutely sure, but it almost seemed that he'd slanted her a quick wink.

She noticed the older gentleman—Theodore Williams—who moved about the kitchen in ceaseless silence, and after one rapid assessment, she pegged him as the most interesting person in the room.

Appearing rather subdued, the chauffeur located a vacant chair near the bay window overlooking the east gardens, now buried in snow. It was already too dark to investigate just how deeply the ground might be covered.

With an air of reluctance, Mr. Williams sat down. He turned his head to face the window and remained in that position for a time. She watched him for what seemed a solid minute or more, before the man sighed audibly and tendered a faint smile when their eyes met.

What's bothering him? she wondered. Something was, 'twas plain to see. Ach, the weight of the world seemed to rest on the man's slight frame.

Years ago, her Amish girlfriend, Mary, had told her you could tell things about a person's face—whether or not they were telling the truth—when they talked. But this man wasn't saying a single word. She didn't know why on earth it was so important for her to know if he could be trusted. No reason, really, she decided, and went about the pleasant chore of buttering her baby peas, carrots, and baked potato.

The roast pork was so tender, she cut off bite-sized portions with only her fork, paying close attention as Natalie Judah, the sweet-faced nurse, explained what was taking place in Mrs. Bennett's quarters. "Katie and her mother seem to have broken through the first icy layer . . . and I'm not sure what has made the difference."

Panicky feelings surfaced, yet Katherine dared not speak up. Not now. She'd just have to wait and listen. Yet sin stirred within her soul—the sin of jealousy. She did not want an impostor "breaking the ice" with *her* mother, and she didn't want to be sitting here enduring a report about it, either!

Still, she found herself helpless to listen as Natalie continued. "I was beginning to wonder if they would ever click—those two—after their shaky start yesterday."

Katherine caught a curious exchange of glances between Rosie and her husband. What was that peculiar look that passed across the butler's face?

Discreetly, she stole additional glimpses at the husband-wife duo sitting up the table from her. She was not disturbed by the frequency of what seemed to be secretive looks shared. Oh, she'd seen her Amish parents do the same thing, and often. People connected by love often passed silent intimacies with their eyes.

She knew it to be true, for she and her darling Dan had experienced something quite similar in their teen years. Especially during house church, while sitting on those hard wooden benches for three hours on a Sunday morning. A rather bittersweet circumstance for a girl who could scarcely sit still, yet a girl in love. The sweet part was that the men sat segregated from the women, which made it possible for Dan's doting blue eyes to dance for her, offering love messages only sweethearts cherish. . . .

Attempting to rid her mind of past lovely things, she tore her bread in half before buttering it. She savored the first bite, thinking how nice and even she'd cut the loaf tonight, with the aid of electricity, of course.

Natalie was talking again, and Katherine found herself hanging on every word, occasionally peering down the table at Mr. Williams. Why wasn't *he* entering into the conversation about the mistress and the Amishwoman?

Naturally, if someone wanted to be rude, they might be asking *her* the same question. But it had been drilled into her—her whole life—to "fade into the woodwork," so to speak, when elders gathered at the table or any other time. And with a quick look round at her new friends and colleagues, it was clear she was the youngest person present. Not only that, but she was a woman.

Rebecca had taught her total submission to a man's authority—under God, of course. Sitting here, enjoying Christmas Eve supper in the house of her natural mother, Katherine supposed even though she was a woman grown and out on her own—that she was still attempting to throw off deeply ingrained practices. Customs so much a part of her, she could not shake them off at will or on a mere whim, either one.

Had she not been a paid employee, she might've had the nerve to speak up and enter the conversation. Especially when it came to the part about Katie's leaving the room so suddenly this evening. "And lo and behold, if Mrs. Bennett's daughter didn't turn around in the hallway and return with a tray of hors d'oeuvres," said Natalie. "I couldn't believe it!"

"Well, of all things." Theodore broke his silence, looking up, then wiping his face with his folded napkin.

Katherine sat spellbound. Oh, she wanted to explain the situation. Tell them—all of them—that Katie Lapp, or whoever she was, had pulled the tray out of Katherine's own hands and flounced back into the mistress's room with it. That the young woman hadn't understood a stitch of Pennsylvania Dutch, not even a simple comment about the weather being bitter cold.

She wanted to tell them she thought Katie Lapp was an impostor, wanted to holler it out into the frigid New York air.

Tonight, though, the cat had her tongue, no getting around it. So she sat there, enduring perpetual speculation about this and that and thus and so till she thought she might burst.

It was moments later she realized Mr. Williams had spoken, as much as to agree with Natalie Judah that the Amishwoman *had* done something completely out of order. Katherine worried that what might follow could be a reprimand, and rightly so. Would the old man turn and speak to her next?

She was fairly sure he didn't know it was she who'd been assigned the tray of hors d'oeuvres. Relieved, she reached for her glass of ice water and sipped slowly, letting the coolness soothe her throat as it trickled down.

Due to the snippets of information she'd overheard in the past twenty-four hours, she had come to understand that Mr. Williams was the mistress's favorite chauffeur. Rosie had even hinted that the gentleman was also Mrs. Bennett's confidant. This knowledge intrigued her, for the man had grandfatherly qualities. Some of them even reminded her of Dawdi David, her mamma's father, long deceased.

Pondering this, she wondered: *What secret things does Mr. Williams know about Laura Mayfield-Bennett?* Had Katherine been more confident of her place in the household, she might've taken him aside and pumped him full of questions.

When dessert was served, she focused her attention on the couple with the ongoing parade of darting glances. Jah, Rosie and Fulton Taylor seemed to know something they weren't letting on to anyone. Might be, *they* were just the folk to help her.

❖ ❖ ❖

Laura realized, much later, that Dylan had not returned home from his supper outing. Strange that Katie had been the one to mention it.

"Dylan's in good hands," she reassured her daughter. "We hire only the best of help, drivers included."

That seemed to suffice, and they went on talking about casual, carefree things—becoming more and more comfortable with each other.

Rosie hurried in from the hall and began to clear away the holiday dishes. "You've had a long day," she warned, cocking her head in that concerned way she had.

"Long but happy."

"But tomorrow will be another full day—exchanging gifts and dining."

Smiling at her daughter, Laura replied, "I wish to soak up every minute I have left with my girl."

Then, not wanting to put a damper on things, she did not bring up the matter of her husband's delay. Never said a word, even though her personal maid appeared altogether eager to engage in small talk. Especially with Laura's daughter. So eager was she that Rosie slipped once and referred to Katie as Katherine.

Laura promptly reminded her of the woman's nickname. "She wants to be called by her Amish name."

"Yes, I'd just forgotten." Rosie blushed. "Please, do forgive me, Katie."

The young woman nodded agreeably. "That's all right. I've been called many things in my life."

Except Laura Bennett's daughter, thought Laura, grateful for this day. And for the love.

The hour was late when Natalie came to check on her. "You seem to have enjoyed yourself," the nurse said, preparing to take her back to the dressing area.

Smiling at her daughter, Laura reached for Katie's hand. "I'd say one of the best days of my life."

Katie smiled sweetly. "For me, too."

She felt her throat constrict with emotion. "We'll have another lovely time tomorrow. The best Christmas ever."

"I'm counting the hours," Katie said, standing to leave.

The women hugged briefly, then Laura watched, with failing eyes, her dear one depart for the Tiffany Room upstairs.

Tomorrow's the day, she decided. *I'll tell Katie about my family—her grandparents—and all that is to be hers . . . on Christmas Day.*

CHAPTER SEVENTEEN

❖　　❖　　❖

Dylan Bennett, sitting in the plush armchair of a hotel lobby, gazed about him at the crowd of stranded travelers mobbing the area, arranging for a room. Just his luck—lousy timing to boot!

Not to worry, he told himself. His aspiring New York actress could handle herself quite nicely, with or without him at the estate. He smiled, commending himself on a choice pick. The girl could go far—maybe even Hollywood, after this stint.

Now, if he could just obtain a luxury suite—the kind he'd first requested. Because of crowded conditions, the place was packed, the best rooms taken. He might've easily succumbed to the offering of a simple room for himself and Rochester, the bumbling idiot who'd driven them into a snowbank. But given the circumstances, he'd rather lounge . . . and fume in the elegantly furnished sitting area. In the meantime, he would consider his options: either wait out the storm, or hire a tow truck to pull the Mercedes out of the ditch. Anything to keep from sharing cramped quarters with Rochester.

Fact: Apparently, no end was in sight for the ferocious Christmas Eve blizzard, howling lionlike as it dumped a record-breaking blanket of snow on the city. No hope of obtaining even the most primitive of tow trucks at this hour. Had he not just heard from the bellhop that roads east of Canandaigua were impassable—County Road 10 having been blocked off moments earlier by highway patrol—he might have seriously entertained the notion of summoning Theodore, his senior chauffeur, to retrieve them.

Alas, he was stuck . . . trapped only a few miles from home. And to top it off, the phones in the entire place were tied up. All of them. He could kick himself for leaving his cell phone back home. So here he sat, a man of means . . . displaced, unsettled, and waiting, waiting for some loser to get off the phone.

Glancing across the atrium, he noticed Rochester lingering near the phone booths. Present assignment: to signal Dylan when a telephone was available. Just reward for the young, inept chauffeur. The lad had much to learn, he decided.

He checked his watch. Nearly midnight. Was his wife resting now, happy as a lark? Had she enjoyed a satisfactory evening, become comfortable enough with Katie to reveal the generous plan for her daughter's future?

Knowing how Laura adored Christmas—her religious beliefs being what they were—he suspected that if things had gone well, tomorrow might be the day he'd been waiting for. Waiting was the name of the game—in business and in matters of life—and legacies.

Annoyed that he might have to spend the holiday marooned, he reached for *The Wall Street Journal*. Rochester would just have to call to him when the next phone was available. In the meantime, before he dialed up the estate, before he disguised his voice to address whomever answered, and before he spoke with drowsy Miss Katie Lapp, impressive impostor, he'd have a look at a few stock prices, just to pass the time.

❖   ❖   ❖

The clock on the mantel chimed twelve times, wakening
Dan Fisher out of a deep sleep. He'd drifted off at his desk,
and although the angle of his head in relationship to his neck
was creating an annoying crick, he stayed put for a few more
minutes.

In spite of this being the night before Christmas, he'd
spent the entire evening composing a letter to his sister. Had
he not been thoroughly exhausted afterward, he might've
headed upstairs to bed. But emotionally spent, he'd fallen
asleep with his head resting heavily on his hands.

Slipping back into a half dream state, the images before
him were as real as the day the sailing accident happened.
And always the same. . . .

He found himself face down, regaining consciousness on
a sand reef, having been swept up by the ocean below. How
he'd gotten there, he did not know, but he knew one thing
sure: he was alive when he should have drowned!

Swimming to shore had been excruciating . . . he
thought his arms might give out after more than an hour in
the swirling waves. Attempting to make headway toward
shore, yet not seeing, not knowing where he was in the
midst of the vicious storm, at one point he thought of allowing the ocean's fury to roll over him, bury him at sea.
He contemplated merely breathing in the deadly salt water,
receiving the ocean into his bursting lungs . . . succumbing
. . . relinquishing the will to live, to stop the pain, the horrid
wrenching in his chest.

But he had survived. By God's almighty hand, he was
alive!

The half-hour chime jarred him to life again thirty minutes later. This time he picked himself up, left the study

lamp lit, and ambled toward the stairs.

He looked back at the letter.

The letter.

The startling message would change everything, would rearrange his family's very existence—maybe even alter the lives of the People.

Shatter yesterday, awaken truth.

With the fracturing of years would eventually come the Ban and Meinding—excommunication and ultimate shunning.

His.

By returning to confess to his father his grave deception concerning his accident, yet at the same time refusing to return to the Amish community—by doing that, he would be setting himself up for high jeopardy. Exposing himself to an Amish bishop's decree. This by the mere mailing of a letter.

The envelope, contents inserted, lay diagonal on the desk, unsigned, and as of yet, undated. Still, he was certain of one thing: *This* message must be the one mailed to Annie. None of the previous rough drafts were acceptable to him. Yet he wondered how his sister would take the news, worried that quite possibly, after reading and discovering he was alive after all, she might faint . . . or worse, fail to believe the honest words he'd written.

He hoped rather she might study the handwriting. Look past the words, the English-sounding phrases learned from his years out in the world, find her "deceased" brother buried between the lines. The one who'd long loved her, missed her, wished things had turned out far differently for all concerned.

Falling into bed, he knew what to do about the timing of the letter. It was imperative Annie receive it when she might be most likely to fully concentrate on his request—to consider meeting him face-to-face. He must not procrastinate further. Each day counted, in God's eyes and in his own. Too much time had passed and there was much to set right. Yet he was reluctant to disrupt his sister's Christmas, would not intrude upon it for the world.

For him, the most difficult part—composing the letter— was finished. He would wait and send it immediately after New Year's Day.

Settled about his decision, he slept, conjuring up joy-filled dreams of his former sweetheart girl and the bitter-sweet Hickory Hollow days of yore.

❖ ❖ ❖

Along about one-thirty, Katherine awakened with a start. Somewhere in the house, a telephone jangled. At last, it stopped, and she sat upright, uncertain of her precise whereabouts for a moment.

Commotion outside her bedroom door followed shortly, and she crept out of bed to lean her head against the door.

"Miss Katie," someone was whispering. "Can you come downstairs? You're wanted on the telephone."

Curious, Katherine opened the door a crack. She saw the phony Amishwoman emerge from her room at the end of the hall, far removed from the servants' quarters.

"Who's calling at *this* hour?" the impostor said sleepily.

There was more whispering, and, although Katherine wasn't totally certain, she thought it was the butler who was delivering the message. When the man turned, she saw Theodore Williams' face instead. The old gentleman lumbered down the hall to the long, grand staircase.

What on earth is going on? she thought. It was the middle of the night, for pity's sake!

Closing her door a bit more, allowing for only the slightest of a crack, she waited for the senior chauffeur's footsteps to fade before opening the door wider again. Just in time to see the strawberry blonde, in a flurry of flaming red slippers, hurry down the hallway, turn, and dash down the stairs.

Katherine closed her door and rushed over to the dressing room where a walk-in closet swallowed up the few items of clothing she'd brought from Lydia's. There she donned a blue terry cloth bathrobe and slip-on house shoes.

Directly, she passed through the dimly lit hallway and made her way down the stairs. Not to appear nosy, and to avoid being noticed, she sat halfway down the steps, near the landing, listening. But the house was silent as the moon.

She held her breath in hopes of lessening the noise of her own breathing. Then, getting up, she tiptoed farther down the steps, straining to hear.

In the distance, coming from the library, perhaps?—she heard the faintest of sounds. Someone's voice.

Grateful for Garrett's guided tour that first day—pointing out the mansion's corridors and general layout—she knew enough to enter the opposite side of the enormous library room, there being two separate entrances. She slipped in without being noticed, glad for the dark hue of her blue robe.

Bookshelves, housing hundreds of volumes, loomed tall above her, like windmills, their vanes breathless in the darkness.

She listened as the impostor spoke. "You expect *me* to pull this off by myself?" came her peppery words. "I'm only here because you hired me."

Hired?

Katherine was aware of her own heartbeat. Not only did she feel it pumping inside her chest, she felt the pulsing . . . no, the *throbbing* . . . in her ears.

"Yes . . . yes, I can handle Christmas dinner, but I'd feel better about things if you were here . . . at least in the house."

The pause was much longer than before, as though the

person on the other end had much to say.

Who's calling this late? Katherine wondered.

Then the revealing words pierced her through—words that made the hairs on the back of her neck prickle. "But I can almost feel it—I'm *that* close. Tonight your wife told me, in so many words, she has some big news. Probably about the money."

Your wife? Who was Katie Lapp talking to?

Suddenly, Katherine knew. The fake Katie was on the phone with Mr. Bennett! But . . . what did she mean about "the money"?

Her heart pounded wildly, though she refused to stand by, privy to a possibly wicked, greislich scheme. An innocent, dying woman's money must surely be at stake. Letting herself out, Katherine waited in the darkest corner of the hallway for the woman to finish her loathsome chat.

No wonder, she thought. No wonder Dylan Bennett had had such a chilling effect on her when first she'd called here.

Her mind spun in all sorts of directions. Such connivings and finaglings! Something, something must be done to set the record straight. She must move in where angels fear to tread. Yet what could she say or do to prove she was truly Laura's daughter—and Katie was not?

She had no proof. Or did she?

She remembered the little lilac sachets she'd brought from Hickory Hollow—so like the ones she'd found in the bureau drawers here. Would they be enough to persuade the mistress?

How she wished she could sit down with the Wise Woman. Ella Mae would gladly help her decipher the situation, if only Katherine had not been shunned.

She couldn't leave New York and return to Pennsylvania. No, she must stay put, stay here in her mother's house. Protect Laura Bennett's money, estate, or whatever it was, from falling into the wrong hands. Do something to bring a black-hearted soon-to-be-transgression to a screeching halt.

Do something. . . .

Just ahead, in the darkened hallway, a figure emerged from a curtained entryway. She wondered who on earth was lurking in the corridor. When the shadow evolved into a man—a man with a determined stride—she was reminded of the senior chauffeur, Theodore Williams.

What was the old gentleman doing? Snooping?

She stood glued to the spot, unable to think of what she might do to get his attention without alerting the imposter. Well, by the looks of things, she wasn't the *only* one who'd just overheard a most suspicious telephone conversation.

Katherine waited until the hallway was completely clear before heading back toward the stairs. As she was about to reach for the banister railing, she stopped and thought of her ailing mother, the dear, unsuspecting woman. What lay in store for her?

Turning, she made her way toward the south wing, in the direction of Laura's suite of rooms.

Wide awake, with no hope of falling back to sleep, at least not tonight, she tiptoed down another long passage-way. Her destination was the tall French doors. As she crept through the darkness, she thought of the artist's portrait and knew she must see the canvas for herself.

At once, Katherine realized she was standing on the spot where she'd first encountered Katie Lapp, the "Amish-woman" who hadn't understood even a few simple words of Dutch. The woman who was concocting something evil with Laura's *husband*, of all things!

Silently, Katherine moved through the open glass doors and into the formal sitting area. A lovely dinner table, displaying two crocheted place mats, was situated off to the side near a fireplace, embers dying fast.

To her right, she spied an easel where a large canvas, now

draped, had been erected. Wondering if this was the commissioned work Rosie and Garrett had spoken of yesterday,
she stole over to it, careful not to bump into several brushes
drying on the floor.

With a steady hand, she pulled back the sheet and
peered at the unfinished painting. Stepping aside, she allowed the window's snowy reflection to cast a silver glow
over the canvas.

She caught her breath as she studied the art. Off to the
right side of center, Laura's outline was evident. What
seemed odd was the hollow space directly in the middle.
Was this to be the spot for Laura's daughter? If so, why
hadn't the artist sketched in at least *something* there?

Katherine tilted her head, wondering what it would be
like to pose for a portrait. To be painted alongside her natural mother. Her rightful place!

Anger rose up in her. Ach, she must devise a way for Mr.
Wirth to paint the *correct* person in the designated location
on the canvas: Laura Bennett's true daughter—Katherine
herself. Otherwise the portrait would be a lie. As deceitful
as the man named Dylan D. Bennett, she recalled from the
phone book in Lydia Miller's kitchen.

Thinking about Mr. Bennett's name, she wondered if the
middle initial might not stand for Devil. She couldn't imagine what sort of man would plan to hurt his own bride in
such a way, a desperately ill wife at that. A wicked, wicked
man, for sure. Not in the sense he would dish out harsh
treatment according to a religious ruling, as Bishop John had
done, not *that* sort of man. But a sneaky, conniving person.
For sure and for certain.

Shivering with emotion, she redraped the canvas, remembering she had been accused of being that way herself—more conniving than any of the People in all of Hickory Hollow.

But not anymore. She was different through and through

because of who she was—Katherine Mayfield, the upstanding daughter of a kindhearted woman. She figured that because of Laura Bennett's close connection with the Almighty, she, too, was somehow linked to righteousness. Hadn't this been the real problem all along—trying to measure up to the Ordnung without knowing who she really was?

She thought of her Amish mamma, how gentle and honest Rebecca had always seemed. Yet how sadly mistaken Katherine had been, discovering that the woman she thought of as her angel-mother had in all truth been a liar, had kept from her supposed daughter a secret so painful it gouged out an instant wedge between them.

Jah, Rebecca Lapp had been a wonderful-gut storyteller, all right, in *every* sense of the word. The secret of Katherine's so-called "adoption" had been so devastating, it jolted her right out of the place she'd called home.

Now she lived *here*, safely under her birth mother's roof, and she resolved to do everything in her power to halt this treacherous scheme. That horrible thing Dylan D. Bennett was cooking up with the impostor Katie, even at this very moment!

She left the large parlor room silently and hurried back upstairs to her own quarters. Then before going to bed, she gathered up the potpourri sachets from each of the drawers and placed them on her pillow. The smell of lavender sweetened the dreary wee hours and soothed her soul.

CHAPTER EIGHTEEN

❖ ❖ ❖

Theodore slept fitfully that night, tossing about, even punching his pillow off the bed at one point. His dreams were anything but good ones; nightmares best described the visions of villainy he experienced.

Upon arising, he thought nothing of traipsing across the hall to the room where Fulton and Rosie Taylor made their marital love nest. Lightly, yet firmly, he knocked on their door.

The sleepy-eyed butler came promptly. "Theodore? Is everything all right?"

"Not on your life. I have to speak with you . . . immediately."

Fulton put his hand on the doorknob, pulling the door closed behind him. Wearing his white nightshirt and nothing on his feet, he stepped into the hallway. "What *is* it, Williams?"

"How quickly can you dress?"

Fulton nodded as though he understood the urgency. "Give me three minutes."

Satisfied his friend had taken him seriously, Theodore added, "I'll wait for you in my room, and don't bother to knock." He sighed. "What I have to tell you must be kept in strictest confidence."

❖   ❖   ❖

"I could use your help presenting the Christmas cake during dinner at noon," Rosie told Katherine. "You'll light the candles. Of course, you'll be careful not to utter a word either to the mistress or her daughter—attend only to your duties. Do you understand?"

Katherine cringed at hearing the phony Amishwoman being referred to as Laura's daughter. Still, she couldn't believe her luck—being asked to look after dessert in the grand dining room. "I'm to light the candles . . . on the cake?"

"Yes, Mrs. Bennett has been enjoying this tradition for several Christmases now; in fact, she's the one responsible for it in the first place." Rosie went on to explain that the cake was to be in commemoration of Christ's birth. "A birthday cake, so to speak."

"Oh" was all Katherine could say. Such a thing was strange to her—not having been given birthday cakes as a child growing up. Still, Lydia Miller had made them for her sons, and sometimes Katherine, along with the rest of her Amish family, would be included in the Mennonite frolic, enjoying a piece of cake—ice cream, too—with candles representing the appropriate year of celebration. So it wasn't as if she were completely in the dark about it.

Smiling, she realized again her natural mother seemed to possess a childlike heart and a flair for fancy things. *Just like me.*

After all, birthday cakes were for children—English children—weren't they? She was delighted Rosie had asked her to serve Laura Bennett on this special day.

She went about her routine work, grateful she had not been appointed the task of cleaning the Tiffany Room, where the dreadful impostor was staying. Surprisingly, Rosie had assigned the room to herself today, in spite of the fact that Rosie Taylor was clearly the mistress's personal maid.

◈　◈　◈

Before Laura's breakfast was served in bed, she received a telephone call. The estate operator answered, patching Dylan through. "Merry Christmas, darling," she heard him say.

"And to you," she replied happily.

"You may have heard I wasn't able to make it home last night."

She nodded silently. Many nights her husband's whereabouts were suspect. Nothing new.

Yet she listened as he continued. "Rochester and I have been holed up downtown—snowbound—waiting for the roads to open. Minutes from home but stuck all the same."

"You're *stranded?*" Instantly, she felt sorry for him. It was Christmas, after all. "You stayed in a hotel, I trust."

"Yes, and I'm awaiting a tow at the moment. Should be home in time for the holiday dinner, though. At least, that's our intention."

"Well . . . I do . . . I do hope you'll make it all right." In spite of her faltering speech, she thought of telling him how lovely her evening visit with Katie had been, but she thought better of it.

"How are you feeling today, Laura?"

He sounded genuinely concerned, and she found her heart lifting, daring to hope her Christmas miracle might include some kind of reconciliation between the two of them. "I think I may be improving. It's most extraordinary what's happening . . . it's the discovery of Katie, I believe. Getting acquainted with my daughter is putting me over the

189

top, giving me a new lease on life. And I have *you* to thank for it, Dylan."

She sighed, pulling the bed comforter close. Tears welled up unexpectedly. "I do so appreciate what you've done for me . . . about locating Katie, I mean."

Anticipating a reply, she waited. Strangely enough, the line seemed to have gone dead. "Dylan . . . are you there?"

"Ah yes . . . yes," he sputtered. "Glad to hear of your improving health. I'll be home very soon." And without saying good-bye, he hung up, giving the impression of being terribly rushed as their conversation came to a close.

Rushing home to *her?* She sighed again, choosing to dwell on Dylan's timely present. A true and glorious Christmas gift.

◈   ◈   ◈

"Please, tell us a story, Mam," Elam pleaded. "Just a short one'll do." He sat next to his wife, Annie, leaning elbows on his parents' kitchen table. His younger brothers, Eli and Benjamin, were finishing up their desserts, helping themselves to seconds and thirds of ice cream. They'd had the noon meal early, at their usual time, in spite of Christmas.

"Ach, my stories are for the womenfolk," Rebecca replied, waving her hand the way she always did.

"No, no," Annie chimed in. "Not necessarily true. You've told many a story right here round this table, Mam."

His mother looked downright haggard and pale, far different from the rosy-cheeked woman he knew. Her hazel eyes had always been clear and alert; today they seemed cloudy and, jah, sad.

If only his sister hadn't gone and gotten herself shunned, none of this would be happening with Mamma. *Katie's fault,* he thought as angry thoughts crowded his mind.

Benjamin spoke up. "Tell us about the time the horses ran off with ya. Now, that's a gut one."

The rest of the family, even Samuel, joined in the chorus, attempting to get Rebecca to loosen up her tongue. Too long since any of them had heard her go on and on with one of her stories. Much too long.

Elam was worried. From everything Annie had told him, he wondered if his mother might not be losing her mind. Still, he had to try to get her talkin' 'bout the past . . . *any* part of her life she deemed worthy to recite.

" 'There was once a girl named Rebecca,' " began Elam, prompting her. " 'She was out in the potato field, doin' the plowing for her Pop when—' "

"Elam, now stop right there! You daresn't trick me into storytellin' thataway."

His face stung with the rebuke. "Sorry, Mamma. I just thought—"

"Don't be getting yourself into trouble by thinkin'. Do ya hear?"

"It's all right, Rebecca," his father spoke up. "Our son meant no harm."

"Dat's right. Honest, I didn't, Mamma."

"My storytellin' days are behind me," declared Rebecca. "And nobody, not you, not any of the family, can make me start again."

Elam was silent, hoping she might go on to explain herself, to tell the family gathered here what was so awful troubling to keep her from sharing the stories she'd always held dear. But his mother clammed up right then and there, and that was the end of the discussion.

Eli and Ben got to talking about Jake Stoltzfus, Mary's uncle, who'd headed out to Indiana somewheres already, even before the holidays. While they gabbed, Elam daydreamed, watching Annie snuggle their baby son close.

Out of the blue, Mamma leaped clean out of her seat,

ranting on about hearing a baby crying. Annie shot him a concerned glance, and he caught the bewildered looks of the others, too. It was as if their mother had gone daft before their very eyes.

"Baby Daniel's sound asleep," Annie said softly, reassuring her.

"No, it ain't my grandson I heard," replied Rebecca. She cocked her head, listening as she stood in the middle of the kitchen floor. "There . . . don'tcha hear that?"

Elam shook his head. "Why not sit down and rest a bit, Mamma. No one's crying."

By now Samuel had gotten up and gone over to wrap his long arms around the glassy-eyed woman. "Come on, now, Becky, let's have ourselves a little chat."

"No, no . . . no," came the frightening reply. "There's a baby upstairs a-cryin'. I hear her, Samuel. I do!" She was pushing her husband away now, the glazed look spreading across her tear-streaked face. "My little daughter needs me, don'tcha see? Ach, my baby needs me so."

Elam fought back his own tears, hot vexing ones. Just look what Katie had done to their precious mamma. Look what she'd done to *all* of them.

CHAPTER NINETEEN

❖　　❖　　❖

As far as Fulton was concerned, Theodore's plan was splendid. They'd simply wait for the master of the house to return. If he was marooned somewhere in town, as his phone call to his wife had indicated, Master Dylan would be fidgeting about now, anxious to get home to oversee his underhanded plot. And, no doubt, to enjoy the lavish Christmas feast.

Meanwhile, Rosie had decided to do some plotting of her own, astute woman that she was. In the last-minute preparations, she might inadvertently question the woman who called herself Katie Lapp.

"Do be careful, my love," Fulton said in the privacy of their quarters. "I'll not have anyone scolding or picking a fight with my sweet pea."

"Oh, now, you mustn't worry. Miss Katie Lapp, whomever she is, has nothing to say to me!" And she was off down the hall to tend to her duties.

When he encountered the artist coming down for breakfast, Fulton greeted the man with generous praise. "I hope you won't mind, but I had myself a peek," he admitted. "Last evening."

Justin Wirth smiled, his blue eyes shining. "It's not always possible to keep a project under wraps, I've found."

"Especially at Christmas?"

"The most fickle of seasons, unfortunately." The young man was as cordial as he was comely.

"Do keep up the good work," Fulton said with a knowing wink, excusing himself. He was eager to assume his tasks today—the Lord's birthday. To assist God almighty with some "housecleaning"—well, just a bit. To help right the wrongs of this manor, he and his good wife, Rosie.

◈　◈　◈

Mary Stoltzfus thought it would be nice to deliver her home-baked sweets *before* the bishop's family had their Christmas dinner. She'd heard through the grapevine that the meal was set for twelve-thirty sharp. Later than many of the holiday meals served up at dairy farmers' homes in the Hollow.

Somehow, she would plan to make an honest excuse to run an unexpected errand, tell her parents and grandmother she'd be back in a jiffy. 'Course, they'd all know what she was up to, but that wouldn't do no harm, really. Most everyone in Hickory Hollow felt mighty sorry for John Beiler and his five motherless children. Woe be it unto her not to help spread Christmas cheer to the only widowed bishop around these parts.

So, trying not to think much about her best friend and all that Katie had gone through to keep from marrying the good Bishop, Mary selected several dozen each of angel gingerbread and sour cream chocolate cookies, packed them carefully, and took them in her father's carriage to the bishop's.

Little Jacob answered the front door. "Hullo," he said, letting her in, eyes wide. "Merry Christmas to ya."

"Same to you, Jacob." She stood there in the front room,

feeling mighty awkward now that she was here. Still holding her basket of sweets, she smiled down at the beautiful boy with wheat-colored hair and the bluest eyes she'd ever seen.

"Didja bake somethin' for me?"

"Jah, for you and your brothers and sisters."

"*Daed* too?"

She nodded.

" 'Cause my father needs some gut home cookin', ya know. He needs to find us a mamma awful bad."

"Oh?" The youngster's words surprised her.

"Jah, 'cause after Katie went down to you-know-where, we just kept on waitin' round for the Lord God to send us someone else. So far, we ain't seen no one pretty as your girlfriend."

"Jacob!" The bishop came rushing in the room to snatch up his young son and carry him back into the kitchen.

She heard bits and pieces of the reprimand but was glad to know the little fella wasn't in too terrible much trouble, bein' only four and all.

In a short time, she was handing over her basket of goods to Bishop John, saying, "Merry Christmas to all of you."

"It was gut of you to pay us a visit, Mary. Thank you kindly." The bishop's voice sounded softer, more compassionate than at any Sunday Preachin' service. Soft as a breeze in summer. She wished ever so much she might stay and linger in its tenderness.

❖　❖　❖

"Ousting Katie Lapp is the least of our worries," Theodore whispered to Rosie in the hallway. "What'll we tell Mrs. Bennett?"

"Well, I'd hate to add to her misery, poor soul," she said, brushing back a strand of graying hair. "But, according to the nurse, the mistress seems to be improving . . . ever since she

195

and the young woman started getting on so well. Even *I* can see the progress she's made. So you have a point. Running the impostor off may not be such a wise move at the moment."

Theodore mulled it over, stepping back to lean on the banister railing. "We may not have long to work out the details—that is, if you plan to confront the Amishwoman this morning. Do you?"

"That's just it—she's not Amish," Rosie informed him on a triumphant note. "She's an actress or model from New York City. Can you imagine?"

Theodore scratched his head. "You took some liberties with the master's files, I do believe."

Rosie nodded sheepishly. "Fulton and I happened upon a random file marked 'Katie Lapp'—and . . . well, we couldn't resist a peek."

"Unscrupulous rogue," he whispered.

Turning to go, Rosie called over her shoulder. "Better wait to decide until after I have a chat with Natalie. She'll know what best to do for the mistress."

Heart sinking, Theodore walked down the hall and into the kitchen. They'd had their chance while Dylan was out. Could've sent the Amishwoman packing right after breakfast. A delay could cause unnecessary tension among the domestic staff for the holiday. In fact, he was most certain it would.

Already this morning, word had spread through the ranks that Mr. Bennett and Rochester had gotten themselves stranded in town somewhere—the best limousine thrust into a snowbank.

He stifled a laugh, thanking the Good Lord. It might've been *him* stuck overnight with that snake, Dylan Bennett.

Time was of the essence. He scurried to his post.

◈   ◈   ◈

It seemed providential, almost. Katherine had gone outside to shake rugs from the butler's pantry when she'd happened upon Theodore Williams. He was whistling as he worked, shoveling the snow off the back steps and walkway.

When he noticed her, she was surprised that he stopped what he was doing to speak. "A fine Christmas morning, isn't it?"

"Yes, and a good thing to see that the worst of the storm is over." She shook one of the smaller rugs a bit longer than necessary, wondering if the old gentleman would return to his work.

She was pleasantly surprised when he struck up a real conversation. "It's high time we got better acquainted, you and I. Yes"—and here he seemed to mutter to himself. Then he came out with it. "I do believe I owe you an apology, Katherine."

"Whatever for?"

He offered her that faint yet grandfatherly smile. "For not properly welcoming you to the Bennett estate."

"Thank you." How truly good of him, although she could see no reason for him going out of his way to say such a thing. For a moment, she thought again of her Dawdi David. Mr. Williams' words rang out as soundly and confidently as those of her Amish mamma's father.

The gentleman struggled to pull up his coat sleeve with a gloved hand, studying his watch. "I best keep shoveling. It'll be dinnertime before we know it. Season's greetings to you," he said, as though dismissing her.

"Merry Christmas, Mr. Williams."

He chuckled. "Please, call me Theodore."

She said nothing in response, only smiled back at the man. The pitch of his voice, the way he looked at her—all of it—unnerved her more than she cared to admit.

❖   ❖   ❖

Dan Fisher thought it terrific to have been invited to dinner at the home of the boss and wife. Owen and Eve Hess were his dearest friends in all of Jersey. No finer Mennonites around. He felt blessed of the Lord to have been privileged to work alongside such genuinely devout and caring people.

Sharing office space in Owen's firm had been a godsend from the start. Not many established architects would've given a farm-boy-turned-draftsman a job fresh out of college. Yes, Owen had been kind to him all these years, assisting Dan in establishing an ever-growing clientele. Yet as generous a man as Owen was, Dan had never spoken of his Amish background. Or of the sailing accident that had triggered the ripple effect in his life.

Thinking he ought to ask ahead for some time off after the New Year, he'd volunteered to work overtime during the holidays. And the good man had agreed. "You haven't missed a day since you came to work for me," Owen had pointed out.

So everything was in order to return to Hickory Hollow for a visit. Only one problem could he foresee: telling Owen how to get in touch with him while there. He'd rehearsed various ways of revealing where he was going. To visit old friends . . . to see his only sister . . .

What could he say without divulging his past? He didn't know exactly how to handle the situation. Perhaps it was time to reconsider the long-kept secret. Not that he was ashamed of his heritage, not in the least.

But things *were* complicated, did not appear on the surface as they truly were. Nothing about that day five years ago could be described in black or white; nothing about his impromptu decision was simple. . . .

The storm had come out of nowhere, else he would've stayed ashore—never even rented the sailboat. Mercilessly, the squall had tipped the boat, tossing him overboard. From that point on, everything had become muddled up in his mind.

The very reason for going to Atlantic City had been to give himself opportunity to think. To contemplate his future with the Hickory Hollow church. And even though it was a relatively common thing for a baptized Amish boy to hire a Mennonite van driver to take him to the ocean on a birthday spree, he'd felt somewhat awkward going it alone that day.

Thankfully, the driver had known of him from his birth, being Peter Miller's brother-in-law, a God-fearing Mennonite who lived only a few miles from Hickory Hollow. And oh, how they'd talked—practically the whole way to the shore. Mostly about religion, especially in regard to Dan's points of contention with the Amish church.

It wasn't unheard of for professional drivers to take Amish folk here and there in their fancy cars or vans. For a price, of course. And Dan had paid dearly, but not so much in terms of the cents-per-mile quote to his final destination. *His* payment had come in costly denominations of love lost: relationships with dear ones, family and extended family—church members he'd known and loved all his life. Paid for with a single report from the Coast Guard.

Gone . . . his former life. Gone, his future with Katie.

Pinning a gold clasp to his tie, Dan wondered what Samuel Lapp's only daughter would think of him now if she could see him dressed this way. "Fancy like the English," Katie would say. A sobering thought, to be sure.

Would he never stop thinking of the girl he'd left behind? All these years, the one thing that had kept him going was the hope that his sweetheart girl must have surely found happiness with another man. A good fellow in the Amish church who embraced the same faith as her forefathers.

Yet thoughts of Katie—sweet, headstrong girl that she

was—married to someone else tore at his soul. He was caught in the middle, with no way out.

Outside, the noonday sun made ribbons of gold on the deep, deep snow, and as Dan left his home, most of the house lights shone out from the windows, upstairs and down. Giving no thought to the huge electric bill sure to follow, he drove his fine car through icy streets, his heart as heavy as the new-fallen snow.

CHAPTER TWENTY

Tall tapers were flickering on the dining room table when Dan arrived at the Hess home. In spite of the snowy brightness outside, Owen's wife had set a festive table, complete with candlelight.

He and his boss settled into comfortable chairs in the living room, visiting, doing their best to avoid "shop talk" while Eve worked in the kitchen. "It's good you're taking some time off here soon," Owen commented.

"I'm looking forward to it. Hope to visit relatives in Pennsylvania."

"Oh . . . whereabouts?"

"The Lancaster area. Ever hear of a place called Hickory Hollow?" A lump constricted in his stomach. Even speaking the name of his birthplace brought on a mixture of emotions—both stress and bliss.

"Can't say I've ever heard of it, really. Must be a little hamlet somewhere off in the hills."

"That's right." He paused.

"What relatives do you have living there?" came the curious reply.

"Actually, my entire family lives there. My parents and

brothers—all married. And Annie, my sister, she's a married woman now, I hear."

"Well, you should've asked off for her wedding," Owen said, smiling. "I'm an understanding man."

Dan leaned forward, feeling the tension knotting in his neck. "It's been over five years since I've seen any of them." The realization brought renewed sorrow. "It's time for a visit."

"I should say so." Wearing a serious expression, Owen folded his arms across his chest. "I think you've been working too many long hours here lately."

Dan sighed and plunged in. "I suppose . . . well, there's a reason why I work so much." And he began to unravel bits and pieces of his secret past.

When his chronicle was through, he sat back and let out a deep breath. He'd purposely left out a few sacred details. Couldn't bring himself to verbalize everything—the wounds still so raw. Couldn't just blurt out the reason why he'd let the People—Katie, too—think he'd died in the sailing accident.

Owen sat up, folded his hands, and expressed a desire to pray. "Let's ask the Lord to go before you, to open the doors for you to speak to your father. We'll pray that God will soften the hearts of your people . . . your family."

Owen had not mentioned a word about Katie. But then, Dan's friend wasn't the type of man to risk embarrassing anyone. Not in the least.

❖   ❖   ❖

"Do I have time to make a phone call?" the impostor asked as she and Katherine passed in the hall, a few feet from the library. The woman looked well rested, Katherine thought, after having been up all hours the night before.

She shrugged. "Dinner will be served any minute now, but go ahead."

"Then you'll cover for me?" The woman sounded much too demanding, but before Katherine could reply, Katie Lapp scurried off into the enormous room filled with many, many books and one telephone.

Not interested in listening to another disgusting conversation, Katherine stayed put, waiting outside as the young woman placed her call.

Fortunately, the phone chat didn't last more than a few minutes. Katie rushed out of the library, her eyes bright. "I haven't missed anything, have I?"

"Not a thing."

"That's good, because I was dying to talk to my boyfriend. He's really put out with me that I'm not home for Christmas."

Katherine decided to take a chance. "Oh? Where is home?"

"Pennsylvania."

"Really? I'm from there, too."

The smile faded instantly. "Small world," mumbled the woman, and Katherine thought she heard a groan.

"So it is." Unconsciously, she reached up to adjust her cap. A mere habit, a reflex born of the Plain years. Instead, her hand found the ruffled maid's cap, the fancy thing that marked her new life.

❖   ❖   ❖

It had been harder to deal with his wife than Samuel Lapp would ever have thought possible. Rebecca was pretty near hysterical.

"I *said* I was sorry about the baby crying and bothering everyone's dinner. I *knew* I shouldn't have let her sleep all by herself upstairs," she sobbed in the front room.

Samuel had no idea what to do or say to get his wife calmed down. She'd caused such a scene at the table, and Annie, dear girl, was left to clean the kitchen alone.

Elam, Eli, and Benjamin, much to his relief, had vacated the house. But now here *he* was, with a dilemma on his hands: how to help Rebecca get ahold of herself.

He took both her hands in his. "There's no baby upstairs, Becky, honest there ain't. There's only one baby in the house right now; it's little Daniel, and lookee here"—he guided his sniffling wife over to the doorway, and they peered through to the kitchen—"he's sound asleep over there in the cradle Elam made."

His wife's eyes were dark, unusually so, and the look in them was alarming. He thought about riding over to see the bishop after a bit, have a quick, quiet talk. On second thought, he didn't want to disrupt John Beiler's Christmas with his family. Didn't want to let on anything was wrong in front of the children, neither.

Rebecca was crying more softly now. "I want my baby girl back. Can't live another day without my Katie girl."

He took the sobbing woman in his arms, held her close. There was no rebuking her now. She'd spoken their shunned daughter's name, not out of willful disobedience. Rebecca was clearly out of her mind.

"I'll see what I can do," he said, groping for something to ease her pain. "We'll keep on a-praying for her soul."

It had been the only approach to take. The weeping ceased and his wife pulled away. A smile broke across the tear-streaked face. "Ach, you *will* help bring her home, won'tcha, Samuel? You gonna help me get our baby girl back?"

He leaned down and kissed her wet face. "I miss her, too, Becky . . . I do." And he brushed away his dear wife's tears gently with his thumbs, wondering if and when she'd ever be right again.

❖   ❖   ❖

Dylan let himself in the front door, catching the aroma of roast duck. "Splendid," he whispered, ignoring the fact that Fulton was not at his post.

He kept his overcoat and scarf on until after arriving in his upstairs office, where he removed both, draping them over the leather couch. How good to be home again, he thought and wondered when he ought to seek out his Amish impersonator.

Quickly, he located his files—his secret copy of Laura's last will and testament. He was pleased. Everything was in order, where it belonged.

A loud knock came at his door, and he jumped, startled. "Who's there?" he called.

"Fulton, sir."

"One moment." Dylan gathered up the papers and stuffed them back into the file drawer. Then moving around to his desk, he sat down, folding his hands in front of him. "Come in."

The door opened and in walked the butler. "Christmas dinner will be served in ten minutes, sir."

"In the dining room?"

Fulton nodded slowly, then paused for a moment. "Mrs. Bennett and her daughter plan to join you there as well."

"Ah . . . good." He'd guessed the three of them might share this special meal. "Together at last," he quipped.

"Indeed." Fulton stood there, waiting to be excused, his eyes set in a cold, unforgiving stare. "Will that be all, sir?"

"One more thing. How are the mother and daughter getting along, would you say?"

"Famously" came a stony reply.

"I see. And what of Mrs. Bennett's health?"

"Sir?"

"Is it safe to assume the mistress will be comfortably sedated for the meal?"

"Nurse Judah is better prepared to answer that question, sir."

He rubbed his chin, waiting, yes, taunting the tall man. "I see, but what is *your* assessment of the mistress's overall demeanor?"

Obviously annoyed, Fulton shrugged. "I'd say she's quite delighted, sir. Happy to be celebrating the Good Lord's birthday."

Dylan cringed. Why must the man bring the Lord into it?

"But what of her illness? Is she improving?" he pressed further.

An eye-opening smile played across the butler's face. "With God's help, I pray Mrs. Bennett might outlive us all."

Suppressing a curse, Dylan excused the butler immediately.

❖   ❖   ❖

Katherine held the box of matches in her hand, gazing down the hallway for a long moment. Mr. Bennett was home; she could hear his deep voice, mingled with Katie Lapp's and Rosie's, who was most likely feeding the mistress her dinner.

Apprehension gripped her, threatening her resolve.

This is what you've been waiting for. Now is your moment.

But she wasn't ready to seize it. Couldn't get her confidence back, for one thing. She thought of the sachet link between herself and the mistress, the color and thickness of their hair . . . everything and anything to encourage herself. Boost her spirits.

But it was the painting, and her rightful place in it, that made her blood pressure rise. She would move heaven and earth to see that the phony Katie never, *never* showed up in that mother-daughter portrait!

When Selig burst through the kitchen's double doors carrying a two-layer cake perched high on an elegant silver cake stand, she was ready and eager to follow him down the hall and into the luxurious dining room.

Inside, Rosie was seated to Laura's left, feeding her a spoonful at a time. The sight of it pained Katherine greatly, and she had to look away. Yet doing so forced her to view either Mr. Bennett or Katie Lapp. Neither a worthy subject.

With a flourish, Selig set the elaborately decorated cake in the center of the long table, between two candelabra— directly across from the masquerader. Mr. Bennett and Laura sat at either end, and Katherine was surprised to hear both of them join in when Rosie started up the "Birthday Song."

That was her cue to light the candles. She took several steps toward the table, and leaning over opposite the impostor, she struck the first match, willing her hands not to tremble. Not to cause the slightest mishap in the lighting.

❖ ❖ ❖

Dan pulled his gaze away from the candle flame positioned in front of his dinner plate on the Hess table. How he longed to see his sweetheart again. If only for one glimpse.

When he visited Annie, he would plead with his sister to tell him of Katie's marriage. This, only after they discussed thoroughly a plan to approach their father for Dan's confession.

Yet he wondered, when the time came to hear the truth, could he take it like a man? Could he bear the pain?

If only he could arrange to observe Katie discreetly from afar. Across the barnyard, perhaps? As she hung out the week's wash on the front porch clothesline, maybe. She'd never have to know. . . .

"Can I get either of you some more coffee?" Eve asked as she snuffed out the candles and turned up the dimmer switch.

"Not for me, thanks." Dan watched the spiral of smoke as it curled toward the modest chandelier overhead. "Everything was delicious, Eve. Thank you for sharing your Christmas dinner. I really appreciate it."

"Oh, anytime." She smiled at him and turned to go into the kitchen.

"We mean that, you know." Owen wiped his mouth with the napkin. "Now, about the young woman you mentioned earlier. How will Miss Katie take the news of your being alive?"

Dan wished his friend hadn't mentioned it. "It's hard to say, really, but I don't plan to be around when the People find out about my confession. Katie included."

"So you'll leave Hickory Hollow without seeing her?"

He felt very nearly ill. Never before had he allowed himself to consider how he might handle things.

"She's better off hearing it from Annie. My sister's her oldest brother's wife."

"Ah . . . so you're nearly related, then," offered Owen.

Dan hadn't thought of that. Hadn't wanted to. There'd been enough of a love-bond between them without having to look the present facts squarely in the face. He didn't need his and Katie's past tied to an extended-family relationship in order to reconnect them.

Anyway, it was cruel to anticipate such a reunion. He wouldn't taunt himself, wouldn't entertain the hope of having Katie back. No, Elam's little sister was long married. He was almost sure of it.

CHAPTER TWENTY-ONE

❖ ❖ ❖

As it turned out, Laura hadn't gotten around to telling her daughter about her grandparents—the original owners of the estate. She'd planned to inform Katie of the will earlier this morning. This she felt to be a wise move, since who could tell what Dylan might do to get his hands on the young woman's inheritance after Laura's death?

A violent contracture of her ankle and lower leg had occurred after breakfast, and much to her dismay, Nurse Judah had had to notify the doctor. He, in turn, had ordered an hour of physical therapy. Excruciating as it was, the procedure had limbered up her muscles, easing some of the cramping, as well. But she'd completely missed out on her time with Katie.

Now as she sat in her beautiful dining room, she wondered when the appropriate time might present itself. Between bites of lemon cake, she tried to draw Katie out, to get her to share more of her life in Amish country.

"Perhaps she'd rather not talk about it in front of everyone, dear," Dylan piped up.

From the corner of the room, she noticed the blurred shape of Justin Wirth turn and face this way, curiously. "Oh, but I find the Plain lifestyle fascinating," the artist remarked.

Laura had nearly forgotten the man was even in the room, he worked so effortlessly, so silently. "Yes," she said softly, the word sticking in her throat. She was having much more difficulty swallowing. More so each day that passed.

"Where is it you come from?" Justin asked Katie.

"Lancaster, Pennsylvania. About five hours south of here."

"Nice place," he remarked.

Laura made another attempt at communicating. "Yes . . . it was beautiful even . . . even when I visited many . . . years ago." She was not about to reveal the truth of her most *recent* journey to Pennsylvania Dutch country. Besides, it was an effort to get the words out today. Sheer frustration had come with this untimely speech impediment where, always before, her enunciation had been precise. She was mortified.

Most upsetting of all was the humiliation of having to be fed in front of her husband and daughter. Still, she would not give up hope. Not until after she'd spoken with Katie in private. Then, and only then, would she allow the disease to run its terrible course.

❖   ❖   ❖

Here lately, Benjamin Lapp had been spending more time with the family pony, his shunned sister's pony, really. Funniest thing, he couldn't get the animal to come when called. Didn't seem to know his name—Tobias. But it was, after all, the name Katie had given him, long before she'd up and gone ferhoodled disobeying the bishop over a guitar and some ridiculous tunes she'd made up.

Truth was, he couldn't get Tobias to eat much, either. The beautiful animal had turned downright dumb. Ben had told his father and Eli about it, but he guessed they'd decided to pay him no mind, 'cause nobody but Ben seemed to care a hoot about coaxin' the poor thing to eat or drink.

Today he'd decided to try something new. Something sweet, straight from the dinner table. A sugar cookie, with extra sugar sprinkled on top.

He held the treat under Tobias's nose, letting him have a whiff, then crumpled it into the feed trough below. "There now, have yourself some dessert mixed with hay." He stroked the pony's mane. "Katie ain't here to spoil ya rotten, but I am. Now, please, won'tcha eat?"

He heard the scrape of work boots behind him. Turning, he saw his father's scowling face, and the angry words spewed forth. "Benjamin, didn't I tell ya weeks ago not to be mentioning your sister's name in my house? That goes for the barn, too. Your sister's under the shunning, have ya so soon forgotten?"

"No, sir."

"Well, then, what do ya mean by talking to this pony about that . . . that . . ." His father slumped down, bent his knee to the dirt floor.

"Dat? What's-a-matter?" He ran to his father.

Weeping, Samuel leaned his elbow on one knee and smothered his face into his big callused hand. "Your mamma's going crazy, Ben . . . and I can't just stand by and watch . . . watch her. . . . She's not herself no more."

"Aw, Pop, it'll be all right," he managed to say. "The bishop did the right thing, shunning my sister . . . didn't he?"

Shaking his head, Samuel moaned like he was in terrible pain, then he blurted out a whole slew of words in German, hurling profanities into the bitter cold air.

Tobias seemingly understood and began to whinny over and over, shaking his head again and again. But Ben couldn't bring himself to weep along with his father or to have a temper fit with stubborn Tobias. Still, his innards sure felt tore up, but good.

◈ ◈ ◈

When it was time, Katherine returned to the dining room with Garrett to clear away the dainty dessert dishes. She took Laura's plate and fork, handed to her by Rosie, and stopped in her tracks when she glanced over at the easel. Mr. Wirth was beginning to sketch some Amish clothing, the impostor's, probably.

She wanted to rush over and set him straight, tell him that not even the fake daughter's clothing represented any of the Lancaster orders. Truth be told, *nothing* about the woman was honest or decent.

Just when she thought she might disregard Rosie's request and actually speak to the artist while assisting at the table—just at that moment the fork slipped off the plate in her hand, and embarrassed, she bent down to retrieve it. When she did so, her maid's cap fell off and Katherine's hair cascaded over her shoulders.

Justin Wirth turned and looked at her, acknowledging her with a nod, staring at her hair. Their eyes locked for a long, long moment; he released her at last by turning to study his own painting, then glancing over at Katie, who was chattering away to Laura.

"Katherine," prompted Rosie, "you may take the dishes to the kitchen, please."

"Yes, ma'am," she replied, holding her hair back from her face with one hand. She escaped into the kitchen to repair the bun and replace her cap, then hurried back to the dining room.

When she returned for the crystal goblets, she knew she dare not look in the artist's direction. Those scrutinizing blue eyes . . . ach, how they haunted her. Disturbed her no end, for they reminded her of Daniel's.

"How do the Amish celebrate Christmas?" Mr. Bennett spoke up.

Startled for a moment, thinking it was *she* the man was speaking to, Katherine opened her mouth to reply. Thankfully, she caught herself in time to remember she was no longer Amish. In time to overhear a pathetic, inaccurate account of Plain folk running around with handsaws, cutting down trees, dragging them out of the forest to their homes to be decorated with quilted homemade ornaments. She almost laughed at the ridiculous spiel. And something about the way it all tumbled out, something about the way the impostor's lies seemed to roll off her tongue, told Katherine the whole thing had been very well rehearsed.

"Excuse me, but that's not the way it is," Katherine blurted out. "Amish people don't celebrate Christmas with decorated trees."

Rosie and Garrett gawked at her, but she couldn't stop. Had to explain things the way they truly were.

"How would *you* know?" the false Katie accused.

"I know" was all Katherine said, turning her full gaze on the woman in her Amish costume.

Mr. Bennett stood up suddenly. "Who *is* this woman?" he demanded.

Katherine cringed. Himmel! She'd spoken out of turn, should never have given in to her emotions. Now she was done for.

Rosie made an attempt to gloss things over. "This is our new maid, sir. Fulton signed her on two days ago."

"Does the woman have a name?" he bellowed.

She spoke up quickly. "Katherine, sir."

His face flushed bright red. "Yes, well, may I see you outside?" He gave a nod toward the hallway.

"Excuse me," she said, especially for Laura's and Rosie's sake. But she kept her eyes on the floor when it came to Katie Lapp, sitting so smug in all her glory. Puh!

"So . . . it's Katherine, is it?" He purposely lowered his

voice, hoping for a chilling effect.

"At your service, Mr. Bennett." She curtsied.

"What is the requirement for servants' communication at the table?" he drilled her, captivated by her stubborn yet refreshing naiveté.

" 'Speak only when spoken to in regards to table or food needs,' " Katherine recited.

"Very well. You broke the rules of the house, and what?—during your first days of employment? Not a good beginning."

Would she break down? Cry for him? he wondered.

"I'm sorry, sir. I'll try harder next time" came the meek little voice. Much like a child would address her parent.

He had to suppress a laugh, lest he be heard in the dining room. Initiating their movement down the hall, he led her farther away from the gathering. "We'll certainly see about that, won't we?"

"No, sir . . . I mean, yes, sir," the young woman stammered.

She couldn't be much older than his New York model. Still, he looked her over, up and down, surprised that she was still casting an innocent gaze back at him when his eyes fell on her face once more.

This woman . . . what was it about her? So very different from the brazen, even seductive Alyson Cairns he'd brought here to deceive his dying wife.

"I shouldn't have said anything about the Amish, sir."

It would seem she was begging . . . pleading with him not to reprimand her further. Remarkable!

He added, "You will be placed on a probation of sorts."

"Probation?"

It was clear the woman had no clue of the word's meaning, and he chuckled. "Where've you been all your life?"

"Hickory Hollow, sir."

"I see." He wouldn't let her unsophisticated demeanor

rub him the wrong way. Yet what was it—that look about her?

"Hickory Hollow's an Amish community, sir," she continued. "I know about the Amish ways because I grew up in the Old Order."

He felt his eyes narrow into judgmental slits. "What did you say your name was?"

"Katherine, sir . . . from Hickory Hollow, Pennsylvania. I called you up on the phone not too long ago. Don't you remember?"

And he'd thought she was merely a misinformed yokel! How could he have miscalculated so?

"Pack your bags this instant," he hissed, glancing over his shoulder.

"I'm your wife's true daughter" came the amazing reply. "You mustn't force me to leave, Mr. Dylan D. Bennett. I've come such a long way!"

"What's your proof?"

"I have her hair." Katherine ripped off her maid's cap, auburn curls once again tumbling about her face, then turned her profile toward him. "And her chin. See?"

"You have nothing, you conniving little tramp!" He restrained her when she tried to push past him. "I'll have you arrested," he threatened. "You'll *never* set foot in this house again!"

Struggling, he clamped his hand over her delicate mouth and forced her to the stairs.

The commotion in the hallway disturbed Laura. She kept looking to Rosie for some explanation. "Dylan seemed terribly upset just now."

But the maid could only shrug her shoulders. "Something's got Mr. Bennett riled is all I know."

Even Justin had abandoned his brush to peer out the doorway. Such a bellowing. And for what?

Laura supposed it had to be something out of the ordi-
nary to ruffle Dylan's feathers so. Possibly the new maid's
outrageous comment. How did *she* know about Amish cel-
ebrations?

With the stress and the worrisome questions, came another attack. This time the pain shot through her face, accompanied by tremors in her throat. When she tried to
speak, to cry out, only the most guttural sounds emerged.

Natalie was summoned, and before she could be excused, Laura found herself being whisked out of the dining
room.

Christmas Day . . . oh, her heart went out to her daughter left sitting there alone at the table.

She prayed silently that the Lord might allow something
beneficial to come of the exodus. Perhaps *now* Justin could
focus on Katie, on painting her into the mother-daughter
portrait.

❖   ❖   ❖

It was late afternoon by the time Katherine checked into
a roadside motel, having arrived by taxi. She stopped crying
long enough to pay the lobby clerk for two day's rent. What
she would do after that, she didn't know. Acquiring a job
should be ever so easy, though, for a former Amishwoman
who could cook, keep house, care for children. . . .

But landing a job was the last thing on her mind.

She dried her tears and set about the chore of unpacking
her bag, then put her guitar away last of all. Sitting at the
desk in the small, musty room, she clenched her fists against
the thought of having been thrown out of the estate . . .
threatened, too, by that vicious man, Laura's husband! She
thought too, of her brief stay at the Bennett mansion, re-
gretting having no time or opportunity to say her good-byes

to the servants. For in such a short time, they'd become friends.

She thought of Rosie and Fulton, how they'd taken her under their collective wing, so to speak. And Mr. Williams—she did believe the old gentleman was just beginning to warm up to her.

Everyone had been so kind. Everyone except the master of the house. *He* had acted like the devil himself, and she wasn't all that sure that he wasn't.

After her unpacking was done, she realized the potpourri sachets had been left behind in the corners of the bureau drawers. All of them, even her own lilac ones.

The thought of having abandoned her own handmade creations caused her to cry all over again. But in the sadness—the pitying of herself—came the surprising answer to Mr. Bennett's accusation.

What's your proof? he'd roared at her.

Suddenly, she knew . . . realized fully what she needed for evidence, as sure as she was Laura Bennett's daughter, she knew. Now . . . how would she go about getting it? Who did she know in Hickory Hollow with a telephone?

Lydia Miller, of course! For the first time in several hours, Katherine smiled. Smiled so hard that half a dimple popped out on one cheek; she spied it in the wide mirror over the dresser.

There *was* proof. The kind of proof Mr. Bennett could never dispute. The rotten-to-the-core man would drop his teeth. For sure and for certain.

Now . . . how to get her hands on the satin baby gown?

Part III

The Lord is my light and my salvation—
whom shall I fear?

Psalms 27:1

CHAPTER TWENTY-TWO

❖   ❖   ❖

Lydia Miller went about the living room, gathering up crumpled wrapping paper amidst toys and games—Christmas presents to her young grandchildren. She was truly surprised when Edna summoned her from the kitchen wall phone. "I think it's long distance," her daughter-in-law said, covering the receiver. "Sounds like it might be Katherine."

"Katie Lapp?"

Edna nodded, and Lydia swept loose strands of hair into her covering before taking the phone. "Hello?"

"Cousin Lydia . . . it's me, Katherine, calling all the way from New York."

"Well, Merry Christmas to you. How nice to hear your voice."

There was a slight pause. "Lydia, uh, I was wondering . . . well, I need your help."

"Are you all right?"

"I'm fine, really I am. But I wonder if you could drive over to my mamma's house. I need you to talk to her. Today."

Lydia wondered what could be so important on a busy Christmas afternoon. But as the sketchy details began to unfold, she felt the weight of responsibility begin to settle on her shoulders. Still, she wasn't at all unwilling to do Katherine's bidding. "I'll see what I can do," she promised.

"Remember to ask Mamma gently. You'll do that, won't you, Cousin Lydia?"

"Of course I will." She sighed, wondering if she oughtn't to mention that Katie's mother and Ella Mae Zook had dropped by for a visit.

Stepping out in faith, hoping what she was about to say might help things, not hinder, Lydia told Katherine about the unexpected visit.

"Mamma . . . and the Wise Woman, really? They came to see you?"

"I know . . . I was surprised, too."

"Well, how's Mam doing?"

Lydia stared at the lights on the tree. "I'd say she must be awful preoccupied. She's suffered a terrible loss."

"True," came a tentative reply.

There was an awkward pause.

"So . . . you want me to get your old baby dress from her, then?"

"That's right. Only please tell my mother you want to *borrow* it. See what she says about that."

"I won't lie, Katherine. You know better than to ask me to." She wondered if the world had begun to rub off on her cousin's daughter.

"It wouldn't be a lie," Katherine insisted. "She'll have it back . . . in all good time."

Lydia sat down on the wooden stool near the wall while the caller continued. "Once you have it, I'll need you to mail it . . . by overnight mail, please. To me." And she gave the address of the motel.

"Aren't you staying at your natural mother's place?"

"Not now. It's a very long story, and I hope to share it with you someday, but . . . well, I'm paying for long distance."

"I understand, but I hate to think of you being at a motel somewhere, especially on Christmas Day. Bless your heart. Why, Rebecca would be worried sick if she knew."

"Oh, but she *mustn't*! Please don't tell Mamma that part. I'm fine here, Cousin Lydia, really I am. But getting the baby dress will solve everything. So if you'll save the receipt for the mailing, I'll pay you back. Please . . . this is ever so important to me."

Lydia could hear the longing in the young woman's voice. "I'll try, Katherine. But I'm telling you it may not be easy. Word has it your mother's not well."

"Mamma isn't?"

"Well, she's not herself, to say the least."

"Ach, no!"

"It's been a real blow, losin' her daughter both to a bishop's decree and then to a fancy, worldly woman."

"Oh, but you're wrong. My natural mother is anything *but* worldly. She's a good, honest woman. And I think she's about to be hoodwinked, possibly out of a lot of money. Maybe even her entire fortune."

Alarmed, Lydia promised to do her best to get the baby gown mailed up to New York. Fast as she could.

Nothing about the visit to the Lapp home was easy. To start with, Samuel almost didn't let her in—"because Rebecca's lyin' down just now," he apologized.

"Oh, I can come back later," she said.

At that, he seemed to open the door a bit wider even as he stood there making excuses for Rebecca who "ain't in any shape to be comin' downstairs for company."

Unconsciously, Lydia fixed her eyes on his tan suspenders, the sound of Katie's pleading over the phone echoing in her mind. The poor displaced girl was counting on her. And it was odd, but something inside her—a surprisingly powerful resolve—wouldn't let Lydia back off this first attempt at seeing Rebecca Lapp. Not without trying harder, at least.

"Maybe I could run up and see her. That way she wouldn't have to get dressed and all . . . unless she's sleeping."

Samuel shook his head. "No, no, she ain't asleep, but she's been through a horrible, awful time today." A long pause. " 'Tis our first Christmas without . . . without the girl. You can imagine. . . ."

But, no, she *couldn't* imagine. Her children were all grown and gone, true, but to have one of them leave the community because of some age-old ridiculous shunning practice! No . . . never.

She noticed the man's sunken eyes. One look at his forlorn countenance and Lydia could readily see the aftermath of grief. He, too, was suffering great loss.

"I'm so sorry . . . wish Peter and I could've helped Katie out more." She'd struggled off and on with guilt, having opened her home to Samuel and Rebecca's runaway daughter.

"You did all ya could," Samuel replied, and with that, he motioned her inside, took her coat, and led her upstairs.

When Lydia first laid eyes on her cousin, she felt near like crying herself. Rebecca was all doubled up on the bed, as though she was experiencing tremendous pain. She lay on her side, clutching a rose-colored baby dress in both hands.

The part that evoked tears was seeing the Amish-woman's lips move as if she were talking to the little dress; yet not a sound escaped her lips. Only Samuel's hard, frightened breathing could be heard in the room.

Lydia searched her pocketbook for a tissue. What had gone wrong? she wondered. How had her cousin slipped from yesterday's semidetached behavior to *this*? Had the severe shunning of her daughter pushed the woman over the edge?

Lydia could easily see there'd be no approaching Rebecca about giving up the beloved gown. Not today. Not with her clinging to it as if it were a lifeline to Katie, somehow.

Even if she went ahead and asked for it the way Katherine had suggested—to *borrow* it for a while—even then she knew the plea would be refused or misunderstood. No, borrowing the only threadlike connection to Katie—a symbol that might well be preserving the confused woman's sanity—well, it was out of the question completely.

How long she stood there, Lydia didn't know exactly. But when she turned to whisper to Samuel—that she'd best be going—Rebecca stirred a bit.

Startled, she hurried to the distraught woman's bedside. "Rebecca . . . it's your cousin Lydia. Is there something I can do for you?"

Rebecca's eyes were empty, dazed, and she began to moan—long, low-pitched groans, as if in travail.

The glassy-eyed look took Lydia by surprise—she was that shook up. "You don't have to speak, Cousin, but maybe a nod of the head?" She hated to inquire this way, as if she were talking to someone other than her own blood kin. Someone completely unrelated. "Are you in pain?" She had to know.

It was then that Katie's mamma placed her hand on her breast and tried to sit up.

"Are you in *physical* pain, Rebecca?"

Her cousin stared back blankly.

"Can you hear me?" she tried again.

Unexpectedly, there came a nod. "I must get up . . . must take care of Katie. Don't *you* hear my baby crying?"

So baffling was such a question, Lydia knew she couldn't bring herself to follow through on Katherine's request. Per-

haps someone else, someone *closer* to the Amish community, might be able to pry the baby dress away from the fingers of a brokenhearted mother.

Who would be willing to help Katie? Who in Hickory
Hollow could Lydia turn to?

❖   ❖   ❖

Mary couldn't stop thinking about her encounter with
the bishop. How mellow and strangely subdued his voice
had been. Honestly, she'd never heard him sound thataway.
Not at Preachin', for sure not at barn raisin's or nowhere
else, neither.

She wondered, had he softened his voice for her? To let
her know that the same man who'd shunned Mary's dearest
friend in all the world had another side to him? A kind and
gentle aspect to his soul?

Pondering this, she helped her mother prepare fruit salad
and leftover main dishes from the noon meal. She dared not
discuss her thoughts with Mam or Mammi Ruth, though
she'd thought of nothing else since arriving home from the
visit with John Beiler.

Oh, she hoped her sour cream chocolate cookies had
absolutely melted in his mouth—his and the children's. One
good way to a man's heart was through his stomach, her
mamma had always said. Jokingly, of course. But she'd seen
her mother's cooking work wonders with her Pop many a
time.

She thought of the next scrumptious recipe she might
offer to the bishop and his half-orphaned brood. Ach, she
wouldn't be waitin' long, neither. Come next Sunday, she'd
have another mouth-watering surprise for John Beiler.

And . . . she was gonna be listening; comparing, too, the
sound of his "delivery voice" during the sermon, weighing

it against the almost romantic utterances of this most glorious Christmas Day.

❖   ❖   ❖

She struggled to get past the haze in her mind. Fuzzy . . . woolly. *Everything* about Rebecca's thoughts felt that way—like peering through gray cellophane paper.

Fighting off a precarious feeling that if she let herself relax—even while lying in her own bed—if she gave in to the pulling, the all-consuming murkiness, it might swallow her up. Might devour her entirely, and she'd never be right again.

Something in her consciousness told her there was someone standing in the room. Someone besides Samuel. But she couldn't begin to guess who.

Then, intruding on her attempts to think . . . *think* . . . the crying returned. The insistent wail of a newborn baby. *Her* baby.

Frantic feelings pulled at her, deeper . . . deeper into the wailing. Into a tunnel, the corridor long and narrow. The desperate wail of a helpless child—her heart-child who could not receive nourishment.

Crying echoed in her ears, reverberating through the white, sterile passageway. Rebecca closed her eyes, trying to block out the heart-wrenching sound. As she did, the tunnel gave way to people—two women. One, a teenage girl carrying a sleeping baby, the other, the girl's mother.

"I want you to have my baby," said the girl with red hair.

Eagerly, Rebecca's arms went out to receive the beautiful infant. Her arms felt the slight weight of the tiny one, and she offered a warm bottle. But the rosebud lips would not suck.

More crying . . .

What would she do if she could never quiet the infant,

227

never be the kind of mother her baby truly needed?

But when she opened her eyes, longing to see the darling bundle, oh, yearning to gaze on her child, she looked—and Katie was gone.

Sitting up in bed, Rebecca listened, listened with all her might, but heard nothing. She hobbled down the hallway to another bedroom. Ach, the house was still. Dead still.

Sighing, she sat on Katie's bed, holding the satin baby gown. When she'd kissed it, she laid it back in its hiding place.

It was then she realized the infant's crying had stopped.

◈　◈　◈

Mary was caught off guard after supper when a big, beautiful car pulled up in the driveway. "Who's this?" she said to her mother.

They gawked out the window as a woman hurried to the back door. "Looks an awful lot like Rebecca's Mennonite cousin," whispered Rachel.

"Jah, I see whatcha mean."

When the knock came, Mary rushed to the door, welcoming their neighbor inside.

"Can't be staying long," Lydia said, keeping her coat on as Mary pulled up a chair. "I'll get right to the point."

Mary listened carefully as the woman described a phone call. One from Katie. "She called this afternoon, Katie did, needing a baby dress that her mamma's kept around all these years, I suppose. It's made of satin . . . pink, and has the name *Katherine Mayfield* embroidered on the back facing."

Completely in the dark as to what Lydia Miller wanted with either her or her mamma, Mary kept still and paid close attention.

"It seems Rebecca's mighty taken to the dress. I don't

know how to describe it, really, other than to say, she's clinging to her daughter's baby clothing for dear life, like it's all
she has left of the girl."

"What's Katie need the dress for?" Mary asked, wishing
more than ever she could help her friend.

"She really didn't say in so many words," Lydia answered, "but I think it has something to do with her natural
mother in New York. Anyhow, she needs it mailed up there
as soon as possible."

An overwhelming feeling welled in Mary's heart, and
she found herself volunteering out of the blue. "I'll go and
get the dress for Katie."

Lydia's face brightened instantly. "You will? You'll go
over to the Lapps' and talk to Rebecca?"

"I know she's hurtin' awful," she told the woman. "*All*
of us are worried sick about her mental state. But I have an
idea about the dress."

"Oh, I'm so glad I came over," Lydia said, putting her
hand to her throat. "I almost didn't come, almost had to call
Katie back and tell her the bad news."

"First thing tomorrow, I'll pay Katie's mamma a visit."
She couldn't put her finger on it, couldn't have explained it
to anybody if she'd wanted to, but for some unknown reason, Mary could hardly wait.

CHAPTER TWENTY-THREE

❖   ❖   ❖

The morning after Christmas, Laura discovered that her speech had become more distinct again, nearly back to normal. She had even felt confident enough to ask Rosie to invite her daughter downstairs to share a late brunch.

"Are you sure?" Rosie pressed her.

"I *must* see Katie today. It's very important."

"Very well." And Rosie was off.

While waiting for the two of them to return, Laura rehearsed the inheritance information she was about to impart. First, though, there were questions, things she'd reflected on year after year while separated from her baby girl. Oh, she realized such inquiries might have no merit for her daughter. Yet they burned within her, and because life was winding down swiftly, she wanted today—this very morning—to be the moment she finally opened her heart completely. She must hear Katie's answers, give the girl ample opportunity to fill in the missing pieces, the lost heart-knowledge of the years.

After they enjoyed a light breakfast of fresh fruit and tea, Laura and her daughter were alone at last.

"For years, I've wondered about certain things," she began. "About your babyhood and growing up."

"That's understandable," Katie replied, smiling. "What would you like to know, Mother?"

Laura stared at the fire snapping in the fireplace across from them, thinking she must tread lightly, perhaps. "Well, I've always wondered how you were told about your adoption . . . what your family might have told you . . . about me."

Katie nodded, pulling on one sleeve. "I've always known I was adopted. It was something my parents spoke of freely."

"Oh, then you *were* legally adopted at some point?"

"I was adopted right away, as far as I know. As an infant."

"And the birth certificate—was one issued, naming your parents as legal guardians?" Her heart thumped hard.

"They always told me it was as if I was born to them. But, no, they never said who my real mother was, maybe because they didn't know for sure."

"So even though I was never contacted, and no attempts made to locate me," Laura pressed on, praying her voice would hold out, "you're saying that in all legal respects, you are *their* child?"

Katie was silent. She shook her head suddenly, stood up, and went to the window. "I don't know, Mother. I believe I did see some legal documents when I was very young, but I don't remember them exactly. Maybe I never was adopted. Maybe I'm still your daughter . . . legally, I mean."

"But if you aren't absolutely sure . . . ." She paused, desperately worried that her wonderful surprise might well be on the verge of disintegrating.

"I don't think it's a problem," Katie was saying. "Because whatever you have in mind . . . about . . . well, about when you pass away, I'm sure things can be worked out."

Laura stared at the young woman, silhouetted in the window. What was she saying? Did she have some inkling of the revised will? And if so, how could that be?

Theodore had been the last person to see a copy of her

last will and testament. She fully trusted her friend and chauffeur. There was no questioning *his* integrity.

A flood of inquiries came to mind, but she first wanted to look into her daughter's face. Still, the strain on Laura's eyes—having to squint into the light from the window—was giving her a headache. "Come sit closer to me, Katie. My eyesight is failing fast."

Her daughter came quickly. "I'm sorry, Mother. I hope you don't think I'm rude or forgetful. It's just been such a long time since—"

"I know, dear. I know." She sighed. "Now, you must forgive me for prying, but ever since you arrived here, I've wondered about something else. You see, I recently gave a letter to an elderly Amishwoman in Hickory Hollow while I was there . . . searching for you."

"Oh?"

"I've wondered if you had opportunity to read it, and if, perhaps, my letter was the reason you were found and brought here by my husband."

"A letter? Well . . . no, I don't think so. Anyway, everything happened so very quickly."

"*What* happened, exactly, Katie? How was it you came to Canandaigua to be my Christmas gift?"

Katie blew her breath out with force but did not speak for the longest time.

"It's very important to me. I must know how you located me," Laura insisted.

Katie stood up again, this time heading for the fireplace, her back to Laura. "I wasn't found . . . not the way you might've supposed."

Waiting eagerly for more, Laura forced herself erect, instead of leaning against the back of the wheelchair. "Was there a private investigator involved? Did my husband hire someone to search for you?"

"Oh, you could say there was some hiring going on, all

right. But no, not a private eye."

Bewildered, Laura felt her gaze boring into Katie, trying desperately—through distorted vision—to read her expression. What was the girl endeavoring to say?

Laura felt as though her breath wouldn't accommodate her need for it. Struggling as she inhaled, she thought of calling her nurse.

When she was nearly certain the conversation was at a standstill, Katie suddenly turned around to face her. Her daughter seemed tentative—Laura could hear her breathing erratically. "No one discovered me in Hickory Hollow, or wherever it is you think I'm from, Mrs. Bennett." Removing her prim head covering, Katie shook out the strawberry blond hair with the mere loosening of two pins. "I'm *not* your daughter, Mrs. Bennett. But please know that it wasn't my idea to deceive you!"

The truth stabbed Laura's heart.

"I am so very, very sorry I ever consented to come here," the woman said before fleeing the room.

With the emotional pain came shortness of breath and the worst bout of tremors Laura had suffered in weeks.

❂   ❂   ❂

There were always a great many folk visiting in Hickory Hollow during the Christmas holidays, and today was no exception. Mary hurried her horse along the snow-packed lane, meeting up with a whole caravan of carriages heading in the opposite direction. She figured Rebecca Lapp wouldn't be all that surprised to have extra company, probably. Still, she hoped her visit might help her shunned friend . . . someway, somehow.

A blast of warmth from the Lapp kitchen met her as Samuel welcomed her inside. A glance into the next room let her know that Rebecca was up and about.

Gut, she thought. With Katie's mamma up and dressed, well, she wondered if her chat might not go over lots better than if Rebecca were lying flat on her back in bed.

As it turned out, she was wrong. Awful wrong. "Whoever heard of takin' clothes away from a helpless baby?" came the first heated refusal.

"But Katie needs the dress," Mary said softly. "She wanted me to ask you for it. I'll give the baby dress to your daughter."

"I have no daughter!"

Mary shuddered, almost wishing she'd never come.

"My daughter died in a hospital over twenty-two years ago. Stillborn. Dead . . ."

"I'm sorry, Rebecca. Truly I am." She got up out of the chair, then turning, faced her friend's precious mother and spoke the real truth. "But Katie Lapp ain't dead. She's shunned."

"The bishop killed her. John Beiler did it . . . he's the one to blame for my Katie leaving. *He* is."

Mary left the room, heading back to the kitchen. She passed Samuel on the way. "I think she might need a talk with the Wise Woman."

"Jah, couldn't hurt nothin'," Samuel said, stroking his long beard. "Bishop John can't help her now."

"I'll see if Ella Mae won't come over after bit. I'll bring her myself."

"Denki, Mary. We'll be waitin'."

Five minutes with Rebecca had left her shaken to the core. Five minutes. . . . She felt sorry for Samuel. He had to live with Rebecca twenty-four hours a day. Poor, dear man.

The way the storytellin' woman talked just now, you'd think she'd given up on the Lord God Almighty. Almost made Mary herself wanna quit believin'.

❖　❖　❖

When Rosie asked to see Justin's progress on the portrait, he declined. "From now on, the mistress of the house and everyone else must wait for the unveiling," he told her. "Something to look forward to in the New Year." The man grinned, obviously quite pleased.

She left the artist alone with his canvas and hurried back to the kitchen, wondering who should inform him of the most recent events. It was certainly not *her* place. Laura would have to break the news about the impostor's unexpected departure. Laura . . . or Mr. Bennett himself.

Meanwhile, she hoped the time spent painting such a fine portrait hadn't been for naught. After all, wouldn't it be lovely to have a likeness of their kind and loving mistress—the woman who'd brought the Christian faith to this house? Brought the love of the heavenly Father to both Rosie and her husband?

She could visualize the portrait hanging in the library or drawing room. And if Mr. Wirth was the sort of highly creative master she supposed him to be, it might take very little to refine the oil painting, placing the focus on Mrs. Bennett alone.

When morning duties were attended to, she brooded over the woman called Katie Lapp. The actress had exited rather abruptly—similar to Katherine's leaving, with one glaring difference. Mr. Bennett himself had driven one of the limousines, taking the woman to the airport. *Good riddance!* Rosie thought.

Had she been forced to, however, she would have had to confess she was more than a mite discouraged that *Katherine* was gone. She and Fulton had both felt they might be on to something with the responsible, demure maid. And what a cook! Why, she could bake the finest of Amish pies. They'd even toyed with the notion that *she* might be the mistress's true daughter.

But given the opportunity, things between the former

maid and Laura Bennett had never clicked. Besides, if it were true, wouldn't Katherine have spoken up? Declared her identity?

Then why *had* Katherine left? Was it plausible the excuse Mr. Bennett had given? That there had been a death in the family and she'd had to return home quickly?

Whoever had expired so unexpectedly, she did not know. But she *did* wish there had been time for a fond farewell.

As for the so-called Katie Lapp . . . what a revolting situation! Begone with the charlatan!

But the dear mistress was in such a bad way over it, suffering one contracture after another. The stress of the day, unraveling the self-confessed fabricator, had taken its grave toll. Fearing for Laura's life and the future of the manor, Rosie went to her knees in prayer.

❖ ❖ ❖

Her face, though blurred in the mirror, looked gray and waxen, her lips pale. She struggled to inhale, the anxiety of the morning clawing at her with each breath.

Natalie had tried to persuade her to go to the hospital. "You'll be much more comfortable there."

But she had vowed not to leave "until Dylan returns, because I must speak to him one last time."

"Then it is necessary that you lie down, Mrs. Bennett," Natalie urged. "I'll prop you up with pillows."

She refused the nurse's suggestion and continued to inspect herself as best she could. Looking down, she studied the skin beneath her fingernails—dusky. Her hands—clammy and cold.

Natalie began to move the wheelchair nearer the bed, away from the dresser mirror. "I want you to rest now, Mrs. Bennett. It's very important."

"Nothing's important now. Nothing, except seeing my husband again."

The nurse began to treat her as if she were a child, putting her to bed against her will. How she resented it and fought back, slapping at the youthful hands.

Then, unexpectedly, there were more of them surrounding her, people subduing her. And she cried out, using up so much air she nearly passed out.

Despite all her efforts to resist, the horrid nurse gave her another injection . . . no, there were so many others pushing on her now. Forcing her limp and sore body against the bed. Weighing her down, down. . . .

Then, within seconds, came the peace. The lull after a storm.

Later, she thanked Natalie, apologizing for her irrational behavior.

"You don't have to excuse yourself, Mrs. Bennett. I understand that your flare-ups cause you great distress."

She was silent for a moment, then spoke in a whisper. "In the end . . . will I lose control completely?"

Nurse Judah pursed her lips. "You mustn't think that way. Do concentrate on living, Mrs. Bennett. We . . . *I* want you to survive this episode."

Laura was comforted by Natalie's hand on her perspiring forehead. The affectionate touch made the crises of the day somewhat more tolerable, indeed.

CHAPTER TWENTY-FOUR

The next day, Katherine sat alone in her motel room, trying to work the TV remote. "What's keeping Lydia?" she said aloud. "Mamma wouldn't hold on to that baby dress if she knew I needed it. I *know* she wouldn't."

Giving up on the television, it being a tool of the devil anyway, she picked up the newspaper to read the "Help Wanted" section. Though her eyes scanned the ads, her mind was still fixed on her last moments at the Bennett estate.

What a fierce man—Dylan Bennett! She felt horribly frightened for her birth mother, a considerate and sweet lady having to live out the remaining days of her life with such a person.

When she thought of the wonderful-good oil painting, there was rage. The *other* Katie was going to wind up next to Laura Bennett! The thought infuriated her, and she wished more than anything that she'd shouted out her identity to her mother. Instead of that wicked Mr. Bennett.

Even now, sitting in this pocket-sized motel room, cigarette smoke slowly seeping through the cracks, she wanted to do something to change things, with or without the little satin gown. But she'd never get past that monster, Dylan

Bennett. She knew better than to try. Might wind up in jail
. . . or worse.

She'd wait for the package from Lydia Miller, wherever
it was. With the baby gown—sewn by Laura herself—with
that kind of proof in hand, she could walk right over the evil
man. And no one and nothing could stop her!

❂   ❂   ❂

After lunch, Natalie called the doctor, informing him of
Mrs. Bennett's persistent flare-ups, as well as her labored
breathing.

He, too, recommended admission to the hospital. But
her patient seemed completely confused, insisting that she
must wait until her husband returned from the airport. That
Dylan had important business in town—arranging a romantic cruise for the two of them.

Natalie wondered how long before she herself would
have to make the call—decide *for* the sick woman that she
be taken by ambulance to the hospital. Surely no more than
a few hours at the most.

Mrs. Bennett continued to ramble incoherently, and on
occasion even behaved with uncharacteristic irritability toward her caregivers. Yet Natalie offered nothing but kindness in return, nurturing her dying patient.

The instant the choking occurred, Natalie spun into action. Laura had been sipping cold juice through a straw
when she began to cough and gasp for air. In seconds, her
pale complexion had turned bluish.

Natalie knew all too well the dangers present, and as
soon as the coughing subsided somewhat, she listened to
Laura's lungs with a stethoscope and heard crackling. A def-
inite sign of aspiration pneumonia—a deadly complication
she had been expecting.

By late afternoon, Laura had developed a temperature.

Alarmed, Natalie knew the woman needed supportive IV therapy, and because she was having such difficulty swallowing, a feeding tube would also be necessary.

Natalie decided not to say a word to Mrs. Bennett. Instead, she took Rosie aside. "I'm going to need your help, as well as Garrett's and Selig's, when the ambulance arrives."

"Ah, I hate for Mrs. Bennett to leave us this way," the maid said in the tiniest voice. "I'd hoped it wouldn't come to this."

"So had I." Intent on maintaining her medical professionalism, Natalie did her best to hold back the tears.

"How long before. . . ?" Rosie shook her head, unable to finish.

"Hours, maybe a few days . . . if she's lucky."

Rosie blew her nose. "She's ready to go, our Laura is. She knows where she's headed after this life."

"I don't claim to share Mrs. Bennett's beliefs," said Natalie. "But if there is a heaven, it will be a better place when she gets there."

"This *house* has been a better place because of her," Rosie remarked, eyes glistening. "As for heaven—it's always been glorious because *Jesus* is there."

Natalie kept quiet. The maid could say what she wanted to about eternity. But as far as Natalie was concerned, the simple fact was she would miss her patient, and yes, she honestly hoped there *was* a heaven, for the sake of a fine Christian lady named Laura.

◈   ◈   ◈

The sound of a siren rang in her ears, and before she could protest, she felt her body being lifted up and onto a wheeled cot.

She sensed they were taking her away—to a place where she did not want to go. These cruel people in white. These people who could breathe freely at will. Without worry that the next breath could be their last. For though she pulled hard, she found no air.

Where was Dylan? Why hadn't he returned with their plane tickets? Their plans would be useless now. All their future hopes and dreams—Dylan's and hers—dashed to pieces. . . .

❖   ❖   ❖

Mary hitched up her father's best horse and drove the carriage over to visit Ella Mae. But it was Mattie, her daughter, who came to the door of the Dawdi Haus, the small addition for aging relatives, connected to the main house.

"Oh, hullo. I guess I was expectin' to see your mother," she said, stepping back from the door.

"She's sick in bed with the winter flu."

Mary's heart sank. She thought about going upstairs to speak to Ella Mae but figured there was no use risking her own health, not if the Wise Woman wasn't able to help her out today anyway.

"Well, I'm sorry to hear she's sick. But can ya tell her I stopped by?"

Mattie smiled. "Seems my mam's second only to the bishop around here. Sure, I'll tell her."

Mary turned to go, hoping Ella Mae's illness wouldn't keep her down for too long. 'Cause she knew if Katie's great-aunt couldn't help her out—and soon—there'd be nobody else.

Nobody knew how to patch things up between people or give advice like the Wise Woman. You'd've thought she was hooked up with the Lord God Himself.

Seemed odd, really. When it came right down to it, Ella Mae Zook never actually preached if you went to see her about a problem. No, sometimes—*most* of the time—she'd quietly quote a psalm or a proverb from the Bible. Or she'd just sit and listen to what you had to say. Didn't even tell you what you should or shouldn't do. But when you walked away from her little house, you'd most always feel like you knew the answer. Felt better for having gone to see her.

Thinking about all that, Mary realized the Wise Woman was a lot like herself—wanting to do what was right, yet not ever wanting to step on folks' toes. And something else she'd learned from visiting Ella Mae—holding grudges weren't gut for nobody. Made your heart fill up with blackness, crowding out the spaces for love.

"But some of us just ain't never content with what the Almighty sends our way, t'ain't so?" the Wise Woman had told her days before Katie was supposed to marry the bishop but didn't.

Mary had agreed. Some of the People—folks like herself—were always wishing for more than their lot. 'Specially when it came to wanting a husband and a good, loving marriage.

Still, she wouldn't give up on the bishop. Wouldn't give up on a man who'd filled up quite a few of those heart spaces inside her, in spite of her friend Katie's harsh shunning. In spite of all that.

She hurried home and told her mamma how sick Ella Mae was, hoping the old woman would shake off the flu bug in record time. Hmm. Maybe she could help the illness run its course a little sooner.

What *would* the Wise Woman think if she showed up tomorrow with a batch of freshly stewed prunes?

CHAPTER TWENTY-FIVE

❖ ❖ ❖

More than a week had passed with no word from Hickory Hollow. Katherine stewed and fretted, in a constant state of panic, wondering what to do next. She had found a part-time waitressing job at a fifties-style diner nearby and, in the early morning hours, created one frenzied or melancholy tune after another on her guitar. All in a sad minor key, notating each one, just the way Dan had shown her. This, she believed might keep her sane.

After dark, she'd hire a taxi and have the cabbie drive slowly past the Bennett estate, her eyes fixed on two large windows—the bedroom she knew to be Laura's. Her thinking was that if light poured out from the windows, chances were her mother was still alive.

In addition to the nightly treks, she would dial up the Bennett mansion, disguising her voice, trying her best to get some word of her mother's condition. But the estate operator never put her through to Rosie or Natalie. In fact, this voice was different from the one she'd heard when calling for the first time over two weeks ago.

There was so little time. Might be too late already.

Honestly, she'd just assumed that with Lydia Miller in charge of things at home—her being such a responsible woman—she would have managed to locate the tiny satin dress by now.

Katherine had no idea what was holding up the process, but she couldn't sit by and wait any longer.

Lydia answered on the first ring and seemed relieved to hear Katherine's voice on the other end of the line. "I thought of calling you, more times than not," her cousin explained.

"Oh? Is there a problem?"

"I'm really sorry, but I've had no luck. And that's not to say that I—*we*—haven't tried." And she went on to tell how Mary Stoltzfus had gone to see Rebecca, too. "Your mamma's mighty attached to that baby dress. No one, not even Samuel, has been able to talk her into loaning it to you."

"Not Dat, either?" She could hardly believe it. "So my father must know that I called you, then."

"Yes. And he's not the only one. Several others know now." And Katherine listened as Lydia spelled out the latest holdup. "It's Ella Mae, your great-aunt . . . she's been sick with the flu for days."

Feeling as though the whole idea was a lost cause, Katherine sighed into the phone. "Well, guess I should've been praying about all this before now."

The voice on the other end was silent for a moment. "Peter and I are praying, Katie. We're praying for *you*."

Katherine almost corrected her, wanted to remind her that she wasn't Katie anymore, but she let it go. "Well, since you're talking to God about me, here's something else you can tell Him. It's about Laura Bennett—my natural mother. She's awful sick, you know. And I can't be sure, but I wouldn't be surprised if she's in the middle of some evil scheme. Can't go into it, but there were some terrible, dreadful things going on while I was there."

"And you're not with her now?"

"No. But the minute Ella Mae's well again and gets my old baby gown, soon as that happens, I'll be on my way back to Laura. Then I'll prove I'm Katherine Mayfield—I'll march right in past her horrid husband and see her again. Oh, I want to know her, Lydia. Want to spend time talking with her before she dies."

"Well, then, I'll send the dress the minute I receive it," promised her cousin.

Katherine wanted to believe Lydia, because all she had now was hope. Hope . . . and the bold English prayers of her mamma's Mennonite cousin. Without any of that, she might've felt truly alone.

❖ ❖ ❖

Dan hurried into the church where Owen and Eve met him in the foyer. "Slow down, you're not late," teased Eve.

He checked his watch. "Just wanted to get a good seat for the concert."

The three of them settled into a pew near the middle of the sanctuary. The evening's presentation was to feature both vocal and instrumental music.

During the first number—a female soloist accompanied by gentle guitar chords—he thought of Katie. This music, this harmonious music, filled him with joy . . . sadness, too. And he wrestled with troublesome doubts as he sat in the Mennonite church, knowing beyond all question how right his sweetheart girl had been for him, yet—even then—not wanting to influence her against the Old Ways. Still, thinking back, he *knew* he'd let things slip out. Things that haunted him to this day.

He wished he could apologize to Katie, confess to her, along with his father. But he would never do anything to threaten her present . . . or her future, by bringing up his past misdeeds. No sense in piling another mistake on top of all the others.

The jubilant hymn being performed spurred him on, giving him courage for the task ahead. His sister would've received his letter by now, he figured. And tomorrow he'd write the follow-up letter, asking Annie to round up some Amish clothing in preparation for his visit to Father.

How he longed to share his newfound joy—his Christian witness—with his father; his mother, too. Yet he suspected that Jacob Fisher, terrified by the consequences, would be obligated to report him to the bishop once Dan made it known that he'd been saved and had joined the Mennonites. The irony of it—and the renewed heartache his confession surely would cause—all of it, had discouraged him from making amends.

Now hearing the music—especially the guitar background—spoke peace to his soul. Tomorrow he'd follow through with his plan to mail a second letter to Annie. That way, at least he wouldn't be accused of dampening Hickory Hollow's holiday spirit. For that, he was thankful.

Come what may, his sister—his entire family—was soon to see him. Alive and well . . . face-to-face.

❖   ❖   ❖

"Rebecca, someone's here to see you," Samuel called, leading Mary and Ella Mae into the front room.

Hoping that *this* visit might turn things around, Mary followed the Wise Woman through the kitchen.

"Well, hullo there, Rebecca," said Ella Mae, touching the woman's hand. "I've missed ya."

Rebecca began nodding her head in a most curious way, and Mary felt a sting in her stomach, observing Katie's mamma. So unlike the cheerful Rebecca Lapp she'd always known. Unlike anyone she'd ever known in Hickory Hollow.

"I hoped you'd be showing off that little baby dress ya made for Katie," the Wise Woman began, her voice crackling like always. "Thought maybe we could try it on your baby today."

Mary nearly dropped her teeth. What on earth was Ella Mae saying? Is *that* how Rebecca was thinking these days?

"Can't find it no more," said the daft woman. "Been a-lookin' and can't seem to find it."

"I'll help ya. Honest, I will," said Ella Mae, reaching for Rebecca's hand and leading her around the house. They looked like two young children playing a game of hide-'n-go-seek.

So while Ella Mae began to shape a story, one she might be telling to a group of women the way Rebecca often had, Mary sat and talked to Benjamin.

"Didja ever hear of an animal refusing his own name?" Ben asked her.

"You talkin' about Satin Boy?"

"We call him Tobias now."

"Oh . . . well, maybe that's why he doesn't come," she said. "Ya know how . . . well . . . could be that's the reason he's not respondin' to ya. Try calling him by the name *she* gave him."

Ben shook his head, chuckling softly. "Himmel, what trouble that girl's caused . . . even the animals don't know which end's up."

She let him finish jabbering on about the pony. Then when he was quiet for a bit, she spoke up. "I was wonderin' what ya might think of something, Ben."

"Think of what?" His thick blond hair lay flat against an oily scalp, showing the ring mark where his winter hat had sat on his head.

"I've been thinking about talking to the bishop."

"What for?"

"Oh, I just a wanna ask him some questions . . . about

the shunning. Do ya think he'd shun me, too, for talking to him about it?"

Ben laughed. "Doubt it. 'Cause everyone's a-thinkin' you may be his next wife, Mary."

She gulped hard and tried to cover it up by coughing, leaning off to the side of her chair. "The bishop . . . and me? Married?"

"And why not?" he said. "Don'tcha think it's a gut match?"

Secretly, she was elated. But, of course, she'd be keepin' those kinds of thoughts to herself. Deep inside, where no one could guess how she felt about Bishop John Beiler. Or so she'd thought.

When Ella Mae came downstairs, she came alone. "Rebecca's havin' herself a nap." She pointed toward the ceiling. " 'Speck we best be goin'."

Mary hopped up and went to get their coats. "Didja get it?" she whispered, helping the Wise Woman into her wrap.

"Is the bishop *standhaft* . . . unyielding?" replied Ella Mae, wearing a crooked smile. Then out from the old woman's basket came something shiny and pink.

"Is that *it*? Is that the baby dress . . . uh . . . *her* real mamma made for her?" Mary couldn't bring herself to speak Katie's name right out loud, but she could think it!

Ella Mae looked Mary straight in the eye. "Never you forget it, honey girl. The *real* mamma's right upstairs."

Even though she tried repeatedly on the ride home, Mary never could pull it out of the Wise Woman how she'd got ahold of the baby garment. Jah, she tried asking many different ways, even though she felt it wasn't the right thing to do at all—trying to trick someone into telling you something against their will.

By the time they arrived at Peter and Lydia Miller's house, though, she didn't much care anymore *how* Katie's

infant gown had ended up in Ella Mae's basket of sewing and
stitchery. The main thing was, this being Saturday, Katie'd
have it by Monday morning.

"Before noon, guaranteed," Lydia informed her after
she'd run up the front porch steps and delivered the dress.

"Hope this makes her happy," Mary remarked, not
meaning it sarcastically, though it might've sounded that
way.

"Oh, she'll be mighty happy, all right," said Lydia, grinning broader than Mary'd ever seen her.

Then the smile faded and Lydia folded her hands as if in
prayer. "You must ask the Lord to protect your friend. She's
off by herself in a motel room somewhere. But . . . something tells me . . . that's not her biggest worry. . . ."

Of course, Mary had to know what on earth Lydia meant
by that, and the two women whispered their confidential
chatter until Mary had to rush off and get the Wise Woman
home to a warm fire and some piping hot coffee.

CHAPTER TWENTY-SIX

❖ ❖ ❖

On Monday, January fifth—before noon—Katherine received a UPS delivery. Heart pounding, she studied the package the man had brought her, recognizing Lydia's handwriting immediately.

Tearing open the parcel, she found the rose-colored baby gown wrapped in tissue paper. "Oh," she whispered, and hugged the tiny garment to her cheek, remembering with absolute clarity the first time she'd ever laid eyes on the shimmering fabric.

She sat in silence, struggling not to cry lest she stain the little dress. Then, remembering that, before ever leaving Hickory Hollow, she'd once found a single mark on the garment. Believing it to be her mamma's teardrop—she searched for it. Finding it, she wept.

After a time, she called a cab. Staring at the name embroidered on the facing, she ran her fingers across it, feeling the stitching, still intact after these many years. Rewrapping the dress, she bundled up and waited for her ride—the short ride back to her mother's estate. As she waited she prayed, in German, that the Lord God heavenly Father might keep Laura Bennett alive, at least for a few more hours. That He'd protect her from the wrath of Dylan Bennett, as well.

Katherine asked the cab driver to drop her off around the east side of the estate, closest to the servants' entrance. That way she could slip past anyone who might try to detain—or arrest—her, so strong was her need to see her mother, to reveal the truth to the person it mattered to most.

Bold with determination, Katherine crept through the outside doorway, checking to see if anyone was near, then hiding in the first room she came to—a spacious storage closet. Inside, she paused, listening, straining to hear the slightest sound. Perhaps Garrett or Selig. Anyone.

When it seemed the corridor was clear of servants, at least, she opened the door, moved quietly into the hallway, and tiptoed down past the grand staircase, toward the south wing—her mother's quarters.

Once again, she stood to the side of the tall French doors, peering around them to see into the sitting room. Odd, she thought. No one was there. Not even Natalie Judah, the live in nurse.

Suddenly frantic with worry, she rushed past the love seat and comfortable chairs arranged near the fireplace, past the cherry sofa where tiny matching Christmas trees had brought gaiety to the room.

She was standing in her mother's private bedroom now, her heart in her throat. There the bed had been stripped bare of all coverings and sheets.

"Rosie?" she called. "Nurse Judah?"

There was no answer, so she called the louder.

Still no reply. Even Mr. Bennett's presence might've been welcomed at this moment. Yet there was no one.

Seized with a choking terror, Katherine dropped to her knees beside the empty bed and began to cry out to God in English, abandoning her familiar German rote prayers, praying for the first time the way Peter Miller had taught her to.

"Oh, dear Lord Jesus, please, please don't let my mother be dead. Please . . ."

She heard the scuffle of feet and turned to see Theodore Williams coming into the sitting room.

"Katherine?" he called to her.

"Oh, Mr. Williams, where's my mother?"

The old gentleman's face went ashen and he muttered something under his breath.

"My mother . . . Laura . . . is she dead?"

Afraid, so afraid, of his response, she looked down at the UPS mailer—knowing what wondrous thing she'd hidden there—and she cried. She cried so hard that Mr. Williams came over and offered her his own handkerchief.

❖   ❖   ❖

Samuel had his hands full taking care of his wife. Sitting next to her, talking softly to her, watching her writhe in their bed, he figured he must've been out of his mind to let Ella Mae come and take the one and only thing Rebecca had cherished so.

Now his dear spouse could speak of nothing but Katie's baby garment. Yet she had it no longer. Without the fancy dress to hold, to stroke, to whisper to, her world seemed to have fallen near apart.

He didn't know what on earth to do about it, 'cept summon the bishop. Maybe if John Beiler could see what his pompous ruling had done to Rebecca, maybe then he'd see the error of his standhaft ways. The unbending ways of the Old Order.

The minute he began to reflect on these defiant thoughts, though, he was filled with remorse. Still, he wondered if it might not do the community some good knowin' what the shunning had done to the wife of Samuel Lapp.

◈   ◈   ◈

He'd see to it personally. Katherine—*Miss* Katherine, it was now—would be driven safely to the hospital. "Mrs. Bennett's life hangs by a thread," Theodore told her as they headed for the limousine. "The doctors don't give her much longer."

The young woman wiped her tears and, of all things, insisted on riding in the front seat opposite him. The next thing he knew, she was showing him an exquisite baby gown.

"This is the dress I wore on the day Laura gave me away," she said. "See the name embroidered in the back?"

He glanced over to consider what looked like tiny stitches forming the name *Katherine Mayfield*.

"It appears that our missus was most creative, even as a teenager," he commented. Then he broke the news delicately to the young woman. "Not long after you left, your mother discovered the truth about that woman parading around as Amish. Katie Lapp, or whoever she was, has left town . . . and so has Mr. Bennett."

Katherine frowned. "He has? When?"

"Days ago, and no one has heard from him since."

"I wonder why," Katherine said. "Wouldn't he want to stay around . . . until . . ." She choked back tears.

Poor girl. How could he tell her? Drawing a deep breath, he began. "There is strong evidence to indicate that the man was . . . in cahoots with one of his partners, as well as the New York model-turned-actress. Evidently, they'd planned to swindle your mother out of the estate . . . and possibly more."

"How awful evil." Katherine tucked the baby dress back into the tissue paper.

"Yes, and we're still trying to piece things together.

Thankfully, the estate will not fall into the wrong hands upon Mrs. Bennett's death."

"What do you mean?"

He realized he'd already said more than was prudent. "I believe it is Mrs. Bennett's place to discuss her affairs . . . at the proper time."

And that was all he would say.

❖   ❖   ❖

Because she was Laura Bennett's only living relative and had merely to say so to the head nurse—without even showing her the baby dress, none of that—Katherine was told she could see her mother for fifteen minutes at a time, every hour on the hour.

The initial visit was most painful. Katherine tiptoed into the private hospital room, holding her breath as she saw before her a woman wired up with tubes going every which way. Clear oxygen tubes in her nose and intravenous therapy connected to the veins in her arms, one of the nurses was kind enough to explain.

Katherine clutched the UPS parcel and willed herself not to faint. Truth be told, the sight frightened her no end, made her weak, as if she might need to sit down.

And she did. Sat there on a chair beside the bed and stared at the woman who'd given birth to her nearly twenty-three years before.

At one point, Laura's eyelids fluttered, and Katherine stood up slowly. But she stepped back a bit, hoping her mother might be able to focus her eyes on her, for the nurse had explained that Laura's vision was severely impaired.

"Mother? It's Katherine, and no, you aren't dreaming. I really am here."

Laura's eyes closed quickly, and Katherine couldn't

blame her for that—so viciously had her dear mother been duped.

She crept over to the side of the bed. Standing there, patiently waiting for Laura to give her a second chance, she pulled out the satin baby gown.

When her mother did not respond after a time, Katherine reached down and placed the little dress under Laura's right hand, her fingertips resting lightly on the folds of the garment.

"This is the dress you made for your baby girl," she whispered. "My Amish mamma—Rebecca Lapp—saved it all these years. There's some lovely embroidery stitched in the back facing. Do you remember sewing my name there?"

She stopped talking and waited. What she saw broke her heart—and began to heal it—all at the same time.

Big tears rolled down either side of the pallid face. "Katherine," she heard her mother whisper. "Oh, Katherine. You're here at last."

She didn't want to hurt the dear lady or disturb any of the numerous tubes going in and out of her body. Oh, but she wanted to be near her. Hug her—not hard—just embrace a part of her.

Two thin hands came together, slowly grasping the satin baby gown. It was then that Katherine leaned over and kissed the hand nearest her, letting the tears flow freely.

"I've missed you all my life," she managed to say. "I've never been truly Amish, not through and through." Then, so as not to tire her mother unduly, she picked the choicest portions of her life to talk about. Things like her cravings for beautiful music and fine, fancy clothing, jewelry, and different types of hairstyles. She told about the letter Laura had written to Rebecca, Katherine's adoptive mother, and how it had gotten burned up before she'd ever laid eyes on it. About living in Hickory Hollow, always wondering what she might be missing out in the world.

Sometime before the nurse came in to let her know fifteen minutes was up, sometime right before then, Katherine told her mother about the boy with blueberry eyes. Her one and only true love, Daniel Fisher.

"What . . . a wonderful boy," her mother said. "I wish he were . . . still here."

"All of us—all the People—were sorry, too. It was the most dreadful time of our lives." She said it without holding back her love feelings for Dan, so free she felt with this woman. *This* mother. And hoping her first mamma might forgive her. Someday.

CHAPTER TWENTY-SEVEN

❖   ❖   ❖

Two days later, Laura was still alive and wearing thick glasses so she could see Katherine more clearly. The new lenses had given her spirits a tremendous boost. Furthermore, she'd felt a quickening in her, a most unusual feeling. She was convinced she was getting better. And she told her daughter so . . . the nurses, too.

She'd felt something similar upon first meeting that vile impostor of a woman, and she'd heard that such occurrences had a tendency to induce a kind of remission sometimes. She could only hope *this* one might last, though, that she might beat this disease, once and for all.

But she was bright enough to know she mustn't put her trust in physical improvements alone, not when it was her emotional health that had seen the biggest lift. Her daughter had come home. The girl had moved heaven and earth, as she'd put it, to search for Laura. And what things she longed to share with her. Fifteen minutes here and there during the course of a day simply wasn't enough.

When Natalie Judah—who was no longer responsible for her care—came for a quick visit, Laura implored her to get the hospital visiting rule lifted.

"I'd love to do that for you, Mrs. Bennett, but I believe

it would be futile to try," the nurse said.

"Please, see if someone will listen to you," Katherine pleaded. Then when Natalie had left to do whatever she could, Laura's daughter told her something her friend Mary Stoltzfus had always said, growing up in Hickory Hollow. "Ya never get if ya don't ask."

When Laura asked her to repeat it in Dutch, Katherine laughed and obliged her, putting on the thickest German accent she'd ever heard. But she loved it, every minute spent with her adorable Katherine.

Not long after, Natalie returned, sporting a broad smile. "I guess I should've pleaded your case before this. The hospital has consented to give you unlimited time together— the two of you. That is, if Mrs. Bennett agrees to rest periodically."

Because of the new glasses, Laura noticed happily that Katherine appeared as delighted as she.

❖   ❖   ❖

The drive to Lancaster seemed much longer than Dan had remembered, even without a horse and buggy. It may have only *seemed* long because of the many boyhood landmarks along the way, especially once he made the turn off Highway 340.

The closer he came to Hickory Lane, the more he found himself slowing down to savor the rolling hills, the tall, tall trees, the way the sun played on blanketed white fields. Even in the dead of winter, this part of Pennsylvania was rich with beauty. And the memories . . . how they beat a path to his brain.

Fighting off the impulse to drive past the Lapps' red sandstone house—see for himself if Katie still lived there— he turned onto a narrow road, leading to Weaver's Creek. It was here that he and Katie had written a love song together while sitting on a boulder. They'd watched the creek ripple past them that day, and he'd tried to tell her of his doubtings, his questionings about the Amish church. He had tried, but the only thing he could even begin to say, really, was that no matter what happened, no matter if he got himself shunned, he'd still always love his Katie.

Of course, if his recollections were true, about the only thing he *did* do that day, at least when it came to declaring his love, was kiss her. Again and again. Till she had to wriggle free from his arms and take him on a walk toward the bridge and the creek below.

There, perched on a boulder in the middle of the stream, he had pulled out some folded staff paper and a pencil from his pocket and shown Katie how to notate music for the first time.

The music. . . . How he'd always longed to share it as a gift to his People, to his precious Katie, so full of melodies and lovely lyrics herself.

Yet the Ordnung forbade it.

Over the years, prayer and fasting had brought him to his knees in holy communion with his Lord and Savior. But it was the music and spiritual worship within the church walls, like a balm of Gilead, that had soothed his splintered soul.

He wondered how Katie had ever survived without it, for he questioned whether anyone might've come along to fill his disobedient shoes in that regard. Who else would've offered her the same sort of bonding—the love of music they'd shared so intensely? Still, it was sin, according to the Amish church. And for her sake, he rather hoped she hadn't pursued that particular interest, especially if she wanted to remain in good standing with the People of Hickory Hollow.

Checking his watch, he realized the appointed hour was upon him. For in his second letter to Annie, he'd asked her to meet him near the old one-room schoolhouse, knowing it would be vacated well before four in the afternoon. It was the perfect place for him to change into Amish clothing, too, and he hoped she wouldn't disappoint him in this.

Annie was right on time, and he waited in his car for a bit before getting out, allowing her to pull the carriage into the school lane.

Spying each other at almost the same instant, they literally ran into each other's arms, laughing and crying. "Daniel!" sobbed his sister. "I can't believe it's really you." And she pulled back to look him over. "You're so tall, ach, you're a grown man, ain'tcha?"

He picked her up then and twirled her around. "I've missed you, Annie!" he shouted into the frosty air.

Holding hands, they ran together toward the Amish school, letting themselves inside. "I didn't know what on earth to think when I got your first letter," Annie began. "I thought it was some kind of horrid joke at first. But then, before long, I knew it was you." Her voice grew softer. "By reading it over and over again, I *knew*."

She was full of questions, so many it made his head spin. But what she wanted to know more than anything was the truth of what had happened in Atlantic City five years ago.

He pulled in a deep breath, then began, praying she'd understand, could forgive him. "I ran away on my birthday, angry at Dat," he explained. "It started out to be an innocent outing—a sailing expedition, all by myself."

"Just you, alone?"

Dan took it more slowly, gave her a moment to digest his news. "I needed time to think . . . to think where my life was headed. So much of what I knew about religion and God had been passed down to me from our parents—their parents before them. I know you may have trouble with this, but I needed something in *writing*, something I could read for myself. For another thing, I wanted to be sure I was

260

saved, so . . . I was secretly studying, even memorizing parts of the Bible."

"You were?" The light left her eyes.

"I wanted to spare you, Annie. Wanted to protect you and the rest of the family from thinking I was sinning." He didn't go on to tell her that he'd had the same reason for shielding Katie Lapp, as well.

Continuing with his story, he recalled the unexpected storm. "A severe one . . . I was knocked overboard. Almost drowned swimming to shore."

Dan told the truth, all of it. In the end, there had been ample opportunity to explore a faith to stand on—not one built on tradition or man-made rules. Now for him, he told Annie, the Ordnung had long since been replaced by the Word of God. Many long hours of personal Bible study and fellowship with other Christians had convinced him, had served to boost his confidence and faith in the Almighty.

"Ach, I don't know what to say," Annie spoke in a near whisper.

"I don't expect you to understand, Annie, or forgive me—neither one, for that matter." He shrugged sadly. "I was a foolish nineteen-year-old boy, terribly immature. But I've come home to repent."

"Well, you'll be needin' these if you're to meet with Dat." She held out a bag of clothing. "And don't forget this." She handed him a black felt winter hat.

"Thank you, Annie. I appreciate your help."

"Ach, my husband has plenty of hats, ya know." Then she told him about her marriage to Elam Lapp.

The Lapp name touched a nerve. For the life of him, Dan couldn't bear to hear Annie spill things about Samuel's daughter . . . Katie. Who *she'd* married, where she lived . . . things like that.

The huge lump in his throat made it difficult to speak.

He cleared his throat. "I hope to see you again before I leave."

"Leave?" Her eyes widened. "But you just got here."

"I'm Mennonite now," he told her.

"Then why'dja come back?"

"To confess my wrongdoings, to come clean before the Lord and Dat. I had a spirit of rebellion in me back in my younger days. Our father needs to hear that I am truly sorry."

Annie appeared stunned, as though she couldn't believe her ears. "But don't you know that if ya leave, you'll be shunned?"

"I've come to face it like a man . . . at last."

She burst into tears. "Oh, we've got the harshest bishop ever!"

"Who?"

"John Beiler, remember?"

"But he's *always* been hard on the People."

Annie shook her head. "I never thought much about it, till here lately." She began to cry again. "Oh, I wish ya didn't have to go through the Meinding, Dan."

He reached for her, wrapping loving arms about his sister. She sobbed bitterly, and when he thought she might never quit, she looked up at him through wet lashes. "Don'tcha see? It'll be like losin' ya twice. Like you're dead *again*. Oh, Daniel, can't ya stay? Can't ya come help Elam work the farm for a bit . . . live with us? Just don't leave again. Please, don't."

Her pleas tore at his heart.

"We have a baby son," Annie said suddenly, as if telling him might make him change his mind. "We named him Daniel . . . after *you*."

Drawing a deep breath, he touched his sister's chin, realizing, as he stood near the desk where he'd learned his ABC's, that if he didn't change into Elam Lapp's clothing soon, if he didn't drive over to his father's house, he might never be able to go through with any of this. It saddened him that much.

"If ya hafta leave again, will ya at least come say good-bye?" beseeched Annie, and she told him how to get to her and Elam's house.

"Yes, I'll come," he said. "I won't leave this time without saying 'God be with you,' sister."

❖   ❖   ❖

It had been an awful selfish thing not to tell Daniel about Katie Lapp's shunning—that his former girlfriend was off in New York somewhere, searching for her birth mother. Annie pondered the problem while driving the horse back to the house.

If she *had* told her brother about Katie, if he knew his sweetheart no longer lived here in Hickory Hollow, well, she could almost predict how Daniel would react. And then, even if her father did talk some sense into Dan after he offered his confession, even so, she understood the drawing power of love. *Their* love—a love so sweet, so strong, that if truth be known, she'd have to say she'd envied it through the years. Oh, she hadn't committed the *sin* of envy. No, it was more like the wonder in a child's heart on Christmas morning. It was *that* kind of feeling she felt when she saw them together.

'Course, Bishop John might not think so if he knew about it, but she didn't care. Main thing was, she had high hopes of Daniel returning to the Amish church. And by keeping this one little secret from him, least for now, it was the best thing she could do. For Dan, mostly, but also for herself.

CHAPTER TWENTY-EIGHT

❖　　❖　　❖

Katherine was shocked when she heard the news.

"You'll . . . be the mistress of the manor, darling . . . after I'm gone," Laura Bennett gasped out.

Shaking her head, Katherine could only reply, "I'd rather be poor and have you alive, Mother. . . ."

"Nevertheless, what's mine today . . . will be yours . . . soon."

With growing horror, Katherine realized that the deadly pneumonia was squeezing the life out of her mother's lungs. There'd be no more talk of the inheritance—not now. She must hear Laura's story—how it came to be that she'd decided to give her newborn infant to an Amish couple. Still, when that moment came—later in their conversation— she'd be very, very careful how she phrased the question. The subject was much too painful—for both of them.

Meanwhile, sitting here beside the hospital bed, Katherine realized how very similar they must appear. Hair color and texture, even their noses matched . . . and the bold, determined line of their chins.

Catching her studied appraisal, her mother smiled. "I'm afraid I'm not looking . . . my best," she managed with a wry look. "My hair . . . so thin now . . . probably the medication."

Katherine took the fragile hand, like a bird's wing, it seemed. "Did the boys ever tease you about being a redhead?" she asked in a lilting tone, hoping to steer the conversation to more pleasant paths.

"Your . . . father did sometimes . . . your *birth* father."

The comment caught her off guard. She hadn't considered another man—other than Samuel Lapp—as her father. Strange, how she'd felt so instantly at home with her natural mother, with not a thought for the young man—her real father—who'd loved Laura as a teenager, then left her pregnant and brokenhearted.

There was a pause when the nurse came in to check for vital signs and see that her mother's IV and oxygen tube were in place. Immediately after that—when they were alone again—Katherine began to ask more questions. Several that had remained lodged in her recollection ever since the day she'd first spied the baby dress.

"Why did you pick satin fabric for the dress?" she wanted to know.

"Perhaps it was because . . . I've always loved the feel . . . the swish of satin."

There were other such questions—favorite foods, whether Laura had a craving for sweets. . . . Then—how it was that her mother had happened to be in Lancaster on the day of Katherine's birth.

At that, Laura's face blanched pale as death, followed by a pained expression. "Oh," her mother moaned. "Quick . . . the nurse!"

Katherine ran to the door to summon help. "My mother's in terrible pain. Please help her!"

A rush of nurses swept through the door, one politely asking her to leave the room.

Had her never-ending questions set off her mother's illness . . . caused undue stress? Katherine fretted. Why couldn't she have been content to sit beside Laura's bed, letting her mother talk only when and if she chose to.

Why must I be so bold, so curious?

Standing outside the hospital room door, she prayed that if this flare-up was to cause her mother's passing—*if* it were—that the dear Lord Jesus, Savior of the world, of Lydia Miller and Laura Mayfield-Bennett, might ease the pain and cushion the tug-of-war between life and death.

Recalling the past hours of intimate conversation, Katherine counted up her blessings. Not only had her natural mother desired to pass on a vast fortune to her only offspring, but her strong faith as well. Laura had explained her relationship with Christ Jesus—in glowing terms of love and acceptance—such things Katherine had never heard.

The idea that God's Son should come to earth and die for *her*—hardheaded and conniving as she was—made Katherine stop and think. Really think about her place in "God's kingdom," as Laura had put it.

As she waited in the hallway, hovering close to her mother's door, she recalled the sweet moments spent talking about spiritual things. It was then, while thinking back over this part of their conversation, that she began to comprehend how unimportant it was to know *who* you were—her biggest hang-up in life, it seemed—but *whose* you were.

Her natural mother had had it all—wealth, the most stylish clothing, the finest foods, even golden combs for her long auburn hair. There were mirrors galore and the best furnishings money could buy, but it hadn't been enough, Laura had told her. Laura Mayfield-Bennett needed something—Someone—greater in her life. Someone who would never run off and leave her or betray her. The Lord Jesus.

Tears sprang to Katherine's eyes, and she wondered suddenly if this was what Daniel had tried to explain to her five years ago. Could it be that Dan, too, had come to know

Laura's Lord? Really *know* Him . . . before he died?

❂   ❂   ❂

Dan knocked on the back door of his father's house. He'd probably made a mistake by not asking Annie to warn his parents. What if they couldn't handle seeing their dead son's "ghost"?

He stood far enough back so that they might see him fully, not merely his face pressed close to the storm door.

For a brief moment, he was glad that it was his mother who appeared at the door but watched in dismay as the blood drained from her cheeks.

"Jacob!" he heard her call out.

"Oh, Mamma, don't faint!" Quickly, Dan opened the door and held on to her until his father came to assist him— this stranger with the beginnings of a beard and a borrowed Amish hat. But he kept his head down, not letting Dat see his face.

"Ah, Elam," said Dan's father, "what didja do to your mother-in-law?"

By now Daniel found himself inside the utility room, helping his mother into the kitchen, where she fell into the big old hickory rocker. He wondered again why he hadn't thought to fine-tune this plan. After all these years—some of them spent in a trade school—shouldn't he have had more sense than to burst in on his loved ones this way?

He found himself sputtering out an apology. "It's not Elam, Father. It's . . . I'm your own son, Daniel."

"Who? What's that ya say?" his mother shrieked and stared, long and hard.

But Dat promptly grabbed both his wrists, squeezing them in a viselike grip. "But you're dead! We thought you died years ago . . . drowned in the ocean!"

He let his father lash out at him. Let him spend his fury.

"How could you go off and let us think you were dead?" the old man bellowed. "Didja know how awful hard your mamma would mourn and grieve your death, till the tears in her eyes all dried up?"

Standing in the middle of the kitchen, Dan did not budge an inch, even after his father released his arms. Then, trying to reckon with his own pain, Dan watched his father pace the floor like a distraught lion. Every now and then the gray-haired man glared back at him, his eyes red-hot with righteous indignation.

Dan was taught as a child to believe that the eyes of his father were near sacred, that they could emanate such emotions as anger, displeasure, and disapproval—yet without sinning.

Truth be known, Dan felt as though he had been transported in time, back to his late teen years, during one of the daily "preaching" sessions his father had imposed on him.

At last, Dan, still standing as if on trial, spoke up. "I've come home to confess, Father. I want to make things right between us."

His anger dissipated, Jacob pulled out a straight-backed chair and sat down near his wife. "The Lord God almighty is sovereign and just," the man said, not sternly, but with conviction. "Welcome home, son."

Then, removing his hat, Dan knelt at his father's knee, praying silently for grace and forgiveness. "I come to you, carrying the memories of my past sins," he began with folded hands. "Transgressions I committed against *you*, Father. And I'm here to ask you to forgive me."

❖ ❖ ❖

"Can you ever . . . forgive me?" Laura begged, struggling to speak. A suffocating cloud of heaviness weighted her chest. "I wish I had . . . kept . . . you as my own, Katherine. I wish. . . ."

She could not finish. The air was gone, and she could not consume enough to say more.

Lying there, hooked up to a lifeline of whirring machines, she longed to hear Katherine's answer. Waited for the words that could free her, those precious words to fill up the past emptiness, the pain-filled years alone without her child.

"Please, Mother, don't be worrying about what you did . . . about choosing Samuel and Rebecca to raise me." Her dear girl stood up unexpectedly and bent down to whisper close to her ear. "I love you. I love you in spite of all the past."

❖   ❖   ❖

"The past is under the blood of Jesus," Dan continued. "The Lord God heavenly Father has brought me home, to offer my confession, full repentance at your knee, Father," he said, using the Amish terminology they would best understand.

Here, he reached for his mother's hand. "Will you forgive me, too, Mam? Can you understand that I didn't intend to fake my death as it seemed I did?"

He didn't wait for either of their answers but went on, recounting the story of the day he'd nearly drowned while swimming to safety. He told them of the Coast Guard boat he'd seen from the reef, watched it comb the raging waters, searching for his body. He repented of his immature behavior, his teenage rebellion, his defiance against his upbringing. And he explained how he'd decided, there on the sandbar, that the easiest, most compassionate way for the People, for his family—for all those who loved him—was for them to presume him dead.

"By not revealing the truth, though, I deceived you. I allowed everyone to think I'd drowned, let them mourn for me. I was only hoping to spare you the Meinding . . . release you from having to shun me."

He paused for a moment, their eyes fixed on him. "Don't you *see*? I thought to save you . . . keep you from having to turn your backs on your son, to treat me as if I were dead. But I know now that I was wrong, Father. It was the worst thing I could've done to you."

His parents listened, their faces solemn and expressionless. Dan stood up and pulled out the wooden bench under the kitchen table. With a sigh, he sat down, facing them. The confession had made his hands clammy, his mouth dry.

Yet, before almighty God, his heart was pure. At least in *His* sight, Dan Fisher was forgiven.

❖   ❖   ❖

She held her mother's bluish hand, unconsciously breathing hard as the dear lady continuously gulped for air. Her color was ashen now, and the death pallor frightened Katherine.

"Don't die, Mother," she whimpered. "I've just found you. Please don't leave me now."

Watching her mother's struggle to breathe, she felt as if she might not survive this crisis herself. She might die along with the fancy English woman who was her real, true mother.

Ach, she'd never witnessed a person die before; didn't think she wanted to even now. Yet she would not abandon the woman who'd given her life.

"My dear Katherine . . ."

"I'm right here with you, Mother."

"Do you . . . know . . . my Jesus?" There was much gasping again, and she felt guilty that her mother had used up so much air for such a sobering question.

What could she say? She wouldn't lie. Not as Laura Mayfield-Bennett lay dying, preparing to meet her Maker.

"God's Son knows *me*," she managed, hoping she believed her own words. "He knows me, and He brought us
together . . . just in time."

"Yes. He knows . . . you, child."

Then without warning, Laura's breathing stopped. And
Katherine began to cry.

❖　❖　❖

"Why, then, does my dead son return home to confess
these things?" Jacob Fisher asked. "What has changed?"

Dan breathed deeply, praying for courage. "So much has
changed. More than you know, Dat. I'm a grown man now,
able to think for myself, to understand God's precepts. I'm
no longer afraid to express my beliefs and compare them
with those of the People. And I can now follow the will of
my heavenly Father and be the kind of son I should've been
to you all those years ago."

"What are ya really tellin' us, Daniel?"

He turned to look at their bewildered faces. "I came here
to confess my sins . . . but I cannot return to the Amish
church. And for that, I am truly sorry."

"So now you give us no choice but to shun you," Jacob
said, frowning hard. "Bishop John will hafta be told."

"My life is in God's hands." Dan stood up, knowing that
if he were to stay longer, his time of confession might very
well turn into a heated debate. One-sided.

"I love you, Dat . . . Mam." He leaned down to kiss his
mother's face. "I wish we could see eye to eye about God's

plan of salvation. It would be so good to be able to share the Good News as a family, to break the Bread of Life together."

Much to his surprise, his father accepted his handshake and did not attempt to refute his parting words.

CHAPTER TWENTY-NINE

It was an endless day, even though Katherine never once resented sharing or bearing the dying experience with Laura. She felt she'd gained something most valuable by sitting there as her mother slipped away, pain gone forever.

But she'd been mistaken about that first moment when it seemed for all the world as if Laura was no longer breathing. Several more times, before the end, her beautiful mother had slipped in and out of consciousness, her chest barely rising and falling.

Laura had made one last effort to speak, and Katherine, in retrospect, was grateful for it. "Look for . . . my . . . journal."

"You kept a diary?"

"While I carried . . . you."

Katherine had wanted to hear more, but she sat quietly, holding her mother's hand. The coolness of Laura's hand in hers let her know that heaven was near. Gradually, ever so slowly, the delicate hand had grown lifeless . . . cold.

Laura's last thoughts had been of her daughter. *While I carried you*, the whisper had come, almost inaudibly.

Long after Laura's spirit had left her body, long after, Katherine sat beside the bed. She imagined her mother

greeting loved ones who'd gone before. Daniel, too, maybe.
Remembering the way he was, she figured her darling would
be one of the first in line to receive Laura Mayfield-Bennett,
just as soon as her mother passed through those pearly gates.

❖   ❖   ❖

Dan had decided long before today that he would not
interfere with his former girlfriend's life. He must protect
his own emotions, as well, and by simply not inquiring, he
could accomplish both. If he hadn't gone back to his sister's
to say good-bye, though, he would've missed hearing about
Katie.

Annie dropped the bombshell almost as soon as he
arrived, after he began telling her that he needed to leave
for New Jersey soon.

"Aw, must ya go?" Tears glinted in the corner of his
sister's eyes. "Can't ya stay, Daniel?"

He reached for her hands. "It won't be long now before
the People will be shunning me. We won't have many op-
portunities like this to spend together."

"Might not even be allowed to talk to each other, neither." She frowned and shook her head as if in pain. "Same
way we treated . . . Katie," she whispered the name.

"Katie Lapp? *My* Katie?" His eyes searched hers, longing
for answers.

"Ach, she's had the harshest Meinding put on her I've
ever lived to see."

"What happened? How'd *she* get shunned?"

"It's not an easy story, really, but it all got started with a
baby dress made of satin that Rebecca kept hidden in a trunk
up in their attic."

Shocking as the story was, he listened to his sister's account of how his sweetheart girl had run away from her
wedding, gotten herself shunned, and left Hickory Hollow

to search for the natural mother she'd never known.

When Annie was finished, he found himself weeping in her arms—not due to Katie's painful shunning. No, the tears he shed were joyful . . . selfish tears.

❖   ❖   ❖

Ella Mae Zook was on the back stoop, shaking out her kitchen rug, when a right fancy English car pulled into her side of the lane. It slowed down, and she squinted, shielding her eyes from the afternoon sun.

When a young Amishman got out of the car, she had a closer look at him—strikingly handsome, he was. But she near lost her false teeth after spying the blueberry eyes.

"Well, whatdaya know?" she said to the January sky, to God, and anybody else who might be listening. Then the Wise Woman laughed right out loud.

❖   ❖   ❖

Mary wasn't seeing things; not hearing them, neither. Sunday morning, after the *Ausbund* hymns were sung, she watched Bishop John and listened to him, trying to decide whether or not his mellow voice—the one she'd heard on Christmas Day—was one of his Preachin' voices.

Then it happened. Right smack in the middle of a sermon on pride and how "one should run from it at all costs," he looked her way, resting his eyes on her longer than necessary. She wouldn't dismiss it as wishful thinking, but when his gaze strayed mostly for the rest of Preachin', she wondered how she might speak to him afterward, during the common meal.

If she *did* get a word with him, she might say that since he'd been put on this earth to save the souls of men, wouldn't he just consider thinkin' about saving Rebecca

Lapp, too? From going insane, that is?

Oh, she'd tell it to him awful gentle, sweet as can be, and if the bishop was the kind of man she figured he was, deep down inside his soul somewheres—if he truly was God's choice for the People, a man who could change his voice at will—well, he just might consider her request. Just might think twice about lifting Katie's harsh shunning. At least so they could talk to the disobedient woman. Use the voices God gave them, all different ranges and tones, for sure, to witness the love of the Lord God heavenly Father himself and maybe even bring her back to the fold.

It was just a thought. Maybe not the *right* thing to do at all. But what with the bishop sending unspoken messages with his eyes during Preachin' and all, in light of that, she could surely hope.

❖ ❖ ❖

By the time she'd climbed two long flights of stairs, the breath in her was gone. Katherine was reminded of Laura's labored breathing at the end—completely ready when the call from heaven came.

Finding the journal her mother had mentioned as she lay dying had proven to be a challenging task. Yet each day Katherine had searched the estate—even several attics— with help from Theodore and Garrett. All to no avail.

Not to be outdone, she decided to meet with the entire domestic staff. Assuming her new role of mistress of the manor had not come easy, perhaps because she was more than eager to share the size and the warmth of the upstairs rooms. Because of this, because she wanted to allocate the space to her friends—Laura's loyal servants, and now hers— she encouraged them to scatter out. They were to choose various guest suites, even Dylan Bennett's former office area—now vacant—for their own private quarters.

So it happened that while Fulton and Rosie, Theodore, and the others were resituating themselves, Justin Wirth came to call, several days after Laura's funeral. "I thought you might consider accompanying me to the unveiling of Mrs. Bennett's commissioned work." His smile was genuinely warm.

She realized, to her amazement, that she'd forgotten all about the oil painting. Someone—Rosie, maybe—had mentioned that the artist had probably salvaged the portrait, since none of them were interested in hanging it anywhere in the mansion. Not with the impostor's face beside that of their dear deceased Laura.

"How about it, then? Would you like to keep me company this Friday evening at the Fine Arts Center downtown?"

Katherine didn't know what to make of this request. It had been a good long time since a young man had asked to socialize with her publicly. She recalled one of the last Singings; she'd gone with her Beloved. But that was years ago.

It seemed rather apparent by the expectant smile on Justin Wirth's handsome face that she might have difficulty saying no. Still, she couldn't help thinking of Dan. Would she feel she was being disloyal to his memory? To their love?

Standing tall and confident, Mr. Wirth grinned down at her as the two of them stood silent in the foyer. When their eyes met, as they had in the dining room on Christmas Day—after she'd lit candles on a birthday cake for the Christ child—she felt something like butterflies flitting around in her stomach. A strange yet lovely sensation. One she'd quite forgotten.

She nodded, returning Mr. Wirth's smile, curious to see how he might have altered the portrait to display her birth mother more prominently. "I'd like to go, Mr. Wirth, I really would," she replied at last. Then realizing she'd almost slipped into her Hickory Hollow speech, she paused and modulated her voice, in a tone more befitting the mistress of the manor. "It would be a pleasure."

She felt mighty pleased with herself, learning to speak the fluid phrases of high society. She'd picked up ever so much from Laura, too, and figured that after only a few more days spent with either Theodore or Rosie, right fine British folk, she'd be speaking and pronouncing the king's English with grace, probably.

Shouldn't take long for her to pick up on doing or saying something right fancy, not when she set her mind to it. And she would, too—for the sake of her natural mother—she would follow through with being Katherine Mayfield. For sure and for certain.

The attractive man nodded. "Please, Miss Mayfield, call me Justin."

"Thank you, I will." Then noticing the genuine warmth in his blue, blue eyes, she thought of Daniel unexpectedly. Thought of him and hoped he wouldn't mind if she got all dressed up and went out on the town with this nice young artist. That is, if Dan just happened to be looking down on her from Paradise.

CHAPTER THIRTY

❖   ❖   ❖

What a beautiful satin gown, Miss Katherine!"

Katherine stood in front of the full-length mirror, making the long dress swish for Rosie. "You don't know this, but once when I snuck away to a little boutique back in Lancaster, I promised myself that someday I would wear a dress like this . . . out in public." She smiled at her reflection. "And just look, here I am!"

Rosie put the finishing touches on the sash at Katherine's waist. "I'd say you look absolutely smashing, love."

"Oh, thank you, Rosie." Then turning, she spun like a top, around and around as she had in her Amish mamma's attic months ago, the day she'd found the little satin baby dress.

Remembering, she went over to the dresser, feeling a bit dizzy but giggling near like a schoolgirl. "I wonder if Justin could paint me a picture of *this*." She held up the tiny infant gown. The garment that had caused so much heartache yet brought so much joy.

"Might be, though I rather think he prefers to work with *live* models for his inspiration." Rosie looked her over, grinning broadly. "And inspiring you certainly are tonight, Miss Katherine. Now, we'd better get you settled in the drawing room."

"Is it time already?"

Glancing at her watch, Rosie nodded. "The evening awaits you . . . Miss *Marsh*field." And they laughed together over the fancy made-up name.

But when Justin, looking right fine in his tuxedo, arrived to fetch her, there was more than admiration shining in his eyes. No, at least for the space of a heartbeat, Katherine thought she could see something *more*, something beautiful for them both. To her surprise, she felt the coldness in her spirit begin to dissolve—that powerful-strong numbness that had never quite left her since the shunning.

Arriving at the Fine Arts Center in Justin's rented limousine, Katherine was breathless with excitement. Assisted by a uniformed doorman, she stepped through a canopied entryway into a foyer, enchanted with her elegant surroundings. Under her feet, the plush pile of carpeting the color of ripe plums. Fine paintings, cleverly lit up by overhead lamps, lining the walls on either side of a long hallway. Lush green foliage and arrangements of forced blossoms—tulips, jonquils, and narcissus—their heady perfume a sure promise of spring.

Her hand tucked into the crook of Justin's arm, Katherine floated beside him toward the main gallery where the unveiling was to take place. Such a gathering it was, too. Important-looking people with important-sounding titles.

"Good evening, Mayor Bledsoe," Justin was saying in his deep, velvety voice. "May I present Miss Katherine Mayfield."

Following Justin's polished lead, she smiled and murmured, "How do you do?"

His Honor was a portly man with silvery hair and a walrus-style moustache. But he seemed pleasant enough as he shook her hand, then inclined his head toward the stunning blonde in his company. "My wife, *Mrs*. Bledsoe."

The woman, her silky hair swinging about her face, seemed young enough to be his daughter, Katherine couldn't help thinking. And when a cool gaze swept her from head to toe, then settled on her left cheek, she was flustered to the point of distraction. *What if I've put on too much blush!* she fretted. *But surely Rosie would've told me, wouldn't she?*

There was no time for further speculation, however, for Justin was introducing her to yet another couple, and Katherine found herself parroting a few well-rehearsed phrases in her new English voice. Still, with Justin never leaving her side, his hand cradling her elbow protectively, she was soon feeling much more at ease, meeting his friends—some, elected officials; others, artists-in-residence who made Canandaigua their home.

Honestly, she couldn't say she wasn't relieved when they finally made their way past the many well-wishers to the main exhibit hall for the unveiling. Immensely pleased, too, with the wonderful-good seat Justin had arranged for her in a row of plump cushioned chairs up at the very front.

As she took her seat, she noticed right away the heavily draped object resting on an easel before her. A pair of spotlights beamed down on the folds of ebony velvet.

For a moment, there was a wave of apprehension as Katherine pondered. How would she feel when the gold-tasseled cords were pulled, and the curtains parted to reveal the portrait? How would she react to the sight of her mother's face depicted on canvas? Would it bring tears to her eyes? The unveiling so soon after the funeral and burial services?

She bolstered herself by remembering that the dear lady was in Glory . . . no pain there, she was most assured. And she hadn't known Laura for all her life as most daughters know their mothers, so maybe the grieving wouldn't be as painful, she hoped. Still, Justin was known for "bringing people to life" on canvas. . . .

Just as the string ensemble ended their number, he stepped forward. Katherine held her breath, bracing herself for whatever feelings might be stirred up by the revelation of his artistic rendering.

But she was *not* braced. Not really. *Nothing* could have prepared her for the startling yet splendid oil painting. For there on the large canvas were depicted *two* women. Two auburn-haired women. Laura Mayfield-Bennett and Katherine, her real, true daughter.

She found herself breathing again, wanting to laugh and shout for joy. But she did the ladylike thing. She sat there, applauding the work, wondering how on earth the artist knew to put *her*—not the impostor—alongside her mother. Not Miss Alyson Cairns—New York actress turned Katie Lapp!

Later, while they mingled with others around the buffet table, she asked Justin about it. "Was it physical similarities between my mother and me that you noticed first?"

He chuckled at that. "Not many people have the privilege of wearing the rich colors of autumn all year long."

She knew he was referring to her hair, delighted that he hadn't called it "red."

As for her chin line and nose, "There are more important qualities than looks when it comes to relationships," he told her. "Even if I hadn't known, I would've painted you next to Laura."

"Oh? Why is that?"

His eyes shone with understanding. "Because, Katherine, you and Laura Mayfield-Bennett shared each other's hearts."

On the drive home, the present mistress of the newly named Mayfield Manor and her friend, the award-winning artist of Canandaigua, shared with each other their childhood backgrounds and interests. During the course of the ride, they discovered a variety of things they had in common, so much so that it was difficult to bring the evening to an end.

"Would you like to stop somewhere for coffee?" Justin asked.

Katherine consented to the after-hours coffee bar, delighted. She never would've guessed the two of them would find themselves so attracted to each other. Or that the evening would hold so many surprises, especially the portrait of herself and her natural mother.

It was much later, when the limo driver stopped at a red light, that she noticed a tall man crossing the street just ahead of them. Briefly, he glanced at their fancy car, and it was then she saw his face. She stared, intrigued.

This man—had she seen him before? In Lancaster . . . at market, maybe?

The more she thought of it, the more she assumed the untrimmed beard was the reason for her curiosity, probably. Maybe he was a member of one of the Old Order Mennonite groups, certainly not Amish, for he wore a handsome fur-trimmed overcoat and leather gloves.

When the light changed, she glanced back and watched the young man walk to the streetlight and pull something out of his coat pocket. It almost looked like a map, the way he unfolded it, and she remembered when she, too, had felt overwhelmingly lost . . . not in the midst of a new location, but among her own People.

She couldn't be sure, really, and it didn't matter anyway. She and Justin were on their way to have coffee and talk away the hours. Her future as Katherine Mayfield was brighter than any star that shone that night. Brighter than either the buzzing white ceiling lights in Cousin Lydia's kitchen or the crystal chandeliers in Katherine's own elegant dining room.

A verse from Ecclesiastes came to mind just then, for she'd heard the Wise Woman quote it many times. *Truly the light is sweet,* she thought.

And Katherine felt she understood. For the very first time.

EPILOGUE

It was long past midnight when I found myself sitting at my birth mother's dressing table with only the moonlight to keep me company. I couldn't help thinking about the mighty exciting evening I'd just had. Such a refined gentleman my new friend was, and, ach, so terribly English. Yet a sensitive sort for sure.

"Must be my artist's temperament," he'd joked as we had sipped black coffee in a cozy corner of the restaurant.

Well, whatever an "artist's temperament" was, I didn't rightly know, but there was one thing I *did* know. I liked Justin Wirth, and even though we'd spent only one evening together, I had a wonderful-good feeling that he liked me, too.

His face was before me now as I sat staring at the frosty windowpane, snowy reflections mingling with my memory of his facial features. Quite unexpectedly, I began comparing the artist to my deceased Amish boyfriend, and, next thing I knew, the two handsome faces took shape in my mind's eye, clear as day.

Justin seemed to smile back at me, and I hugged myself, thinking, *Oh, glory, such a night!* Then his image began to fade and Dan's grew ever so much stronger, blocking out Justin's cheerful expression.

To my dismay, I saw the light go out of the blueberry eyes. So awful sad Dan seemed, looking down at me now, and my heart went out to my long-expired loved one. In that moment I wondered if dear ones who'd passed on *could* see what things we do down here on earth.

Surely he would understand; surely he knew that I'd loved him, and he alone, for all these years. That I'd been ever so loyal—yes, and lonely and heartsick.

"Oh, Dan," I whispered, almost like a prayer, "please . . . can ya forgive me? Can you forgive your Katie girl?"

I surprised myself by uttering my former name—first time I'd spoken it since leaving Hickory Hollow—and I brushed back the tears. "Please, my darling, won'tcha put away your sadness and . . . and see my heart? See my *joy?*"

Silent then, I dismissed the mental picture by out-and-out willpower, hoping for a good night's sleep. And in that moment, I thought of my Amish mamma and wondered if Rebecca's beautiful eyes—those heavenly hazel eyes— might also behold me with sorrow if she knew of my English life now.

Katherine Mayfield, Mistress of Mayfield Manor.

I stood up, noticing as I headed into the bedroom that Rosie had turned down the coverings on Laura's bed—now mine. This room, where my first mother had suffered so, where she'd prayed for me, desperately hoping that I might come to her before she went home to Jesus, *all* of it be-longed to me. Everything around me, everywhere I looked. And to think that my dear, prayerful mother had given this wonderful-good place to me boggled my mind!

Feelings of unworthiness sprang up, but along with that came a sense of anticipation, wrapped up in one trembling bundle. How I missed Laura; how I wished that she'd lived long enough to grow old in her beloved childhood home.

That I might've come to know her better, share her life, her dreams. I wished, too, that I could find her journal, the one she'd written while I was growing inside her . . . so long ago.

"If only Laura were still here," I said to the darkness. Oh, I was for sure and for certain she could guide me through the maze of my future, because I had no inkling what it might hold.

Still, I had always pined for such an English life as this. And a truly good part of me could hardly wait for every speck of it to unfold.

ACKNOWLEDGMENTS

❖ ❖ ❖

Special thanks to Kathy Torley for her professional medical assistance, the Multiple Sclerosis Society of Colorado Springs, and June Heimsoth for her research help.

My appreciation to John and Julie Sullivan—delightful innkeepers of Morgan-Samuels B&B Inn of Canandaigua, New York—for allowing their beautiful, 1810 English-style mansion to be featured on the cover of this book. (Listed in *The Innkeeper's Register*, I highly recommend it.)

I wish to thank Anne Severance, my prayerful editor and friend, as well as Barbara Lilland and Carol Johnson, who offered their faithful editorial guidance throughout the writing process, along with Dave, my dear husband, encourager and friend, and "second eyes."

More From Beverly Lewis

ABRAHAM'S DAUGHTERS introduces readers to an Old Order family. Abram Ebersol and his devoted wife are raising four courting-age daughters on a firm foundation of Plain tradition, and they expect their girls to carry on that heritage by joining the church and making a covenant with God.

However, each of Abram's daughters must come to terms with the Old Ways of thinking and living, ultimately choosing her own path. And sometimes that path has detours and forks in the road with unknown destinations....

The Covenant, The Betrayal, The Sacrifice, The Prodigal, The Revelation

The providential discovery of a postcard written in Pennsylvania Dutch by an "Englisher" on vacation at the Orchard Guest House leads him to the bedside of a woman with a tale of dark secrets and lost love. As Philip unravels the mystery of the postcard, he finds himself drawn to the shy Amish widow he meets. Can he help her over her grief, and find healing for his heart as well?

The Postcard

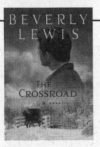

Drawn back to the Amish community over the Christmas holidays, Philip struggles with the vast gulf separating him from the beautiful Plain woman Rachel Yoder. She has suffered unbearable heartache; will his affection for her only bring more of the same? Or must they sacrifice a future together for the sake of all they know and love?

The Crossroad